D1322033

LIMOUSINE

Patrick Conrad was born in Antwerp in 1945. He
is a poet, a novelist, a painter, a screenwriter and a
film director.

Patrick Conrad

LIMOUSINE

TRANSLATED BY
Stephen Smith

VINTAGE

Published by Vintage 2000

2 4 6 8 10 9 7 5 3 1

Copyright © Patrick Conrad 1999
Translation copyright © Stephen Smith 1999

The right of Patrick Conrad to be identified as the author of
this work has been asserted by him in accordance with the
Copyright, Designs and Patents Act, 1988

This book is sold subject to the condition that it shall not by way
of trade or otherwise, be lent, resold, hired out, or otherwise
circulated without the publisher's prior consent in any form of
binding or cover other than that in which it is published and
without a similar condition including this condition being
imposed on the subsequent purchaser

First published in Great Britain in 1999 by
Jonathan Cape

Vintage
Random House, 20 Vauxhall Bridge Road,
London SW1V 2SA

Random House Australia (Pty) Limited
20 Alfred Street, Milsons Point, Sydney
New South Wales 2061, Australia

Random House New Zealand Limited
18 Poland Road, Glenfield,
Auckland 10, New Zealand

Random House (Pty) Limited
Endulini, 5A Jubilee Road, Parktown 2193,
South Africa

Random House UK Limited Reg. No. 954009
www.randomhouse.co.uk

A CIP catalogue record for this book
is available from the British Library

ISBN 0 09 928454 5

Papers used by Random House are natural, recyclable
products made from wood grown in sustainable forests.
The manufacturing processes conform to the environ-
mental regulations of the country of origin

Printed and bound in Great Britain by
Cox & Wyman Ltd, Reading, Berkshire

I saw pale kings and princes too,
Pale warriors, death-pale were they all;
Who cry'd – 'La belle Dame sans Merci
Hath thee in thrall!'

John Keats

Part One

1

'Scorpion fish are seldom aggressive. But I can understand their bad reputation. To the layman they look dangerous, with their malevolent gaze and those poisonous dorsal fin spines, they spread above their head like a deadly fan, when they feel themselves threatened. But believe me, I live with these creatures: they'll eat from your hand. Some of the older specimens even come when you call their name. People are simply reacting to appearance.'

'Usually, yes.'

Commissaris Van Laken is only half listening to the droning explanation of Dr Ambers, the short, balding man who is walking beside him, with brisk little steps, along the gravel path between the stinking cages of llamas and rare gazelles, and who, with his bulging eyes, lipless mouth and peculiar skin disease – as if his skull were covered with scales – himself resembles a fish.

'Here in Antwerp we concentrate primarily on *Pterois Radiata*, by far the most beautiful of the scorpion fish. The rays of its pectoral fin are extremely long, sometimes extending as far back as its tail fin. You can recognise it by the six thin vertical bands which fork out over its back. It changes colour, depending on its mood. And don't go thinking these fellows have no temperament. Given what happened there today, I bet they'll have turned a rosy red.'

It is a quarter to eight and the sultry heat is still hanging among the exotic plants of the deserted gardens. Here and there men in dark blue uniforms are sweeping the lawns clean.

'On hot days such as this, our visitors sometimes leave more than three hundred kilos of rubbish behind,' sighs the director of the zoo, who is waiting for them on the bridge above the little desert with its mangy camels. 'They get mayonnaise everywhere, even in the tails of the macaws. Professor Vandevelde. Pleased to meet you.'

'Van Laken, Criminal Investigation Department. Sorry I kept you waiting. It's practically impossible to drive through Antwerp nowadays, even with the sirens going.'

'I got rid of my car,' Vandevelde reassures him. 'These days it's quicker to walk.'

'Or go by bike, weather permitting,' says Ambers, attempting to enter the conversation, but Van Laken interrupts the talking pangolin.

'To top it all, I had to wait a half an hour at the bridge over Kattendijk lock. It's not my day today.' One of Van Laken's stock expressions. It is never his day.

'Where is it?'

'This way, inspector . . .'

'Commissaris.'

'Commissaris. Your colleague arrived just a moment ago.'

Van Laken follows the zoo director as if he is on a guided tour, as if there is nothing amiss. He thinks: 'This man smells of humus', and blows his nose.

'The inter-regional express for passengers to Mechelen, Brussels North, Brussels Central and Brussels South will be leaving from Platform Six at nineteen hours fifty-two.'

The loudspeakers of Central Station, which are hidden behind the lions, the panthers and the tigers, are still audible at the entrance to the art deco building which houses the tropical salt water aquarium. In front of the pavilion's monumental gate, flying squad officers are talking to a well-groomed young man. When he sees the threesome appear from behind a tall banana palm he bounces towards Van Laken on thick rubber soles. Without pausing, Van Laken introduces him.

'My assistant, Detective Chief Sergeant Courtois. And? Signed?'

'Yes.'

'M?'

Courtois nods. Vandevelde and Ambers follow the conversation, understanding nothing but impressed by the concise efficiency with which these two professionals communicate.

'Public prosecutor's office informed?'

'They're on their way. Only the photographer came in my car. I took him along to the skip this afternoon.'

'Find anything worthwhile?'

'The body of an old black man. In a state of decomposition.'

'Emasculated?'

'No idea . . .'

'Okay. We'll check that later. Gentlemen, I suggest we take a look at those scorpions right away.'

'Scorpion fish,' Ambers corrects him. '*Pterois Radiata.*'

Once inside the hall, it takes them a while to adjust to the half-light. Van Laken leads the way. The mosaic pond, with its goldfish and water lilies, reminds him of the annual school visits of his childhood. At lunchtime he would sneak off to eat his velvety Liège syrup sandwiches, more or less alone, far away from his whooping classmates, and gaze at the fortune in twenty-five centime pieces, coins with a hole in the middle, at the bottom of the crocodile pit. He was already taller than the other children, and therefore did not feel at home in any group.

'She's in the first tank. Down to the left in the Red Sea, Indian and Pacific Ocean section, at the end of the aisle,' says Ambers, wiping the sweat and the dust from the lines in his forehead with a checked handkerchief. The oceanographer's voice sounds hollow, as if in a cave, and mingles with the echo of their footsteps on the concrete slabs. Inside the overheated pavilion, the atmosphere is even more oppressive than it is

7

outside. The sickly smell of rotting plants and fungi is exactly the same as forty years before.

'Who found her?' asks Van Laken, gazing left and right at the illuminated windows, behind which giant turtles and speckled sea snakes hover motionless between concrete rocks.

'The night watchman. He had just started his rounds and came to turn off the lighting above the tanks. He's still in a state of shock.'

'What time was that?'

'After closing. Shortly after seven.'

'How come none of the visitors noticed anything?'

'The pavilion's been closed to the public for a week, because of repair work to the roof.'

'Which has totally confused the seahorses,' complains Ambers. 'Lophobranchii are very highly strung.'

By the time Van Laken and his entourage have traversed the hundred-metre aisle, his eyes have become accustomed to the twilight and he picks out details in the floor that he had forgotten over the years and that remind him once again of his schooldays: lobsters and crabs, inlaid in gold mosaic. After every school trip he had to draw them from memory in art class – he to whom line and form have always remained a mystery.

'Around the corner, on the left,' says Professor Vandevelde. 'But I warn you, it's not a pretty sight.'

'We're used to worse,' Van Laken answers curtly, as he gives Vandevelde an encouraging pat on the shoulder.

The tank containing the butterfly fish and angel fish is the largest in the room because, as Ambers had explained, coral fish are territorial and, if confined to a too limited environment, will turn on their own kind, just like people. It is also by far the most beautiful of the tanks, with its whimsical and colourful coral reef and its fragments of genuine shipwrecks, which provide a daytime refuge for the timorous fish.

'There she is.'

The young woman is naked and floating weightlessly on her side, like a pallid mermaid, in the pale green water. Her long, black hair has become entangled in a flame-coloured coral branch. Her body is slim and muscular, even taking into account Courtois' reasonable observation that the water may be causing a degree of distortion. Her bloodshot eyes are open and the false eyelash is missing from her left eyelid, so that one eye looks larger than the other. The neon light gives her skin a blue-green, fluorescent sheen. Her toenails and fingernails are painted red and her pubic hair has been shaved.

'She's been in there quite some time,' Van Laken thinks aloud, because the fish – which according to Scaly are rather timid by nature – have resumed their tedious, inquisitive ballet around her exquisite body. A dead speckled fish is stuck deep inside her wide open mouth; only its blunt tail is visible.

'A clown wrasse,' observes Ambers. 'Judging from its torpedo shape, a fully grown specimen.'

'Lova Spencer,' sighs Van Laken, gazing at the tank as if at a film screen.

'Who?' asks Courtois, taking out his notebook.

'Lova Spencer. The Esther Williams of porn. Number six.'

'You knew the victim?' Vandevelde asks admiringly.

'Not personally, professor. Not personally.'

Van Laken and his assistant leave the silent zoo, and suddenly find themselves back in reality, amid the beeping, the braking buses and dazed passers-by. The sky above the Astridplein has turned a deep, indigo blue: Antwerp-blue, as Van Laken calls it. There is little point in staying, breathing the musty air of the tropical aquarium, gawping at the drowned film star and listening to Ambers and the public prosecutor babbling. The public prosecutor's team has arrived and nobody needs any further instructions. He has asked the photographer to take a close-up of the letter M smeared on the window of the tank in greasy red lipstick. Lova Spencer's corpse will be sent to the lab for the autopsy and he can question the night watchman tomorrow at police headquarters, when the old man has recovered from the shock.

For a while Van Laken plays with the idea that Lova's murderer might be watching him triumphantly from a terrace across the square. What he would like to do now is to shoot the first shiny-faced shopkeeper who dares to smile at him to ribbons, to free himself from this nagging feeling of impotence.

'Fancy a bite to eat?' he suggests somewhat absently, as he peers up with squinting eyes at Central Station's illuminated clock.

It is a quarter to nine.

Fancy a bite to eat? Courtois knows what that means: queuing under flickering fluorescent lights in the nearest McDonald's, chewing on cardboard and drinking watery iced cola from paper beakers with hands covered in chip fat. It isn't just because he is a metre ninety-five that their colleagues at headquarters call Van Laken 'Big Mac'.

'In this heat, I'd rather have a quick drink. How about the terrace of de Fouquet's? That way we can enjoy the cool of the evening. And you can order the most delicious snacks.'

In the Café Brabant (proprietors Jos and Marina), a drab bar in the Statiestraat with 'rooms for travellers', where he feels inexplicably at home among the scruffy alcoholics and can wolf down his hot-dog with bright orange piccalilli undisturbed, Van Laken sinks down with a sigh at a table next to the pinball machine. After dusting off his chair with his handkerchief, Courtois sits opposite him.

'And don't order Bellinis. They've never heard of them here.'

The waitress is a plump, pallid girl of indeterminate age. She exudes an acrid smell of sweat and has swollen, blue fingers and bitten nails. 'Back on the needle', thinks Van Laken as he looks up at her.

'Two cold colas.'

Big Mac has the irritating habit of ordering what he himself fancies for everybody. But today Courtois just lets him get on with it. The discovery of the sixth corpse in the zoo is clearly perturbing him.

'What did you mean just now: "the Esther Williams of porn"?'

'Didn't you see *Twenty Thousand Virgins Under the Sea*? A Dutch remake of the French porn film *Vingt Mille Verges Sous les Mers*. With a fault in the translation. To the Dutch *verge* seems to mean the same as *vierge*.'

Courtois shakes his head non-committally, thinking: 'Where on earth does Van Laken find the time to look at all those porn videos?'

'Lova Spencer was the only Dutch actress who could give a blow job under water, my lad. Hence M's tasteful little piece of scene-setting.'

'And the dead fish in her mouth . . .'

'Precisely.'

Van Laken glances absent-mindedly at the blue hand which slaps down two warm colas on the formica table in front of him, then at the waitress who has eavesdropped on the end of their conversation. She gives him a sly wink.

'Maria, you stink to high heaven. Never heard of Printil or Rexona?'

'Perhaps we could take a bath together? You don't smell so great yourself,' she replies, turning away with a shrug of her shoulders. Van Laken smiles feebly.

'Tell me about the black man in the skip.'

Courtois takes out his well-thumbed notebook.

'There's not a lot to tell. According to the police physician, he's about sixty years old. Definitely not a tramp. Well cared for nails and teeth. Expensive clothes. Been dead about three weeks – the skip's been in the full sun, you can imagine the stink inside – and as I already said, shot in the back of the neck. No papers. Autopsy tomorrow. Cheers.' Courtois shuts his notebook and empties his glass in a single swallow.

'Who discovered the body?'

'A prostitute, a certain Jeanne Darmon, French, used to work the Burchtgracht, lost her room when they cleaned up the neighbourhood, works the street now, turns her tricks in empty containers. Seems to be a new trend . . .'

'Give the case to the Whore-hopper.'

'Somers?'

'Yes. He knows the lot of them.'

This is not the real reason why Van Laken does not want to get personally involved in this case. Since De Mulder, one of his team, had discovered M's first victim eight months earlier, skinned and hanging from a meat hook among the carcasses in a cold-room at Antwerp slaughter house, Van Laken has known no rest. M is the first serial killer he has ever had to deal with in his well-filled career and the mysterious, elusive murderer has become a real obsession. He has stuck the photo of Lolita Moore, the petite child prostitute, who now looks more like a skinned rabbit dangling from her hook, on the shaving mirror in his bathroom. That bloody hunk of meat is the first sight, beside his sleep-swollen face, with which he is confronted every morning. Deep in her vagina, the lips of which have been sliced away with scissors, Sax, the police physician, had found a wooden Scrabble block on which the letter M was printed. Van Laken has carried it in his pocket as a talisman ever since, fondling it with clammy fingers. He places the polished block carefully on the table, next to a paper plate covered in orange mustard stains, and looks at it. He has tears in his eyes, as if this relic could give him the answer to all his questions. The jukebox is playing 'Een beetje verliefd' – A Little in Love – in the husky blues voice of André Hazes. Beside him sits the only man in Antwerp who is cold this

12

evening. He is wearing a threadbare woollen overcoat with a turned-up collar, and is shivering and complaining about life to a drooling old cow he presumably once adored, when she still had teeth and the hair of Veronica Lake. Such is life. Van Laken's stomach churns.

'When do we leave for Brussels?' asks Courtois, to break the silence.

'Right away.'

2

It is a quarter past nine when Mercury finishes ironing. Applause resounds from the loudspeakers of his Technics stereo.

While smoothing the last creases out of his white linen shirt, he has been listening to the third movement of Brahms' First Sonata for Violin and Piano – the exceptionally beautiful *adagio molto moderato* – in a 1968 live performance by David Oistrahk and Frida Bauer.

He is wearing nothing but pearl-grey, impeccably pressed alpaca trousers, the black leather belt of which he has not yet buckled, so that the trousers are hanging loosely, a little too low, around his hips. His back and his shoulders are tanned. It has been so hot the past few days that he has been able to take care of Ted Harlow's limousine in his swimming trunks.

While the first bars of the *allegro amabile* of the Second Sonata in A major fill the room, now with Suyatoslav Richter at the piano, Mercury steps to the small mirror hanging next to the shower, and studies his angular face at length. He rubs his white teeth with a manicured finger, sleeks his eyebrows, strokes his smooth chin and clean-shaven cheeks, checks the corners of his eyes, snips away a nose hair. He then carefully takes the Ralph Lauren atomiser from the little rack beneath the mirror, sprays his gleaming jaws with a whiff of Polo aftershave, drums with his fingertips on his cheekbones and finds his smile agreeable.

Mercury has only recently moved into this spacious flat, above the garage at the rear of the Brasschaat estate of Flanders' most powerful property developer and pig-breeder, Edward

Vangenechte who, since his move into film production the previous year, now prefers to be known as Ted Harlow. Three weeks earlier, Mercury responded to an advertisement in the *Antwerp Post* and offered his services to Mr Vangenechte as a replacement for the previous chauffeur, who had disappeared, unexpectedly and mysteriously, after ten years of faithful service. His diplomas in art and film history had made less of an impression on Vangenechte than his driving licence, his elegant appearance and his exquisite manners. He had professed a love of beautiful cars, claimed to be a competent handyman and to consider punctuality as something self-evident. Besides, his unusual name, Mercury, sounded perfect for a chauffeur.

'Four weeks on trial,' the producer had suggested. 'Thirty thousand francs a month in hand, plus board and lodgings. Uniform is obligatory but will be provided. Mondays free.'

Mercury would have accepted any offer. The two Porsches, the Lamborghini, the Maserati Bi-turbo, the Testarossa, the Jaguars and the Lincoln Continental Stretch Limo which are standing in the garage shining and ready to go mean nothing to him. There is a deeper, less obvious reason why he had wanted this job, why he would have taken it whatever the conditions. It is a reason he cannot reveal to anybody, and certainly not to the pompous windbag he has to bring to Brussels this evening.

He tightens the knot of his dark grey silk tie under the starched collar of his shirt, moves to the window as he combs back his gleaming black hair, turns off the light and peers out from behind the half-closed curtains at the dusk, at the illuminated beeches in the grounds and, beyond them, behind the rhododendrons, at his employer's tasteless neoclassical villa. In the master bedroom, which opens out on to a balustraded terrace, a light is shining: a yellow rectangle, at which Mercury points his binoculars as if at a cinema screen in the twilight.

He focuses and the interior appears: beige walls, a four-poster bed big enough for six, deep-pile, white fitted carpet through which a Yorkshire terrier is leaping like a hind in a cornfield, a mirrored wall and, on the numerous, superfluous little tables, photos in silver frames and tall vases of white gladioli, like on the yachts in St Tropez. Hollywood in Brasschaat.

On the champagne-coloured satin bedspread, a pair of black nylon stockings are lying beside a nebulous, shimmering rag, probably the lamé evening dress Mercury had collected for her from Armani that afternoon. He begins to breathe more heavily at the thought that he may see her at any moment, and during the brief silence which follows the *andante tranquillo* of the second sonata, she finally appears in the frame. Mercury immediately feels the blood pounding in his temples and the scene begins to quiver. Seen through the binoculars and surrounded by the dusky frame of the falling night, the scene appears even more like a sequence from a silent film.

She – Ava Palomba, a twenty-three-year-old Dutch beauty of one metre seventy-eight, ex-playmate, ex-Miss Malibu, formerly blonde, now auburn – has played small roles in four unreleased erotic art films and the leading role in *Desert Flower*, the long awaited soft porn film in which Ted Harlow has been frantically investing money in an effort to replenish his bank account after three lamentable Flemish flops. According to the tabloids, they had met each other on the set in New Mexico. After the final dub, Ava, God only knows why, had followed her bleached-blond, petit bourgeois pig-farmer back to Europe, where they have now been living together for a month. 'A vision', thinks Mercury. 'A gift from the gods.'

Her image has haunted Mercury ever since her appearance two years ago in the Dutch *Playboy*, crawling naked along the edge of a David Hockney swimming pool with her back arched, in the coppery glow of a Californian sunset. Ava was more than beautiful. She was enigmatic. Seduction incarnate. The sphinx, the symbol, the icon, the unapproachable goddess, the lascivious madonna, the heartless whore, the implacable mistress. After two years of sleepless nights, he had been able to stand it no longer. He had sold his books, his 16mm camera and his collection of original film posters and was just about to leave for Los Angeles when she unexpectedly arrived in Brasschaat, like an angel descending on the city. Now she is so close that he can guess her perfume, can count her beauty spots, can practically hear her breathing, so close it seems all he has to do to touch her with his trembling fingertips is to reach out his arm. The close-up of her tongue curling up over her upper lip seems almost inevitable, as if his silent obsession has mercilessly drawn her towards him. A week after her arrival, he had succeeded in getting Vangenechte to employ him and since that happy day he has spent most of his time caressing the curves of her E-type Jaguar and nourishing his secret passion.

Ava, who is wearing nothing but a minuscule bra and black lace knickers, sits on the edge of the bed and pulls on her stockings, carefully caressing her outstretched calves and her thighs to smooth away the final wrinkles. Then she stands up, holds the lamé dress in front of her, looks at the result in the mirror, lets the dress fall, unhooks her bra and throws it on the floor. The Yorkshire terrier disappears yapping with it under the bed. Finally, she pulls the tight piece of clothing on over her naked skin, like a second, shimmering snakeskin, a costly cocoon, a quicksilver sheath. Like streamlined coachwork, thinks Mercury, swallowing and tasting metal. Does she realise he spies on her at night? Is that why she never closes the curtains? Is that why she leaves all the lights on?

Somebody out of the picture calls to her. She turns around laughing, just like Laura Antonelli in *Malizia*. He sees her dark lips moving: she is talking.

Mercury hangs the binoculars back on the hook, between the photo of Karlheinz Böhm in *Peeping Tom*, his favourite film, and a creased postcard of Max Dungert's 1926 portrait of Kurt Weill, whom he himself resembles, and shuts the curtains. The thought that Vangenechte is probably ogling Ava from another room nauseates him. Moreover, that slimeball could have entered the shot at any moment and ruined everything.

Mercury looks at his watch: it is ten past nine and the second sonata is over. He pulls on his grey double-breasted jacket and his grey suede gloves, puts on his chauffeur's cap, straightens it, and checks himself a final time in the mirror. From a drawer full of car keys, he selects those of the limousine and then, whistling Brahms, he leaves the silent, aftershave-perfumed room.

Moments later, he starts the purring engine of the limousine. He then glides silently along the drives of the grounds in the seemingly endless colossus, gazing with a smile at the smooth water of the illuminated swimming pool. Only this afternoon he had seen her sunbathing naked, floating in a pink rubber Cadillac. Now motionless rhododendrons and azaleas are reflected in the pool. Three times she had let herself slide into the cool water, and he had stopped working. She had then let herself float in the water, weightless, as if hovering, more beautiful than ever. Ava is one of those rare women who are at their most lovely when they are carelessly bored.

A little later he parks the car, exactly on time, at the foot of the marble steps that lead up to the classically fronted villa. This evening he will be missing *Casablanca* on TV2.

3

'You should get out more!' Suzanna calls over her shoulder, as she curls her false eyelashes with iron tongs. 'You get buried here quicker than you think!' Her hand, sown with dark brown freckles between the swollen veins, trembles. Her nails are painted fluorescent blue.

The bare walls of her steel, glass and concrete loft – which looks like an empty hangar with, here and there, a marble pillar or a chair by Starck on which no normal person can sit – reverberate the echo of her deep voice. On the flat screen of the Bang & Olufsen television, Ingrid Bergman is entering Rick's Café.

'Did you hear what I said, Panther?'

The answer comes from far away. From the cellar. A husky, male voice.

'I'm coming, darling!'

Gossip has it that Suzanna Rizzoni is of Italian origin. She has been living in Antwerp for more than twenty years and she still cannot disguise her foreign accent. But it suits her mysterious persona. Nobody knows exactly how old she is and only the best informed, and consequently the most vicious, gossips in the artistic world say that she must be around forty-five. Nor is it easy to guess: Suzanna is exceptionally eccentric, and her appearance changes so often that her age is the last question in anybody's mind. She can thank her more than comfortable fortune to her famous 'zipper fashion' which caused quite an uproar, especially in the seventies. Her collection of dresses, trousers and coats, all consisting of hundreds of zip-fasteners sewn together, had then made the

cover of virtually every major fashion magazine and perma-
nently established her reputation as a major fashion designer.
Since then, success has never left her and each of her shows is
greeted by the press as a miracle of daring and creativity. She
counts both Alice Cooper and Eddy Wally amongst her
clients, has designed costumes for films such as *The Return of
Rocco Mendoza* and *Cybill's Café* and is known as far as Peking,
where she has recently opened a branch. In Antwerp, no
fashionable event can be counted a complete success unless she
attends.

Suzanna never wears her own creations, but prefers old
clothes which have belonged to celebrities. She buys them at
auctions. At this evening's premiere, for instance, she is
planning to appear in the original satin rose and old lace-
trimmed velvet dress and mousseline cape Sarah Bernhardt
wore when she played the role of Marion Delorme.

'Panther! Have you seen my pearls lying around anywhere?'

The young man she calls Panther skips somewhat foolishly
into the room, dancing like a boxer from one foot to the
other.

'Which pearls, darling?'

'The Cees van Dongen pearls, caro. You know the ones!'

'Around your neck, darling. You're wearing them around
your neck.'

'God, I'm hopeless! Come here, you little animal, give me a
kiss!'

The young man seems to have been cast in bronze. He goes
and stands behind her, wraps his oiled arms around her waist,
lifts her up like a porcelain doll, kisses her, growling, on the
neck, then sticks his fleshy tongue in her ear.

'Don't be so wild,' she whispers without conviction,
purring, moaning.

'You smell delicious.'

'Opopanax. Goes with the dress.'

'Stay with me this evening.'

'Panther! You're squeezing me to death!'

Panther has two passions in life: poetry and body building. He has already published a collection of song lyrics at his own expense, under the pseudonym Arthur Rambo. His real name is Jan Wouters and he was born in 1969 in the Zwartzuster-straat. Suzanna met him last year in December, deep beneath the Suikerrui, during the *vernissage* of the avant-garde installation *Art in the Sewers*. She was wearing Jane Fonda's plastic body armour from *Barbarella*. He was earning a little extra by walking around awkwardly with cardboard beakers of luke-warm regional beer, but she continues to insist that he is no less than the grandson of Elmo Lincoln, 'the Tarzan of Tarzans', who triumphed in 1921 in the series *The Adventures of Tarzan*. She claims to have spoken to him for the first time at Sotheby's in London during the auction of the complete wardrobe of the Great Western Producing Company. He had supposedly followed her like a lap dog, slept in front of her door, gone on hunger-strike and even threatened to cut his throat unless she let him in. But everybody knows she is addicted to her athlete and is keeping him, just as she has kept all her former gigolos. This is so entirely in keeping with her eccentric personality that nobody even thinks of objecting.

Suzanna wriggles free and plants her blue nails in his tensed chest muscles.

'Are you sure you don't want to come along?' she asks; while Ingrid Bergman leans on the piano, opposite Dooley Wilson who is dreaming away with a wide grin in a luminous cloud of smoke.

'Play it again, Sam,' she says, gazing with a promising glint in her eyes at Humphrey Bogart, who is sitting a little further at a round table talking to Sydney Greenstreet.

Arthur realises only too well how much Suzanna likes to brag about him to her girlfriends and that he must not always let her have her way, that this profitable relationship will only continue if her desires sometimes remain unsatisfied, if he teaches her to wait, to yearn, to beg and suffer.

'You know how shy I feel amongst all those celebrities. They're your friends, not mine. I don't know what to say to those people.'

'Stop bellyaching. They are all crazy about you.'

'Besides, it's so hot . . . I'm not made for this sort of heat.'

'You seem to be married to the winter!'

He looks at her with his big, misty eyes. Sometimes he hasn't got the faintest idea what she is talking about.

'Anyway, I can feel something bubbling up inside me. An intricate little verse has been buzzing around in my head for a couple of weeks now. Perhaps I'll try to get it down on paper this evening. Or maybe I'll do some stomach muscle exercises. I'm behind on my schedule. Or maybe I'll watch our latest videos . . .'

'It wouldn't do your career any harm.'

'Drop it. Bawling at posh people in the middle of a laser show is nothing for me.'

'We need them, Panther, don't underestimate them.'

'You're the only thing I need.'

She melts. The Bay of Naples looms behind him. She hears mandolins, strokes his broad youthful shoulders, caresses his tattoo: a stalking black panther.

'I won't be late, I promise.'

'Aren't you forgetting something?'

She sinks to her knees in front of him, opens the zips of his leather Rizzoni briefs one by one, closes her eyes and kisses his balls. The cordless telephone rings on the Bang & Olufsen. Without getting up, Suzanna claws for the white receiver and pulls out the aerial.

'Pronto!'

4

'Suzanna?'

'Mmmm . . .'

'It's me.'

Ava wedges the receiver between chin and collarbone while she paints the nail of her left little finger dark red. Paloma Picasso red.

When she had been introduced to Suzanna by the alderman for the port, at a cocktail party in the Osterriethhuis, an eighteenth-century mansion, a couple of weeks ago (Suzanna was wearing the original outfit Faye Dunaway had worn in *Bonnie and Clyde*) Ava had instantly succumbed to the charm of the eccentric fashion designer. Ever since then, the two friends have phoned each other at least five times a day.

'Are you ready?'

'Almost,' Suzanna giggles.

'We'll pick you both up within a half an hour.'

'That's all I need.' She looks up at the swollen veins in the neck of Arthur, who is leaning back with both arms on the television and has closed his eyes.

'Would you believe I'm nervous?'

'You must be crazy! Tonight you'll be the queen. You'll soon be up to your neck in flowers and compliments!'

'That's exactly what I'm afraid of! I hate that film!'

'*Desert Flower?*'

'Come on, Suzanna, the title alone!'

'Now I'm really curious. What on earth is wrong with it?'

'Everything! I'm so ashamed I could die.'

'Shame! That's a feeling I've never experienced.'

'I didn't spend four years at drama school just so I could rush around the desert with a burning candle stuck up my arse!'

'Oh God, sweetie, as long as you're in the spotlight . . .'

Displacing too much air and chewing on a dead cigar, Ted strolls into the bedroom. Beads of sweat are rolling down his crimson forehead from beneath a cropped covering of yellow fluff that looks like a wig. His buttoned-up dinner jacket is so tight that he has difficulty bending his stubby arm to look at his gold Rolex.

'I don't want to hassle you, lamb-chop, but it is nine-thirty. And if we want to arrive there at midnight . . .'

'Suzy, we have to leave right away. Ted is even more nervous than I am. Quickly: what are you wearing?'

'Surprise! You'll see soon enough.'

'We're on our way. See you in a moment!' Ava replaces the receiver.

'I'm not a bit nervous,' mumbles Ted. 'I've never been nervous in my entire life!'

Ava springs up and whirls through the bedroom like a metal spinning top. Her dress is so tight that Ted momentarily has the impression she is naked and has sprayed her body with silver paint.

'How do I look?'

'Much too beautiful,' he sighs, and sinks down into an ivory-coloured sofa.

What he means is: much too beautiful for the others, for the profiteers who will be lusting for her in the darkness for free, for the layabouts, for the toadies and the journalists who will be jostling each other to get into a photo with her, for the ministry lackeys who will be trying to paw her with their clammy hands, for the nobodies, the parasites, the Brussels intellectuals, the stiff-upper-lips, the flatterers, the hypocrites, the worms. Not for him. Nothing is too beautiful for him. He has earned her, just as he has earned everything he possesses. He has sweated blood and tears for her, slaved his whole life long, without ever asking anyone for any help. He has created her and this evening he will be showing her off to the people, to the rabble. He blesses again the day on which he decided to leave his drunken parents and the barracks of Leopoldsburg, to get rich, very rich, and no longer to have to but only to want to, and to see the others crawling at his feet in their turn with their tails between their legs. Revenge, that is what this evening is all about. Revenge.

A slightly dizzy Ava comes to sit beside Ted and cuddles up against him gingerly.

'I'm scared, Ted.'

This is what he loves the most: guarding her, teaching her to fly. Knowing that without his protective wing she would tumble from the nest.

'There's no need for you to worry about anything, pigeon,' he soothes her, stroking her dark hair with his stubby paw. 'Daddy has taken care of everything, like always.'

He has indeed left nothing to chance. *Desert Flower* must be and will be a hit. He has sweetened those who needed sweetening, dined with the press; even Rudy Mentary, the feared columnist and his school fellow at the Jesuit primary school in Grobbendonk, has promised to be mild for once in memory of their hard childhood.

'I've got this strange misgiving.' Her voice suddenly sounds more serious, less girlish than a moment ago. Ted sees how her pale hands disappear between her black, shimmering thighs, a little above her closed knees.

'You're the best.'

'It's not that.'

'So what is it?'

'I know it sounds stupid, but . . . Those horrible murders. You know — you can't open a newspaper without reading about that monster; what's his name again?'

'M. Nobody knows his real name.'

'M, right. How many has he butchered already?'

'I don't know. Five, or so?'

'And it just so happens that all five came from the Netherlands. And it just so happens that all five were in show business, right?'

'More or less. But they were all third-rate actresses, porn starlets, strippers, prostitutes. The bottom of the barrel. Not one of them an Ava Palomba!'

'Oh no? And what about Peggy then? Last week. Slashed to pieces!'

'Peggy was a totally overrated talent. A lousy actress.'

Ava gets up slowly and walks to the window, looks at the motionless bushes and the black, pruned shrubs in the grounds.

'I sometimes feel like I'm being spied on.'

'Impossible.'

'As if somebody's lying in wait for me.'

'You're just imagining things,' lies Ted, who is aware of the impending danger but wants to reassure Ava. Especially on an evening such as this one.

'You can't be careful enough, Ted. A bodyguard wouldn't exactly be a luxury this evening.'

'If anybody has to watch over this divine body, then it'll be me.'

He comes and stands beside her and kisses the tip of her nose with his wet lips. And she doesn't know why, but for the first time she feels something turn to stone in her belly. A cold shiver runs down her back.

'Come on, a real lady always arrives on time.'

Leaning against the bonnet of the limousine, Mercury lights his last cigarette. Soon, during the journey, Vangenechte will not let him smoke. In the distance, he can hear the vague roar of the Antwerp-Breda motorway and closer by, hidden in the crown of the chestnut tree opposite the entrance to the villa, the hooting of an owl. It is going to be a moonless night.

5

With her mask of bilious green dried-up cream, and with two slices of cucumber covering her eyes, Cindy Beaver looks like a dead lizard. She is lying, as if in state, in the middle of the burgundy counterpane of the wide Louis XV bed in the suite she is sharing with her seventy-six-year-old husband, the agent Richard Weinberg, in De Rosier, the Antwerp hotel where the stars stay. The suite of Nureyev, Bowie, Sting, Keith Haring, Marlene Dietrich and a host of other celebrities, Monsieur Bob the owner had assured them yesterday when he had shown them their suite. She puffs on a black Sobranie, purses her chapped lips and blows smoke rings. A sign of life.

In the adjoining drawing room, Richard is sitting in his old-fashioned dinner jacket, white carnation in buttonhole. He is watching the final scene of *Casablanca* – the two raincoats' moving farewell, the aeroplane waiting in the misty background with whirling propellers – and remembering when he met Bogey, in 1955, on the set of *The Desperate Hours*, the film in which he had cast Beverly Garland as Miss Swift. Bogart was already very ill, but they would remain friends until his death of throat cancer on 14 January 1957.

With the neck-brace which supports his head and with which he has been plagued since his fall in 1989, Richard, like all who wear that aristocratic instrument of torture, bears a marked resemblance to Erich von Stroheim. He harbours a burning hatred for everyone who comes trotting out with that predictable cliché.

The fossilised reptile on the bed, twenty-eight years old last week, is his sixth wife and the stylish old man has no illusions about her motivation as far as their marriage is concerned. Her hours of glory are already long behind her. After a promising debut, she had gone straight downhill, aided by what she considers to be a 'fashionable' alcohol problem. She is now working without much conviction on a comeback, in the hope that Richard – on whom in her rare moments of lucidity she lavishes unnecessary and not entirely unselfseeking care, like an ambitious nurse – will again secure a major role for her.

Because Ted Harlow wants Ava to be under contract to Richard Weinberg, he has invited the old fox and his latest conquest to the premiere of the unabridged version of *Desert Flower*, and offered them a suite in the very expensive De Rosier. Richard, who has never been in Antwerp, considers it a unique opportunity for him to go and admire the portrait of Giovanni de Cardida, by Hans Memling, his favourite painter, in the Museum of Fine Art, and has accepted the unexpected invitation.

'Richard?' The mask has spoken and cracks at the corners of the mouth. 'Have you still got a drop of that Parfait Amour?'

Richard struggles to his feet and checks whether there is still a drop of the sweet liqueur in the purple bottle.

'I'm afraid not, bevvy,' he lies and shuffles to the bedroom, where he comes to the disconcerting discovery that his wife is still lying on the bed.

'Cindy! You realise they're coming to pick us up within a quarter of an hour?'

She struggles upright and removes the slices of cucumber from her eyes, which are the same green as the crust on her face.

'No problem, darling. I won't be a moment. I wasn't planning to make much effort anyway. After all, it's not my evening.'

'What do you mean?' Richard asks, caressing a bulbous, milky Lalique vase, which represents a pineapple.

'Don't be such a hypocrite, Rich. This evening all the

attention will be going to that young cow. She's even got you to shift yourself! Because she's what we've come here for, isn't she?'

'For Ava and for Hans.'

'Which Hans?'

'Hans Memling, bevvy.'

'Never heard of him. Is he also in *Desert Flower*?'

While she is saying this she saunters to the bathroom, drops her dressing gown on the rug – a sixteenth-century Kirman – and glides into the marble-floor bath, where she disappears up to her chin in a cloud of light blue bubbles. With a soft sponge, she wipes away the dissolving mask, until her face finally becomes visible between the green smears: she has a perfect, straight nose, high cheekbones and a wide, greedy mouth with pale, full lips. Richard has always had an eye for women who could fade with style. Even without make-up, Cindy is attractive, almost to the point of vulgarity. She also resembles his previous wives.

She toys with the delicate silver chain around her right ankle, a souvenir of her brief relationship with Peggy, who shared a room with her in Amsterdam and who died last week in gruesome circumstances.

'I'd rather not even go!' she calls from her bath. 'What's the point of hanging around there the whole night like a piece of discarded furniture?'

'Here we go again,' sighs Richard, who is used to this sort of caprice from his young bride. After six failed marriages he is beginning to get wise to the mysterious twists and turns of the female soul, and therefore knows how to react.

'Good idea! You have a nice soak in the bath. Shall I ring for another bottle of Dom Perignon?'

'That's right! I'll just drown myself in drink, while the master parades around with his latest discovery!'

'But, treasure, I promised Ted.'

'I'd sooner drown in this bloody bath than spend a single minute in a limousine with that bleached-blond cretin!'

'You're behaving like a child.'

'Of course I am! I'm young enough to be your granddaughter!'

'My granddaughter doesn't drink, doesn't snort, is currently making her debut in the new Almodóvar and I'm going to the bar.'

Richard does not wait for an answer. He winds his white scarf around his injured neck, turns off his hearing aid, enjoying the ensuing silence, and leaves the suite with a deep sigh of relief. Cindy reminds him of Joan Crawford, for whom he had cherished an unrequited passion for years. He therefore knows that within five minutes she will appear in the hall, hidden behind dark glasses, with wet, combed-back hair and a disarming smile, as if everything is simply wonderful. That is why he married her: because she reminds him of love, because he has always been an enthusiastic bridegroom, and also a bit for the down on her thighs.

6

When Ted and Ava finally appear at the top of the steps in the light of the halogen lamps beneath the pediment of the portico, Mercury discreetly stamps out his cigarette, takes off his cap and opens the door of the limousine.

As he is helping Ava step into the car in her tight dress, he catches a glimpse of her breasts in the shadow of her décolletage. He holds his breath in order to retain her scent as long as possible. She smells of the sun and Chanel No.5 and through his gloves, her hand feels unreal, exactly like it does when he touches her in his dreams.

'Thank you, Mercury.' Her voice has never sounded so intimate.

'Good evening, madame. Madame looks divine. I'm sure it will be an unforgettable night,' he whispers, amazed at what he has just heard himself say, as if somebody else had uttered the words that sprang to his lips. She sinks back into the deep seats with a mischievous smile, and he could almost swear that she has winked at him. Mercury steps back two paces to allow Vangenechte – he has never been able to bring himself to call him Ted Harlow – to also step into the car. Then he carefully shuts the door and night falls over the couple in the car behind the smoked-glass window. He puts his cap back on, jauntily, as if he has been doing it his whole life, walks around the eight-metre-long car and takes his place behind the steering wheel. The limousine starts to move, slowly and silently, like a ship laboriously pulling away from the quay, and then glides out of sight through the whispering tunnel of ancient red beeches.

Mercury looks in his wide mirror and sees in CinemaScope

how Ava crosses her legs, how Vangenechte lays his fleshy paw on her garter, how he clumsily tries to kiss her in the neck and imagines with horror the even greater clumsiness with which he sometimes fucks her in the grotesque four-poster bed. The monstrous copulation of a manatee and an Afghan hound. 'I bet he keeps his socks on,' thinks Mercury. He shudders at the thought that, so close to his goal, he will have to watch that revolting spectacle on the back seat powerlessly all the way to Brussels.

'What do you want to drink?' asks Ted, opening the mahogany bar in which some dozen crystal decanters are tinkling.

'Just a Perrier.'

'Ice?'

'Ice. And a slice of lemon.'

'A Perrier with ice and lemon for the lady!' Ted shouts with exaggerated gaiety, as his free hand disappears into the fridge. 'And for me, a cognac. I've earned it!'

Like everything.

Ted pours the two drinks and turns on the CD player with the remote control. Dean Martin's voice resounds from the eight tiny loudspeakers. 'One for the Road'. In the faint light of the ceiling-lamp, he hands Ava her glass with a solemn gesture.

'To your triumph, lamb-chop. A star is born!'

He downs his cognac in a single gulp and immediately refills his glass to the brim.

'Slow down,' says Ava. 'We've still got a long night ahead of us.'

'Don't you worry. I'm from Leopoldsburg. We can take it.'

How high-spirited, self-assured and boisterous he is, as if the whole world is at his feet, simply because he is being driven around with a beautiful woman like some bloated king. Mercury is gasping for a cigarette. To him she is the real riddle in this peculiar pair. What possible reason could Ava have had for moving in with a pompous, pretentious scab like Vangenechte, unless she is just the same as all the others and is only interested in vulgar show, easy roles and a superficial, carefree life. Is owning a castle in Brasschaat, with a swimming pool and some servants, being on the board of a few companies, running a pig farm and posing as a film producer really enough to turn the heads of simple souls? Are money and arrogance truly the ultimate weapons? Does even somebody like Ava have her price? He catches her eye in the mirror. She never looks at Vangenechte like that, he thinks. Either she loves to play with fire, or she is desperately trying to attract my attention, wants to confess her secret, beg for my help. Perhaps I'm mistaken and Vangenechte is blackmailing her, keeping her prisoner and humiliating her daily, just like John Drake, the sombre villain in *Desert Flower*?

The wrought-iron gate at the main entrance to the grounds swings slowly open. Ted picks up the telephone and presses twice on button one. It is the only way he can communicate with Mercury, since in the classic Lincoln Stretch the chauffeur up front is separated from the passengers by a thick glass partition.

Mercury picks up the receiver.

'Sir?'

'First we pick up Suzanna Rizzoni and her latest acquisition. Then we stop a moment at De Rosier to collect the Weinbergs. And, Mercury, we're none too early.'

'As you wish, sir.' Both men replace their receiver simultaneously.

The limousine pulls out of the estate. In the distance, behind the caretaker's lodge, the Dobermanns are barking, as they always do when the monumental gate creaks in its hinges.

'I never perspire,' says Ava, sipping on her Perrier, 'but if I do perspire, then it's under my breasts.'

Ted gazes with bulging eyes at the two dark, horizontal stripes on her dress and turns up the air-conditioning.

7

In the Pepermansstraat, which runs parallel to the high, brick-walled railway embankment alongside Brussels North Station, Van Laken and Courtois are stuck in a shuffling procession of cars. From their red and blue lit windows on the left side of the street, the whores wave like fleshy robots at the anonymous phantoms trudging past in the night, knead their tired breasts, finger their taffeta hotpants, give their index fingers a hand job, suck on their thumbs, press their black fishnet stockinged behinds against the window, point at their arses, caress their generous buttocks, touch the tips of their noses with their curled, fluorescent tongues, stroke their nipples with whips, lick plastic penises – a moving and provocative ritual that Van Laken, leaning up against Courtois, studies from within the car.

'No wonder one of them goes crazy every now and then,' he growls. Courtois, who occasionally leafs through an art book, says that each window resembles a hyperrealistic painting, that the atmosphere reminds him of Hopper, to which Van Laken sombrely and jealously answers that the languid ballet in the overlit rectangles reminds him more of the aquarium in Antwerp Zoo.

'Who knows, perhaps it's that guy in the Volvo in front of us,' he sighs. 'Look at his numberplate: MMM–327.'

Courtois laughs politely. His stomach rumbles. Maybe he should have eaten something in Antwerp.

'Do you really think he'll dare to show himself this evening?' Courtois asks, as he rolls down his window and leans outside, gasping for fresh air. 'On a Tuesday?'

'So far he has always murdered his victims on a Monday. But there is nothing to stop him going out on the other days.'

'To do research?'

'For example.'

'Okay. Suppose M does attend the premiere of *Desert Flower* this evening. How can we recognise him?'

'No idea.'

'He naturally won't be running the slightest risk.'

'You know, a couple of days ago, I woke up screaming and wet with sweat from a terrible nightmare, in which I tied Maartje to a hairdresser's chair and hacked her to pieces. For a moment I wondered whether M was me.'

'Don't worry. Your alibis are rock solid. Besides, you're not the type.'

'That's true. I'm too romantic.' Van Laken lights a new cigarette with the burning butt of the previous one. 'And yet I have this strange feeling I'm going to shake his hand this evening and immediately know it's him.'

'I reckon he's exhausted after his antics yesterday in the aquarium.'

'The actress in the film, what's her name again . . .'

'Ava Palomba.'

'Ava Palomba, thank you, Courtois. Her profile is exactly the same as that of the previous victims. And yet she is still planning to attend the premiere, isn't she?'

'That's why we've come to Brussels.'

'Precisely. And because it's been proved that M already knows the girls he butchers and it is therefore not out of the question that he'll try to approach her this evening. It's that simple.'

'Everyone will be wanting to have a word with her.'

'Don't be so damned negative, Courtois. And watch the road. You could have gone hours ago.'

'Sorry.'

'Besides, this time the orders have come from higher up.

Edward Vangenechte, the producer, is a personal friend of you know who. So mind what you say, later on.'

Courtois is not immediately sure to whom Van Laken is referring, but it sounded important and self-evident enough for him to nod in complicity. Not only will he mind what he says, he won't even open his mouth.

The grey Opel moves off again in the direction of the city centre. On the wall to their right, some inspired artist has painted a giant M in yellow paint and sprayed underneath it 'is watching you, ladies'. But as they drive by, neither Van Laken nor Courtois has time to read this tasteless warning.

8

Five years ago, when no respectable person would have dreamt of living in 'The Island', a slum neighbourhood surrounded by canals and locks to the north of Antwerp, Suzanna Rizzoni, who had seen the rapid rebirth of Soho where she ran a boutique, had bought a draughty, disused sugared almond factory, in a godforsaken neighbourhood full of abandoned warehouses, rusting packing sheds and crumbling storehouses, amongst cafés with bricked-up windows and stinking docks full of the sinking carcasses of redundant tugboats. With the help of the most controversial decorators, she had transformed it into a hyperluxurious, one-and-a-half thousand square metre loft. It is now the Antwerp in-crowd's bleakest and starkest inhabitation, a further testament to her infallible avant-garde taste and proof that she is a relentlessly astute businesswoman. In the same neighbourhood today, even the tiniest and most uninviting bedsit costs the earth.

The limousine makes a wide, stately turn on the paved courtyard of what is now called 'The Rizzoni Factory', and pulls up in front of the brightly neon-lit entrance hall. Above the wide, granite, Perspex and steel portal, the brick façade is embellished with a gigantic, vertical, silver graffito of a closed zip-fastener. It is the work of the young New Zealand conceptual artist Jeff McLover, whose work can also be admired in the permanent collection of the Ghent Museum of Modern Art, which had purchased his world-shaking, six-metre-high 'Thimble of Mink' the year before on Mrs Rizzoni's recommendation.

Mercury gets out, rings the bell – a melodic hum that

reminds him of the first bars of Fauré's *Pavane*, performed by Branford Marsalis – and is just about to talk to the lens of the video camera that is pointing at him, when Suzanna appears in the entrance hall, followed by Arthur who is fastening a roomy, imitation leopard-skin dressing gown over his sculpted stomach muscles.

'That buffoon is not coming with us like that,' hisses Ted. '"Evening wear obligatory", it said so on the invitation.'

In the doorway, Arthur kisses Suzanna on both cheeks without touching her, so as not to spoil her make-up. He then waves to Ted and Ava, who he can see sitting in the car, through the open side window. Mercury escorts Suzanna to the car and opens the heavy door for her. As she gets in, she casts an admiring glance at the young chauffeur.

'Suzy, darling, what a simply enchanting dress!' Ava shouts excitedly, before Suzanna has even had time to sit down.

'Isn't Arthur coming?' asks Ted, feigning deep disappointment. 'What a shame! I was so looking forward to it! The more the merrier, that's what we always say in Limburg. But what the heck. It's his loss, isn't it? So then. Sit wherever you like, Suzanna. And I have to agree, it is a lovely outfit. Incredibly original. Thirsty?'

'Thirsty? No. But I wouldn't say no to a drink.'

'That's what I like to hear!'

Ava has never seen Ted so excited.

'Champagne?'

'With a drop of orange juice, if that's possible.'

'A hydrangea! How delightfully old-fashioned!' he shouts, as he uncorks a bottle of Dom Perignon.

'A mimosa,' Suzanna corrects him, 'not a hydrangea, Ted, a mimosa.'

'You and Arthur aren't fighting, I hope?' Ava asks, as she gazes through the rear window at Arthur, who is disappearing back into the hall of the murky building.

'Of course not, sweetie! But when inspiration calls, he has to write. Poets! Big children the lot of them: sensitive, insecure, dependent creatures, full of contradictions, even when they're bulging with muscles.'

Ted hands her a slender glass, filled with a golden, effervescent concoction.

'That looks absolutely fabulous. Mimosas are right back in fashion,' she says, stretching out her long legs, which almost reach the opposite seat. The interior fills with the scent of Opopanax.

Mercury leaves the courtyard via a narrow alley, just wide enough to allow the monumental limousine to pass. Ava is staring dreamily into the distance.

'You're so quiet, sweetie.'

'I'm looking at your dress.'

'The great Sarah Bernhardt once wore it.'

Ava feels the soft fabric.

'How thrilling; how *poignant*.'

'It fits you like a glove,' says Ted, totally missing the point. 'But of course, you're also great.'

'It took me a while to make up my mind,' Suzanna says coquettishly, 'because at the same auction, I also bought a sublime Redfern evening gown, one that had belonged to Miss Helen Wederburn and that George Hoyningen Huene had photographed in 1931 for French *Vogue*. Long, tight, eggshell-white silk velvet, low cut back, gorgeous, but perhaps just a little too grand for this evening. So, spill the beans!'

'Is there anything you don't yet know?' laughs Ava.

Suzanna points over her shoulder to the driver's cabin.

'I want to hear all about your new chauffeur. Handsome devil! Aren't you jealous, Ted?'

'Handsome but poor!' Ted answers, too quickly, too loud. 'And the most expensive women are the women you don't have to pay for, isn't that right, pigeon?' He bursts out laughing and tries to pinch Ava's cheek, but she slips from the seat and sits opposite him, next to Suzanna.

Mercury is relieved when he sees in the mirror that she is no longer sitting next to Vangenechte. They are now driving along the quays, the car rocking up and down over the subsided cobblestones.

'Can't you turn down that racket?' Ava snaps.

'Frankie Lane?' Ted shouts indignantly. 'The most beautiful voice since Caruso! Outrageous!' But he lowers the volume of the music until it's almost inaudible.

'I can't refuse her anything,' he adds confidentially, grinning stupidly at Suzanna.

'What's the angel called?' The two women are cuddled together, like two giggling school girls in one bed after lights-out in a boarding school dormitory.

'Mercury,' answer Ava and Ted in chorus.

'Nobody was talking to you, Ted!' Suzanna teases. 'This is girl talk.'

'Well,' says Ava. 'He's a quiet, polite young man. A bit withdrawn. I hardly ever see him. He lives alone, in the flat above the garage at the bottom of the grounds, never has visitors and tinkers with the cars the whole day. The last chauffeur, who I scarcely got to know, was warmer, more human. He was more a part of . . . a part of the family.'

'If he ever turns up again, I'll be happy to take Mercury off your hands!' Suzanna laughs, as she takes a small box of cigarillos out of her Poiret handbag.

'I thought you didn't have a car?'

'Who needs one, Ted? I drink when I'm not thirsty, don't I?' Her voice is deep, cavernous, seductive. 'Have you got a light?'

'Ted Harlow never reemploys people who have betrayed him,' he says, as he passes her his Dupont. 'Never! That's a golden rule.'

'Uncle Bens didn't betray you, he simply disappeared,' says Ava.

'Even worse!' Coughing and consequently spilling, Ted refills his glass.

'He left everything behind, his clothes, his personal papers, his souvenirs, everything. Strange. Even that crumpled photo of his mother with the missionaries, in front of their hut somewhere in the Belgian Congo, that he was so attached to . . .'

'Yes. And I had the whole lot burnt. Traitors should be wiped out without a trace. Cheers!' Ted tries to soothe his fit of coughing with a big gulp of cognac.

9

When Courtois tries to turn into the Lomméstraat behind the Madouplein, the car is stopped by a local policeman in dress uniform. All cars going to the Rex have to be checked, for security reasons. Van Laken presses his police ID against the windscreen.

'Excuse me, commissaris. Orders . . .'

'That's all right, lad. Drive on, Courtois.'

The young policeman salutes and allows them to proceed.

The Rex is one of the last of Brussels' local cinemas. Thanks to the passionate efforts of the film-loving, homosexual couple Patrick de Busschère and Sylvain Knopff, it was saved from destruction and did not get torn apart by sledgehammers, or end up as a furniture shop, auction room or supermarket. Over the years, this historic temple of film has taken on a truly mythical aura and it is therefore the perfect setting in which to stage exceptional events, such as this evening's screening. A midnight premiere is unusual in Belgium, but Ted Harlow, who has read that it is all the rage in Hollywood, wants it that way and has therefore spared no expense in turning the Lomméstraat into Sunset Boulevard for one night. The first screening of the uncut version of *Desert Flower* will long remain etched in the memories of the numerous guests: an extraordinary, unforgettable event.

'Glamour! Glamour!' he had shouted in his penthouse office in the Antwerp Tower when the cinema bosses had asked him how he envisaged the premiere.

He has had hundreds of imported Italian palm trees planted in pots in front of the brightly lit, art deco façade of the Rex and for more than two hundred metres the paving stones have disappeared beneath a smooth layer of fine white sand that is supposed to evoke the desert. A red carpet has been rolled out between a double row of burning torches on the stairs that lead up to the foyer. Criss-crossing searchlights illuminate the sky above Brussels. Over the whole width of the complex, the magic words *Desert Flower* are burning in gigantic white neon letters and beneath that, flashing on and off in pink letters, 'starring Ava Palomba', and beneath that, a little smaller, 'introducing Dirk Cools', and under that, even smaller but still striking enough, in golden letters, 'Produced by Ted Harlow'. The line 'Directed by Steve Mendeiros' is not illuminated. Striking but classy, de Busschère, who used to be an interior decorator, had assured him over the telephone.

On the opposite side of the street, the 'fans' – extras hired by Harlow Productions – are jostling each other behind iron barriers to catch a glimpse of the first dolled-up couples that climb the steps to the Rex. There are only five steps and yet most of the guests imagine themselves in Cannes during the festival and clumsily try to imitate its ritual. Stupefied by the blinding light of dozens of flash bulbs young actresses, cooing with delight and almost overcome by emotion, are writhing provocatively for the photographers, striking 'cheesecake poses' and waving to anonymous admirers. They suspect nothing, and above all, they do not realise that M may be waiting in the whooping crowd, motionless, like a spider, calmly choosing his next victim from a distance.

'The security measures are impressive,' Courtois observes, as he parks the Opel in a dead-end alley next to the cinema.

After all, it is only the premiere of an erotic film, even if the cream of the *beau monde* has been invited. If it wasn't for the troubled atmosphere of terror into which M has plunged the film world, such a show of strength would have been unthinkable.

Van Laken and Courtois get out. It is even hotter than in

Antwerp: the humid, oppressive heat that heralds a thunder-storm. In the distance they hear the wailing siren of an ambulance.

'Looks like Sarajevo!' Courtois shouts, hoping a touch of irony will help his boss to relax. 'All that's missing are a couple of lost UN blue-berets!'

'He's here, I can feel it,' says Van Laken, who loves to make such theatrical, barely articulated pronouncements. He lights a cigarette with his noisy Zippo, takes a deep breath, slowly exhales the smoke, narrows his eyes and looks around at the zinc roofs, the dark, moss-covered walls, the dead windows with shattered panes. He gazes at the almost illegible remains of a rusty Michelin advertisement, at the sagging iron garage door at the end of the alley, at the still puddles filmed with blue-green oil in which an ink-black sky, surprisingly full of stars, is reflected.

'Courtois, my lad, we could be in for an exciting night.'

Courtois had already experienced many such unexpected flickers of optimism. They usually meant Van Laken is close to total breakdown and is making a rather crude attempt to keep up his spirits. Since his wife left him to move in with her hairdresser, without a word of explanation and moreover without the slightest warning, Van Laken has become a vulnerable, melancholy man, who sometimes shows human traits which make him appear almost congenial. At such moments he is like a tragic comic book character, a burnt-out hero, and out of compassion for him Courtois would go through fire.

'So,' says Courtois, clearing his throat, 'what else is there on the agenda?'

'You try to find out who is in charge here and whether there's anything to eat. I'm going to mingle with the crowd in the palm grove. And Courtois, remember to breathe in deeply.' Van Laken taps the tip of his nose with his index finger. 'I can smell him!'

Courtois notices how long Van Laken's fingernails have become, now that his wife is no longer there to manicure them.

''im or M?' he answers jokingly.

'Very funny! Rendezvous in ten minutes at the top of the steps.'

Ethereal cosmic sounds and sensual rhythmic panting are resounding from the loudspeakers hidden in the palm trees in front of the Rex: the subtle soundtrack of *Desert Flower*.

10

The face of Mercury, who classes even Gershwin as a variety artist, cramps in a pained grimace when the same, ethereal tones suddenly replace the crooning of Frankie Lane in the loudspeakers of the limousine. Vangenechte has put the cassette of *Desert Flower* into the built-in JVC multi-system colour RGB monitor video recorder and is watching the opening scene of his latest production with a blissful smile: a never-ending asphalt road shimmering in the blazing sun, running straight as an arrow through the desert. To the right of the picture, under a merciless blue sky, Ava stumbles into view in tattered summer clothes, from behind a cactus. Music. Overprint: New Mexico – Almogrado Desert – 4 p.m.

'Pure class if I ever saw it!' shouts Ted. 'Just look at the tension in that shot, at that emptiness, at that black ribbon leading nowhere, the symbol of our schizophrenia! And Ava! Look at that presence, that haughtiness, that pride! And the audience doesn't even realise she has just been raped by eight illegal Mexican seasonal labourers. You only find that out in the torrid confession scene with the bogus priest . . . No, I can't see that saturated sponge, what's her name again, Weinberg's wife . . .'

'Cindy Beaver.'

'Cindy, right, I can't see her doing that!'

'You look really sexy in those tattered shorts,' says Suzanna. 'What are they? Kookai?'

'This is so embarrassing,' mumbles Ava. 'Can't that wait a while, Ted? We'll be seeing it soon on the big screen.'

'As you wish, pigeon, although I myself just can't get

enough of it. You mark my words, ladies. Either I'm very mistaken – which would be a first for me – or this will be the box-office hit of the decade!'

Ted presses a button in the armrest of the back seat and the picture disappears, exactly at the moment that Mercury, sighing with relief, parks the car on the pavement in front of the door of De Rosier.

He gets out and walks through the corridor of the restored cloister, past the Gobelin and Kortrijk tapestries, to the courtyard garden, where Richard Weinberg is sitting bolt upright on a Renaissance chair beneath a golden-yellow ginkgo – according to Monsieur Bob the only tree to survive Hiroshima – reading an old copy of *Knack*. Mercury looks over his shoulder and reads the title of the article: 'M, monster and judge. Profile of a serial killer.' Feeble piece, thinks Mercury, who had gone through it thoroughly the previous week.

'Mr Weinberg?'

The motionless old man is so engrossed in his reading that he does not react. Mercury is obliged to tap him cautiously on the shoulder.

'Mr Weinberg?'

Richard starts, slaps shut the magazine, springs to his feet and turns his hearing-aid back on.

'Excuse me, but Mr Vangen ... I mean, Mr Harlow is waiting for you outside in the car. Would you be so kind as to ...'

Richard casts a quick, probing glance at Mercury, whose stylish manners he seems to appreciate.

'Certainly, young man, certainly.'

With his dignified gait, which is partly due to his fractured cervical vertebrae, he follows Mercury, who opens the door of the limousine for him cap in hand. Ted's hoarse voice rings out from inside the car.

'Richie-boy, you old rogue! Come and join us!'

A sprightly, rotund dwarf springs out of a Renault 5, parked further up on the other side of the street, and begins to take photos frantically as he dashes towards the limousine. Mercury glances uneasily at Ted, who signals to him to let the man continue.

'Those chaps have to earn a living too.'

He has probably hired the photographer himself, thinks Mercury, discreetly turning away so as not to be included in the photos.

Richard, who can scarcely bend over and has to sag at the knees to get into the car, seems to find it annoying to be photographed in such a ludicrous position. He wriggles inside as nimbly as possible, kisses Ava's hand and, groaning and exhausted, plops down beside Ted, who immediately introduces him to Suzanna.

'Suzanna Rizzoni, the queen of the zip-fastener!'

'Weinberg. Richard Weinberg. Honoured to meet you, Madame Rizzoni.' He extends his hand, but they are sitting so far apart that he barely touches her blue lacquered nails.

'Wasn't I right when I said he looked like von Strohalm?' Ted adds triumphantly.

'Von Stroheim,' corrects Richard, tartly but politely, 'Von Stroheim. It's not the first time somebody's made that observation.' Drop dead, man, he thinks, now you can whistle for that contract for your girlfriend.

'You remind me more of Prince Ottokar Ladislaus von Wildeliebe-Rauffenburg,' Richard continues seriously, imitating von Stroheim's Austrian accent, 'his Majesty's Chamberlain, Lord Steward, General of Cavalry and Captain of all the Guards!'

'A prince! Couldn't be anything else!' Ted beams.

'A film prince,' Richard corrects him, 'played by George Fawcett in *The Wedding March*, which I'm sure you know.'

'Wonderful film.' Ted's voice sounds anything but convinced.

'Isn't Cindy coming along?' asks Ava.

'Just a second ago, she still wasn't sure. Migraine. I suggest we wait for a moment. You've come to know her in the meantime, Ted: when she says no, that usually means yes.'

'Like most women!' Ted guffaws. 'Fickle, insecure, not to be trusted, irresponsible! And yet we can't keep away from them! What are you drinking?'

'Nothing for the moment, thank you.' Richard is just about to feign some malaise and escape from the car when Cindy appears in the corridor.

'Well don't wait for me!' Mercury looks over his shoulder, surprised, opens the door again and helps her into the car with imperturbable gallantry. She is wearing tight jeans, fashionably torn just above the knees, Charles Jourdan cowboy boots and a white T-shirt. A supple Fendi shoulder bag is hanging from her right shoulder. Her hair is still wet, as was to be expected, and is combed back flatly. Her eyes are hidden behind large, all-concealing sunglasses. In her left ear sparkles a diamond, the value of which Ted estimates at half of the budget of *Desert Flower*. He finds such ostentatious details the height of vulgarity, but he grins and bears it, because today is a red-letter day, today he is celebrating his triumph and he wants to avoid every jarring note, every occasion for dispute.

'We love simplicity, Ava and I.'

'That's obvious!' answers Cindy, who feels that Ted's strange remark was probably aimed at her. 'I see everybody has already helped themselves! What are you drinking, Ted?'

'Remy Martin VSOP.'

'Well, I'll have the same. With an ice cube.'

'Ice in cognac?'

'Yes. To drown my sorrows.'

Mercury pulls away so gently that nobody notices the car has begun to move.

'Nothing dreadful has happened, I hope?' Suzanna asks ironically, but primarily with hurt pride, because Cindy has so far not so much as glanced at her.

'All depends on how you look at it,' she answers, finally wondering who the extravagantly dressed, cigarillo smoking lady sitting opposite is. 'I'm used to men waiting for me. Even young guys whose neck is not the only thing that's stiff.' She hands Ted her empty glass. She is probably no longer worth it, she whines. For some mysterious reason or other, she is past her sell-by date and that is why she is treated like some secondhand Barbie Doll. Unwanted actresses are barely tolerated in public. Talent doesn't enter into it. It's all about fashion and big money. Everybody knows producers haven't got the slightest imagination, and even less balls. As long as you are bringing in money, they are on your phone all the time, they are grovelling at your feet, but the moment you make the slightest mistake, they drop you like a hot potato, you've missed the train and you can chase after it until the cows come home. Who still remembers her brilliant performance in *Penetrator* or *Draculanus*? Nobody, it seems. She hopes Ava, who is still young and inexperienced and still has to prove herself, will never have to go through this hell. If it wasn't to support her good friend this evening, out of pure concern, then it would never even have occurred to her to attend this sort of carnival once again.

Ted refills her glass, but she tells him she would prefer to switch to champagne, to wash away the taste of the cognac. She lights a cigarette with a trembling hand. Ted telephones Mercury, tells him to get a move on, this isn't a funeral procession, they've only got a half an hour to get to Brussels and, moreover, Ted still wants to buy a pot of honey somewhere. For his cough.

'There are probably a couple of shops still open near Central Station, sir. But I fear we may no longer have time for that.'

'That's my problem, Mercury. What I want is: one, to appear on the steps of the Rex on the stroke of midnight; and, two, to be able to swallow a couple of spoonfuls of honey on the way there if I feel like it. Is that too much to ask?'

'I shall do my best, sir.'

Mercury fastens his safety-belt. Vangenechte shall have his wishes fulfilled, but he shall regret it. By way of revenge, he puts on a new CD: the *Stabat Mater*, by Giovanni Battista Pergolesi, performed by the Liszt Ferenc Chamber Orchestra from Budapest, conducted by Lamberto Gardelli. But it begins so quietly that Ted does not immediately notice.

The limousine skims along the De Keyserlei. The lights in front of the station are on green and the late strollers stare open-mouthed at the black colossus as it squeals around the corner towards the Astridplein, causing Cindy to spill her champagne over Richard's alpaca dinner jacket.

'What's going on?' screams Ava, who is being crushed against her friend with all her weight.

'He's pretty keen,' Suzanna laughs dreamily.

Ted screams through the telephone that Mercury has to stop overdoing it and has to turn off that ridiculous church music.

'Since that kid's been working for me, he thinks he's in some American series,' he apologises, trying to wipe Richard's trousers clean with a white linen handkerchief.

'Leave it. This suit has already been through a lot worse,' laughs Richard. 'Besides, everybody knows good champagne doesn't leave any stains.'

'He's been wearing it fifty years already,' says Cindy, 'here, see these dark spots on his collar: Zarah Leander's snot . . .'

'Zsa Zsa Gabor's tears . . .'

'And here, these disgusting smears in his crotch, a souvenir of . . . what was the name of that inflatable doll again?'

'You're probably referring to Jayne Mansfield, aren't you, bevvy?'

'Mansfield, right! You could always find plenty of time for her! Hours, days, weeks he sat waiting for that cow in foyers! Sometimes I wonder why you married me, Richard.'

'For your irresistible charm, of course,' says Suzanna, her voice cavernous.

'And so I could see the world one final time, in the autumn of my life, through your bewildered eyes, my darling,' Richard adds a little absently, as if he is talking to himself.

'Yes, you needn't worry, I'm sure it wasn't for your money!' Ted remarks with his famous sensitivity.

Arousing general interest, Mercury double-parks the limousine in front of a grocer's shop, where the lights are still burning, and gets out, followed by Ted.

'There's no need for you to come, sir,' he protests for the sake of form.

'Mercury, I've been taking care of my own health for more than forty years already. And I don't just want any old pot of honey, I want the best. And you know nothing about it.'

Vangenechte hurries inside the shop, leaving Mercury waiting on the pavement. A scrawny black man on crutches comes and stands beside him and asks in a broken voice who the rich folks in the limousine are. Through the smoked glass windows it is impossible to see inside the car.

'A famous actress, a film star,' Mercury answers mysteriously and not without pride.

'A film star.' The man sounds sceptical. 'What's her name?'

'I'm afraid I can't reveal that. Reasons of security.'

'Do I know her from TV?'

'Not just from TV.'

'I never go to the cinema anymore. Too expensive.'

'Then only from TV,' answers Mercury, who finds the situation irritating and wants to put an end to this ridiculous conversation.

'Brigitte Bardot?' The man reels with excitement and hangs on to Mercury with a filthy, clammy hand. His breath smells of garlic and medication. Mercury nods.

'But don't tell anyone.'

'This is the first time I've seen her,' says the invalid man with a wide, toothless smile, as he stares at the blind windows of the limousine. 'I used to be in showbiz too.'

Leaning on his crutches, he performs a few clumsy dance steps, reminiscent of step-dancing, while, in an almost inaudible, brittle voice, he begins to sing:

'Brigitte Bardot, Bardot. Brigitte, c'est chaud, très chaud . . .'

Shuddering, Mercury steps back a few metres so that he can check the sleeve the man has just touched, in the light of the shop window, for possible grease stains, and notices that the emaciated wretch is stamping his worn-out, checked slippers in a fresh dog turd. His stomach cramps, saliva floods into his mouth. He locks his jaws together so hard that his cheeks begin to tremble, clenches his fists, screws his eyes shut and imagines himself laying into the poor wretch, knocking him down with his own crutches and thrashing him until he is left lying, twitching and gagging on the pavement in a pool of blood, mucus and shit.

Glowing with excitement, Ted comes out of the shop carrying a bulging plastic bag and walks to the car without looking around.

'And now, put your foot down, Mercury! We've buggered around enough already!'

11

The limo glides over the asphalt of the Britselei like a black arrow. As it passes the Palace of Justice, Richard leans forward to look through the window.

'What an odd building! Some sort of museum?'

Ted bursts into a raw, rattling guttural laugh, which turns into an unstoppable fit of coughing. He wrenches open a pot of lavender honey and sticks in his stubby, pink finger, which he then sticks in his mouth, so that the honey can flow over his tongue into his throat.

'The court-house,' answers Ava in his place. 'Aren't you feeling well, Ted?'

Ted's face has turned purple, making his yellow hair, which is now sticking to his sweat-drenched forehead, clash even more violently.

'I've never felt better,' he pants, 'but Rich sometimes comes up with such questions!'

Nobody understands what has caused Ted to react so hysterically to Richard's innocent remark, unless perhaps it is after all an attack of stage fright.

'I have always been plagued by stage fright,' says Cindy. 'I had to throw up in a bucket before every take. The directors were very understanding. I had my own bucket, with my initials on it. Those were the golden days.'

'It even happens to the greatest,' Suzanna confirms, 'look at Aznavour.' She lays her hand on Ava's knee and gives it a gentle squeeze.

'The only difference being that her nausea wasn't always

caused by nerves,' says Richard, gazing charmingly into Suzanna's eyes, as if Cindy was not present.

'Right, old man. These days it's you that makes me throw up, whereas in the past, it was simply stage fright!' Cindy snarls, trembling with desperation. 'Goddamnit, Ava, say something! After all, I've only come along to support you!' She is on the verge of bursting into tears. Five years of fruitless auditions – not counting a dogfood commercial – have turned her into a wreck.

'I think we should all try to relax a little,' says Ava with a forced, calm smile, looking at the others with exaggerated friendliness. 'We still have a long drive ahead of us. Let's try to make the best of it. That way, we'll look even more beautiful in the photos later.'

'If we get there on time!' With his handkerchief, which now smells of Dom Perignon, Ted wipes away the sweat from his face. The car disappears under Nachtegalen Park, into the Craeybeckx Tunnel. Ted reaches nervously for the telephone.

'Mercury, are you scared of the dark, or what? We've got precisely seventeen minutes to make our entrance at the Rex! And those TV people don't wait!'

'And certainly not for me!' Cindy sobs, as she pours herself another glass of champagne.

'Anybody know any good gossip?' asks Suzanna, who is an old hand at sophisticated small talk and knows that gossip is guaranteed to get even the most deadlocked conversations going again.

12

When Van Laken had been woken from a comatose sleep at around half past six in the morning, eight months earlier, on 7 January, it was as much as he could do to stretch out his arm to pick up the telephone. He had spent the previous evening propping up the bar at The Madonna on the St-Paulusplein, alone with a bottle of J&B and three packs of Gauloises, not understanding why Maartje constantly lied, or stayed away at night, or, when she did sleep at home, lay inertly beside him in bed like a block of wood, with her back turned to him. His neck vertebrae were grating, and the pain in the back of his head was unbearable. His bloodless lips were stuck together. His pasty tongue was like cement, his mouth was glued shut and his throat was so dry that he had difficulty clearing it.

Ten minutes later, unwashed, unshaven and shivering with cold, he stepped into Courtois' car. His assistant, who was sitting behind the steering wheel fresh, perfumed and alert as always, began a sickening story that would have banished even the most stubborn of hangovers. He told of a girl who had been found skinned and hanging from a meathook amongst the frozen sides of beef in a fridge at the Antwerp abattoir. The severed lips of her vulva, her long, blonde hair and crumpled skin were lying in a bloody pile at her feet. The point of the hook that had been planted in her chin protruded through her left eye socket, and the eye, blue-green according to the first witnesses, was dangling in her hollowed cheek from a thin, pale nerve like a clapper in a bell. Her skull, a slippery, oval blood clot, seemed smaller than average.

In the long corner, at the end of the Italiëlei, Van Laken had opened the window of the Opel and spewed up steaming strands of bile, which had immediately frozen and stuck to the door of the car. That very same day, Sax – this was what they called Plouvier, the young police physician who drove everybody at the department crazy by practising his saxophone – had found the Scrabble block with the letter M deep in her vagina, the Scrabble block Van Laken had carried in his pocket ever since as a talisman. Later that same day, the victim was identified as Mieke Zonhoven, born in Groningen on 18 May 1978, and reported missing since December '92. Van Laken soon discovered that she had played a lady's maid, under the name Lolita Moore, in the French porn film *Le Faux Con Maltais*. She had two scenes. In the first, she lost a game of strip Scrabble and was then, as required by the rules of the game, fucked on the table by the winner and his guests, the village notables. In the second, she seduced the lord of the manor in the kitchen, whilst Claude, the lesbian cook, watched with bulging eyes and, squatting in the kitchen sink, masturbated herself with a skinned rabbit. These scenes had undoubtedly inspired the murderer's macabre butchery. Back then, Van Laken had still cherished the vain delusion that the psychopath who had skinned Mieke Zonhoven was also active in the porn world and would be quickly apprehended.

But this evening, amongst the crowd, which whistles and roars each time a new couple steps waving out of a car and climbs the steps of the Rex through the crush of photographers, and whose naïve wonder he shares, he no longer knows what to think. In eight months, M has stage-managed six ritual murders, not counting the five missing youths whose bodies have never been found. And there is no indication that the monster has now been sated. On the contrary, the impotence of the police and his growing popularity seem to be inspiring him to ever-increasing horrors. And an evening such as this, a show-case of female beauty, was certainly not the way to encourage him to come to his senses. Van Laken could not shake the thought that he must be nearby, posing as the most anonymous, inconspicuous, idle gawker, mingled in with the crowd, invisible, unfindable, immune. A time bomb ticking away silently in the languid night.

Van Laken is so sunk in his thoughts that he has not noticed how Courtois has wormed his way through the surging crowd and come to stand next to him.

'The organisers would like to speak to you,' Courtois whispers in his ear.

'What?'

It is as if Van Laken is being torn from a deep sleep.

'Messrs Knopff and de Busschère, the owners of the cinema. A couple. They're waiting for you inside.'

Without answering, Van Laken takes the Scrabble block from his trouser pocket and holds it under the nose of the silent man who is standing next to him watching the ballet of taxis jostling by.

'You never know,' he says abruptly, then crosses the street, followed by Courtois.

'How's the security?'

'Impressive. A dozen plain-clothes detectives, some in evening dress. A few female officers as bait. Gendarmes all over the place. Marksmen on the roofs. Walkie-talkies. A mobile command post linked to headquarters.'

'And who's in charge?'

'Cornelis himself.'

'One of Vangenechte's pals. Same lodge. Doesn't look like we're needed here.' Van Laken stops in the middle of the strutting guests.

'Phone Sax and tell him I want to see him. Now. Today.'

'But it's already half past eleven!'

'At half past twelve then. In the lab. That ought to be feasible.'

'Anything else?' asks Courtois irritably.

'Yes. I want to see everybody who is working on the case in my office at one o'clock.'

'Who is everybody?'

'VDB, the Whore-hopper, the Mole, the Congolese and the Gambler. Drag them out of bed if you have to. Tell them I'm inviting them to a slide show. In the meantime, I'll say goodbye to our two aunties.'

Courtois shrugs his shoulders. The investigation has been going on for eight months already and suddenly it seems that the whole affair has to be solved within a couple of hours. Besides, they must have compared those unbearable photos of mutilated bodies a hundred times without discovering anything new. He is beginning to suspect Van Laken of getting some sort of sick pleasure from the constantly repeated projections. But it does not even occur to him to argue with his hero, the man who has taught him the tricks of the trade. He will phone everybody, just as his boss had asked. Such unexpected, paradoxical decisions are generally indications that Van Laken is exhausted; omens of a deep but fleeting fit of despair.

Courtois gazes compassionately at the tall hunched man who is standing in front of him amongst the dolled-up guests. He knows precisely what Van Laken is going to say to him, what he always says when he is feeling guilty or has no logical explanation for what he is demanding of his colleagues and Courtois is staring at him in dumb amazement: Is anything the matter, Courtois?

'Well, Courtois, is anything the matter?' he asks walking into the cinema and disappearing amongst the cackling penguins without waiting for a reply.

13

'What Richard would like most is to introduce me to that butcher,' sighs Cindy. 'As a matter of fact, I wouldn't be at all surprised if he knows M. You know everybody, don't you, darling?'

Cindy has meanwhile swapped places with Ava, so that she can sit as far away from her husband as possible. They are now driving past Rumst.

'M,' mumbles Richard, lost in his memories. 'David Wayne.'

Mercury, who can listen in on everything that is said via a tiny loudspeaker – there is absolutely no need for Ted to use the telephone to communicate with him – pricks up his ears. In his thesis, at film school, he had discussed in detail the similarities between the two versions of M: Fritz Lang's 1931 original, with Peter Lorre in the leading role, and Losey's wonderful remake twenty years later, with, as Richard Weinberg had said, David Wayne playing the leading role of the child-killer. He had worked on it for six months and knows both films by heart, scene for scene. Even now, five years later, he can still recite the credits faultlessly: Director: Joseph Losey; production: Seymour Nebenzal for Superior Films; coproducer: Harry Nebenzal; scenario: Norman Reilly Raine and Leo Katcher, with additional dialogue by Waldo Salt; based on an original script by Thea Von Harbou, Paul Falkenberg, Adolf Jansen and Karl Vash, from a newspaper article by Egon Jacobson; photography: Ernest Laszlo; sound: Leon Becker; music: Michel Michelet; conductor: Bert Shefter; artistic director: Martin Obzina; sets: Ray Robinson;

make-up: Ted Larsen; production manager: Ben Hersh; executive producer: John Hubley; assistant to the director: Robert Aldrich; editing: Edward Mann. Cast: David Wayne (M), Howard da Silva (Carney), Martin Gabel (Marshall), Luther Adler (Langley), Steve Brodie (Becker), Glenn Anders (Riggert), Norman Lloyd (Sutro), Walter Burke (McNaham) and Raymond – *Ironside* – Burr (Pottsy). Filmed in Los Angeles and released in world premiere by Columbia on 10 June, 1951. Duration: 88 minutes.

It resounds like a melopoeia, like music running through his head, and Mercury smiles contentedly, a little surprised by his infallible memory. He can't see even the erudite Weinberg matching that.

'Does anybody actually know why he calls himself M?' Mercury hears Suzanna ask.

'Perhaps the bastard identifies himself with the M from the film,' says Ted.

'He was a child-killer,' answers Richard, 'who murdered without leaving a calling card and played the flute . . .'

'Powerful script!' Ted is delighted with this cutting, sneering outburst.

'. . . but a blind balloon-seller recognises him by the melody he plays, informs a friend, a billiard player if I'm not mistaken,' – behind the steering wheel, Mercury nods in agreement – 'who writes a big M in chalk on the psychopath's back, so that, without realising it, he walks through the city branded.'

'Hardly at all like our M,' Ava says relieved.

'Our M? Your M, more like! It's fresh, tender, young flesh he's after, pigeon!' says Cindy, washing down two red capsules with a gulp of ice-cooled vodka.

'You're right there,' says Ted. 'M might have less of an appetite for children, but all of his victims so far have been very young women.'

'Who sometimes behave like children!' adds Richard, raising his index finger and looking sideways at Cindy.

'As far as I can see, but of course who am I to say so, we pay the police our hard-earned money to protect us. But after eight months and after five murders, they're not a single step closer to catching this monster. They're just groping around in the dark; every clue leads to a dead end; the authorities are powerless against the ingenuity of the murderer; blah blah blah. It's beyond belief.'

'M is not just any old murderer, Ted, you have to admit that,' Suzanna points out.

'No way! If I'd run my affairs the way that gang of slackers down at police headquarters do, I'd still be up to my knees in pig shit!' says Ted, thoroughly enjoying the sound of his own voice.

'And I wouldn't be shut up in a limousine with this windbag,' thinks Richard, who has spent magic moments in similar cars in the company of Barbra Streisand, Rod Taylor, Willy de Ville, Silvana Mangano, Siodmak and Visconti, to name but a few.

'Perhaps it's just the M of Monday. It said in the paper that all the murders have been committed on a Monday,' says Suzanna, checking in the oval mirror of her powder compact to see if her mascara has run.

'Or the M of Marcel, or of Maurice, or of Michel, or of Manneken Pis, or of . . .'

Suzanna interrupts Ted: 'Or of Mercury.'

A brief silence follows, which she shatters by laughing loudly at the dazed expression of Ted, who is almost on the point of dismissing his brand-new chauffeur on the spot.

'Oh do dry up!' shouts Ava. 'That boy couldn't hurt a fly!'

'Only joking, sweetie!' Suzanna kisses Ava quickly on the cheek.

'Perhaps he's a Moroccan? The M of Moroccan?' asks Ted, who actually appears to mean it.

'Ted, please! Don't be such a Fleming,' Ava answers curtly,

letting the drop of champagne that is dangling from her finger run down between her breasts.

Mercury has listened in to the conversation about M with amusement. Suzanna Rizzoni's remark and the ensuing embarrassment particularly tickled him. This is a woman after his own heart, a woman who makes no attempt to disguise her feelings, a woman who speaks with the voice of Anna Magnani, a woman with sturdy wrists and ankles, just like his mother. He also likes Richard Weinberg, although he wonders what on earth could have inspired this living film encyclopedia to accept Vangenechte's invitation.

As they pass the exit for Mechelen South, the limousine crosses paths with Van Laken and Courtois' Opel, which is racing towards Antwerp with wailing sirens and flashing blue lights in the opposite lane.

'There we go,' says Ted. 'Another pile-up in the Kennedy Tunnel.'

14

'Yes?'

'What has Sax already told you?'

'Nothing. He's waiting for us now in the lab.'

'Wonderful chap. Night owl. Good musician too.'

In Van Laken's eyes, Plouvier is suddenly blessed with every virtue.

'And the lads?'

'They've all been informed. Vandenbos was a bit reluctant, his wife has a rash.'

'Understandable . . . The rash, I mean.'

Van Laken shakes a tiny pill from a glass phial and tosses the medication into his throat with infallible precision, the same jerky motion he constantly repeats with peanuts, whenever they happen to rendezvous in a bar.

'Courtois?'

'Yes?'

'Not too tired?'

'For somebody who's been on the job for eighteen hours, without so much as a cup of coffee, oddly enough I'm not. But I'm dying of hunger. And I wouldn't say no to a hot shower.'

'Did you order sandwiches for the meeting?'

'I've followed your orders obsequiously down to the tiniest letter, commissaris.'

'Talk normally, Courtois. The way you used to.'

Van Laken is usually amused by his assistant's deliberately affected manner of speech. It is, after all, Courtois' only way of giving his colleagues a glimpse of his consciously constructed personality. But tonight Van Laken is clearly out of sorts and nothing will make him laugh. He throws his last empty pack of Gauloises listlessly out of the window and a feeling of infinite fatigue overcomes him, of futility too, of waste, of hopeless loneliness. He misses Maartje. Finds that his clothes stink. Can't feel his teeth anymore.

'Courtois . . .'

'Yes?'

'Nothing . . . It's just not my day today.'

'If it's a cigarette you want, I'm afraid you'll have to wait until the next service station. I'm all out myself.'

'Courtois, I sometimes wonder if you ever have your own opinion.'

Van Laken lowers the back of his seat, until he is lying almost horizontally.

'I think so,' says Courtois, trying to hide his surprise behind an expressionless mask.

'So why do we never get to hear it?'

'Because nobody ever asks for it.'

The lad's right, thinks Van Laken. Over the years, their collaboration has grown into a sort of ritual. Van Laken takes the decisions, hands out the orders, asks the questions, gives the answers and draws the conclusions and Courtois' role is reduced to that of a nodding lady in waiting, or of a faithful lapdog, who listens, says nothing and wags his tail in agreement. Perhaps that was one of the reasons why their investigation had not got any further.

'Tell me, Pol, how do you imagine M? I suppose you've formed some sort of mental picture?'

Pol. This is the first time Van Laken has called him by his Christian name. Courtois immediately forgets the cigarettes and the service station, which flashes by like a brightly illuminated spaceship and immediately afterwards, in his mirror, disappears over the horizon like a shooting star.

'Damn!'

'What?'

'The cigarettes.'

'Forget it. It's not my day today anyway. Give me a profile of M.'

Courtois drives into the Craeybeckx Tunnel without saying a word and turns off the siren. He has tried to visualise M countless times. But he only now realises how difficult it is to describe that vague shadow, to put his fantasies into words.

'I see a man . . .' Courtois begins hesitantly.

'Try harder.'

'I see a man, by which I mean that, according to me, it can't be a woman.'

Van Laken is on the point of yawning ostentatiously, but he changes his mind. Perhaps Courtois' remark, in its very simplicity, is more relevant than he thought.

'Why?'

'Because so far, every serial killer – with the exception of one, Carol Bundy – has always been a man.'

'Carry on.'

'A handsome man, who knows how to use his natural charm to win the confidence of his intended victims. An artist, or at least somebody who moves in artistic circles. Probably white, because all of his victims are white and . . .'

'Zsa Zsa Morgan was as black as the night . . .'

'. . . and according to the NCAVC, the National Centre for the Analysis of Violent Crime, in Los Angeles, a serial killer seldom crosses the racial line. And as far as Zsa Zsa Morgan is concerned, she might well be the victim of a copycat-killer, a secondhand M, who knows.'

'Absolutely.' Van Laken had underestimated Courtois. 'Impotent?'

'Probably. In any case, sexually disturbed. A man who has lost any feelings of tenderness.'

Just like me, thinks Van Laken.

'Religious?'

'More of a mystic. Behaves like some twisted messiah, as if

66

he has been chosen to fulfil some very specific mission of purification . . .'

'What else?'

'An aesthetic, very definitely, with a sense of propriety and theatricality, a man who has a love of order, of the ceremonial, the ritual aspect of life, a man with unfulfilled ambitions who feels himself unappreciated . . .'

'Interesting. Age?'

'Around thirty. Physically strong, because his little tableaux sometimes require a great deal of strength.'

'Lonely?'

'Very lonely. And highly intellectual, a man of sophisticated, eclectic culture, in the philosophical sense of the word.'

'Which means?'

'He constructs his own system from what he sees as the paramount truths of other systems.'

'Right.' This time Van Laken really does have to yawn, but he stifles it, to avoid interrupting Courtois.

'But whose system has for some reason or other become derailed, so that it no longer meets the criteria we consider to be normal, a system that is now solely based upon the confusion between reality and his obsession with purity. In short: we are dealing with a human short circuit, a classic case of schizophrenic paranoia, which has led to psychopathic behaviour. Shall I stop in the Hoogstraat for cigarettes?'

Van Laken does not answer. He is sleeping with his mouth half open, head tilted back, breathing regularly but inaudibly. Courtois looks at his pasty, furrowed tongue, his yellow teeth, his hollow cheeks, his five o'clock shadow, the dark rings under his eyes. He looks just like papa, he thinks, when I found him dead in his deck chair with his bare feet in the ebbing waves. It was the first and last time his father had seen the sea. He therefore decides to let his boss rest and not to wake him before twelve-thirty.

15

Ted had had the three tonne bulletproof 'stretch', as he called it, shipped over from America, and as far as he knows, it is still the only one in Belgium. In his opinion, no film producer worth his salt can travel around in any other vehicle. The jeering comments of his colleague producers, smalltown boys, therefore cannot touch him. Moreover, the limousine is a symbol of power and success, a bit like the Rolls, which he finds too ungainly and above all too English, and hence a vehicle which does not belong in the world of the cinema. In his limousine, he feels safe, unapproachable, insulated from the outside world, raised above the common crowd. That same crowd that feeds on the flesh and the dreams that he sells. That same moronic crowd that has paid for his limousine. It is the perfect moment to light a Romeo y Julia.

On the viaduct, which curves to the left, just before Zaventem, to connect the motorway to the Brussels outer ring-road, a long procession of stationary cars with flashing rear lights blocks their path. Mercury has to slam his foot on the brakes to bring the car to a halt.

'Jesus Christ! Watch where you're going!' Ted shouts from a cloud of blue smoke and picks up the telephone.

'Mercury, could you possibly tell me what's going on?'

'A traffic jam, sir. I fear there's been an accident.'

Below them, on the ring-road, the cars are standing like motionless toys, bumper to bumper in all three lanes as far as the horizon, where a plume of black smoke above an orange glow marks the site of the accident.

'Take the hard shoulder!' bellows Ted.

'That's also full, sir.'

'Very clever. That way the fire brigade can't get through. People are pigs. But that's no news!' Ted gazes ahead in desperation. Such a thing would have been unthinkable with Uncle Bens behind the wheel. 'Okay. Don't panic, Mercury. Just reverse back up.'

But that also turns out to be impossible: dozens of cars are already shuffling behind the limousine across the whole width of the bridge.

'Where in God's name are all those people going at this time of night?'

'To the premiere of *Desert Flower*, of course!'

'Maybe a plane has crashed?' Cindy begins to giggle nervously.

'I'm relieved to see your wife is actually able to laugh, Rich!'

'Come on, bevvy, don't go getting all hysterical.'

'I'm not getting hysterical!' Cindy snarls back. 'I was simply starting to get bored and this has livened things up a bit. Where is the toilet?'

Ted's mouth falls open. He gazes in bewilderment, first at Cindy and then at Richard.

'The toilet? Outside! At the end of the garden!' He can also be witty if needs be.

Cindy gets out, walks to the iron crash barrier, drops her jeans and her tanga to her ankles and squats, amidst the loud hooting of the cars that are waiting behind the limousine in the tailback.

'Watch out for dirty old men!' Ava calls from the car.

'She's working on her comeback,' whispers an amused Richard into Ted's ear.

Suzanna leans over and looks outside through the open door.

'With such an enticing little arse that shouldn't be any problem.'

'Only Madame doesn't want to do any nude scenes anymore. She's dreaming of the classic repertoire. She even wants to change her name – Beaver is a little suggestive, I have to admit. It's par for the course with actresses such as Cindy.'

'No more gratuitous nude scenes,' Ava corrects him, 'and I can fully understand that. Would you still dare to do it, Suzy?'

'I couldn't do that to people!' Suzanna laughs. 'Besides, I've always been rather prudish.'

Nobody knows how long they will be stuck on the bridge, yet the atmosphere has never been so relaxed.

'I suppose people have to have a laugh from time to time, but do you lot realise we're going to miss the premiere?' Ted sounds hoarse. His dreams are collapsing, his world is crumbling. Trembling, he fills the first glass he finds with a generous shot of cognac.

For *Desert Flower*, in which he has personally invested more than a hundred million francs, he has had to sell forty-nine percent of his shares in the pig farm. His three previous films had been showered with undeserved abuse by the press; even the last one, *Hard Labour* – as the ambiguous title suggests, a stylish, erotic, socio-historic fable – which everybody in the industry had originally predicted would outdo *Daens*. The film had run for just one week. In a single cinema. The Roxy. In Strombeek-Bever.

With *Desert Flower*, he has played his final trump card. If this production fails to attract an audience of at least eight hundred thousand, he might as well pack it in and go and live on his savings in some Swiss valley. That is why he followed the American example and spent half of the budget on promotion. This evening's party alone is costing him one and a half million. And here they are, stuck in the traffic on top of a viaduct, whilst everybody in Brussels is waiting for them, so that the premiere can start. And nobody seems to give a damn, not even Ava. And moreover, he has been scared of bridges since he was a child.

Sunk in thought, Ted stirs a honey-covered finger in his cognac.

Cindy flops down beside Richard with a sigh of relief.

'Now that's what I call making the best of a bad situation!'

Ava feels sorry for Ted, who is sinking away into the back seat, like a toad into dark quicksand.

'Cheer up, Harlow. It's not so terrible to turn up last.'

'Quite the contrary. A true star always keeps them waiting,' Suzanna agrees.

'Well nobody'll be waiting for me.'

'Cindy!'

'Not for you either, Richard, rest assured.'

'I'd sooner be listening to the stock market report.'

Ted searches for Radio 2 with the remote control and finds it just at the end of the midnight news.

'. . . And finally: the press agency Belga has just informed us that the body of the Dutch actress Lova Spencer was discovered, earlier this evening, floating in an aquarium at Antwerp Zoo. According to the Antwerp public prosecutor's office, there is no doubt that this sixth horrific murder is the work of M, the psychopath who has been terrorising the film world since last December. Tomorrow, in our midday magazine, we will be examining this dossier in depth, with our guest the American psychiatrist Walter J. Coninck. Meanwhile, despite everything, we wish you all a very good night and sweet dreams.'

'Shut that damned door!' Ted shouts at Cindy, who has left her door open.

Ava wipes away a tear.

'How terrible! In an aquarium! We were at drama school together.'

'Did you hear that?' Cindy shouts indignantly. 'The "actress" Lova Spencer. What a nerve!'

'I don't recognise the name,' says Richard, delving into his memory. 'Did you invite her to the premiere, Ted?'

'I had two thousand seven hundred and eighty invitations sent out. She was probably amongst them.'

'It doesn't surprise me in the least,' says Suzanna calmly.

'What? That she was invited?'

'No, Ted, that she's been murdered. I know one shouldn't speak ill of the dead, but Lova, God rest her soul, led a . . .' Suzanna hesitates, gazes flustered through the black window at an aeroplane that is just about to land in Zaventem. Her voice sounds even deeper than usual. She is breathing heavily. '. . . led a debauched life. She simply couldn't stop; she behaved like a common street whore. You know that as well as I do, Ava. She had nothing left to lose. She even spread her legs in the gutter to get money to support her habit. That slut was the perfect victim for M. She was just begging for it. It was pure suicide.'

'Do you hear that, pigeon? You've got nothing to fear!'

'You'd better give me a cognac too, Ted,' says Suzanna, who seems more shocked by the news than the others.

'I'm afraid the cognac is finished. Whisky?'

'Yes, neat.'

Ted hands her the crystal decanter of twelve year-old Chivas, picks up the telephone and taps in the number of the Rex.

'Ted Harlow here. I want to speak to de Busschère.'

'It's me speaking! I'm so glad to hear you, Ted. Have you any idea how late it is? I was starting to get really worried! And Sylvain is in a right old state.'

'Yes, of course I know how late it is! We're hopelessly stuck on the ring-road. I've never felt so humiliated.'

'I'm all at sixes and sevens, Ted. What do you suggest? Should we start without Ava?'

'Are there many people?'

'Full to the brim!'

'Just as I expected. Keep them occupied.'

'Keep them occupied. Keep them occupied! That's easier said than done! Twelve hundred people!'

'Stop whining, de Busschère! Give a speech, do a belly dance, fuck your partner on the stage, I don't know, think of something!'

'Perhaps I could do my Liza Minnelli impression?'

'Out of the question! I'd sooner you started the film. Tell the rabble that Ava is in the cinema and that she'll be introduced to the audience after the film.'

'So, no Liza Minnelli?'

'No, luvvie, just do what I said.'

'It will be a triumph.'

'Undoubtedly. See you soon.'

Mercury has listened in to the news and the telephone conversation without moving a muscle. He turns off the engine, gets out, goes and sits on the crash barrier, stares dreamily at the dark puddle Cindy has left on the asphalt, and takes a deep breath. The first suite of *Discovery of Brazil* by Villa-Lobos, performed by Pablo Casals, is ringing out from one of the stationary cars. The night smells of exhaust fumes, freshly mown grass, burnt rubber and barbecued meat.

16

Van Laken is still asleep in the car, which is parked with two wheels on the pavement on the corner outside de Fouquet's, when Courtois, who had been in great need of a Salade Niçoise, appears with a satisfied smile from behind the plastic palms in the door opening. He looks at his watch: everything is going smoothly. They still have just enough time to arrive at the city morgue at Schoonselhof cemetery acceptably late. He sits behind the wheel and holds an open pack of Gauloises under the nose of Van Laken, who blinks open his eyes with a groan.

'Maartje?'

'It's me. Courtois.'

'What time is it?'

'Twelve-thirty.'

Still groaning, Van Laken winds his seat back up, rubs his eyes, wipes the steamed-up windows clean with his sleeve and gazes groggily outside at the neon lights of the discos and cinemas in the Anneessenstraat, at the Argentinian restaurants across the street and at the relaxed customers on the terrace of de Fouquet's.

'And might I enquire why I'm lying asleep in an illegally parked car on the De Keyserlei, when there's a maniac prowling around outside who could skin a new victim with total impunity at any moment?'

'You were sleeping so soundly I didn't dare to wake you. And besides, you don't like salads.'

Van Laken cantankerously lights a cigarette and immediately begins to cough, as if this is the start of a new day.

*

Ten minutes later they enter the deserted laboratory between the city morgue and the crematorium, where Sax is waiting for them on a bar stool, practising a solo beneath the flickering fluorescent light.

'"The Peacocks",' says the sallow, dry man, whose white lab coat is covered with blood stains. He holds out a large hairy hand. With his pale bald skull, his stubble-covered chin and his powerful glasses he appears older than he is.

'I'll have to practise a few more nights before they mistake me for Mulligan,' he jokes. 'What can I do for you, Big Mac?'

Plouvier is the only one in the department who dares to call Van Laken by his nickname.

'It's late, I know . . .'

'No problem.'

'I was hoping you could help us examine Lova Spencer's body.'

'Heavenly body!' Sax laughs. 'And in pretty good condition, compared to the others. They can bring in more like that.' He stows his saxophone carefully behind two *sansevierias* on the granite windowsill.

'This way.'

Van Laken and Courtois follow the police physician through a sparsely-lit corridor into a windowless cold-room, the floor, ceiling and walls of which are covered with white porcelain tiles. In the middle of the room there are two marble tables, and on each table lies a long, zipped-up, black plastic body bag. Sax turns on the powerful spotlights above the tables and opens a cabinet, from which, still whistling 'The Peacocks', he extracts a pair of thin rubber gloves.

'That ought to be her,' he says, pointing to the first bag.

Lova Spencer's body had been brought in at around nine p.m. and after a cursory examination, Sax had come to the conclusion that the young 'goddess', as he calls her, must have already been dead when M had submerged her in the aquarium. She had been in the water some twenty hours at the most. According to his calculations, she had been killed yesterday, Monday 18 November, at around seven p.m., approximately twenty-four hours before she was fished out. As with the other victims, he had found no trace of sexual contact, either before or after death.

With a sweeping but exact, almost jovial gesture he unzips the plastic bag, which he then carefully folds open like a sheet on a bed.

'A work of art!'

Sax, who spends most of his free time in jazz clubs, often expresses himself in English.

Van Laken has to admit that Lova is indeed poignantly beautiful, lying there so peacefully, her arms relaxed on her flat belly, her hands folded. Were it not for the grotesque fish sticking out of her mouth, one might even think she was sleeping. Her crimson nails stand out against her colourless skin, just above her shaved, grey vulva. Courtois jots down that somebody, probably Sax, has smoothed her hair and laid it over her left shoulder. A brown label covered in illegible scribblings is dangling from her left foot, an obscene, jarring detail that turns this peaceful body into a corpse.

'Cause of death?' asks Van Laken, gazing seemingly unperturbed at Lova, as if she is a fallen mannequin.

Sax runs his rubber hands over the purple welts on her neck.

'Mundane. Classic strangulation.'

Courtois points silently to the contusions around the liver, on the wrists and the ankles.

'And how do you explain these bruises?'

'She was probably tied up and transported in the boot of a car. We've found traces of engine oil under her nails and here, look, just below the earlobe, that smear: oil.' Sax rubs his finger over the dark smear and holds it to Van Laken's nose.

'Get rid of that ridiculous fish.'

Courtois suspects his boss of hiding his bewilderment

behind a forced professionalism. Even dead, Lova radiates an irresistible charm.

With a pair of slender tweezers, Sax removes the clown wrasse from her mouth. The dorsal fin folds open and catches momentarily in the roof of her mouth behind her teeth.

'This could well be extremely poisonous,' mumbles Sax, as he folds back the spines one by one, the way one shuts a fan, 'and if the gods are with us, M might possibly have been stung.'

'Is the sting deadly?' asks Courtois.

'No idea. Maybe. Perhaps the poison simply paralyses. You'd have to ask a specialist. Professor Ambers, for example. He works at the zoo.'

'I know. Courtois and I already underwent him this evening. But since M always wears gloves – at least, we've never found any fingerprints – I think it's of little importance.'

'Just to be on the safe side, I'll have all the hospitals checked to see whether anybody with that sort of wound has been admitted.' As he is saying this, Courtois jots down his decision in his notebook.

'The question is, why did he choose this particular fish?'

Sax has meanwhile laid the slimy specimen between Lova's breasts. Her mouth is still wide open, as if she is uttering a final, silent cry. Her tongue is blue and folded backwards. Her teeth are like porcelain.

Van Laken sets his half-moon reading glasses on the tip of his nose and bends over the stinking fish. Courtois notices that he is playing with the Scrabble block in his trouser pocket.

'Here you have your answer,' he says without triumph, still in the same, flat tone. 'Look at its head.'

Courtois bends over in turn, so that his chin is almost touching Lova's right nipple.

'I don't see anything.'

'Between the eyes.'

Only now does Courtois notice that the orange markings on

both sides of the fish form an M where they join together at the front.

'Unbelievable . . .' he sighs.

'A very constructive observation,' says Van Laken bitterly. 'And meanwhile, we are not a single step further.'

With a small torch, he illuminates Lova's gaping mouth as far as the back of the throat and sees in a flash the film scenes that had made her famous.

'OK. You can wrap her back up, Sex . . . I mean, Sax.'

'And what should I do with the fancy-dressed herring?'

'Preserve it in formalin, give it a number and file it with the other evidence.'

While Sax zips up the bag and Courtois watches Lova disappear for ever, Van Laken goes and stands with his nose against the cold wall, his hands behind his back, and stares right through the white tiles, as if he is looking outside through a window, at the warm, interminable night in which M is getting ready for his next ritual.

'Who's in the other bag?' Courtois asks Sax, who is throwing his gloves into a rubbish bin.

'The remains of that black man they found in the skip. But we'd better not open it, believe me.' Sax pinches his nose and waves his hairy hand in front of his face. 'In an advanced state of decomposition. I'm leaving that one to Serneels. Tomorrow morning, before he has his breakfast.'

'Old Stinky? He still works here?'

'You bet! He's the only one here who can bear such a stench. He's retiring next year . . . Big Mac?'

Van Laken is still staring at the wall, immobile.

'Big Mac, we're locking up!' Sax turns off the spotlights. Van Laken turns around slowly in the semi-darkness and leaves the room without saying a word. Sax and Courtois look at each other baffled and follow him through the corridor where, compared to the white room, it is sweltering hot. Suddenly Van Laken stops, lights a cigarette and leans with a long, outstretched arm against the wall. Silhouetted against the light, he looks like a stationary stick-insect.

'You know what makes me despair, Courtois?'

'No.' What he really means is yes.

'What makes me despair is that he has no face, but stays hidden away like a worm in an anonymous body, and that he makes no mistakes, never, and that only luck can help us now . . . And having to rely on luck is just about the most humbling part of our profession. It is also so anticlimactic . . .'

'Don't worry,' Sax tries to console him. 'A few hours sleep and tomorrow you'll probably wake up with a brilliant flash of inspiration.' He lays his hand on Van Laken's shoulder – like a spider, thinks Courtois – and pushes him into his office where he starts to pack away his saxophone.

'Have you got any idea why he left her in an aquarium?'

'I'll have a video delivered to you tomorrow. A not entirely unpleasant video. Watch it at your ease, when the family are asleep. It's not exactly a Cousteau documentary, but still . . . well, you'll see for yourself.'

'You're making me curious!'

'What was that piece again, the one you were playing just now?' asks Courtois.

'"The Peacocks". Wayne Shorter plays it on the soprano.'

'I'll have to buy it.'

17

Not a single engine is now still running on the bridge above the Brussels ring road. Attracted by the drama unfolding in the distance below them, most people have got out of their cars for a breath of fresh air. But the night is hot and below them to the right, Vilvoorde lies stinking in its poisonous industrial haze.

The accident is nevertheless inspiring heated debate. Everybody has had a nasty experience in the traffic and the most gruesome stories are being exchanged in hushed whispers. The atmosphere is oppressive and the silence unnatural, as if the earth has stopped turning for a moment and the world has been petrified into a still life for the duration of the hold-up.

Mercury is still sitting on the crash barrier, gazing pensively at the sky, which resembles a fluorescent dome. The detached calm he radiates is getting on Ted's nerves.

'What's that cretin looking at?' He presses a button and opens his window. 'Mercury! Is there anything to see?'

'There should be, sir. After twelve o'clock, that's what it said on the radio.'

'It suits him, that uniform,' Suzanna remarks. 'But of course, that lad could wear anything. All that's missing are the riding boots.'

'Then he'd look exactly like your brother and first lieutenant, Ted,' laughs Richard, 'Prince Nicholaus Erhart Hans Karl Maria von Wildeliebe-Rauffenburg!'

'Who was that again?'

'Von Stroheim himself, in *The Wedding March*!'

'Nice one, Rich!' Ted is completely at a loss, but he laughs along with the others, a pathetic, stupid grimace. He has invited Richard Weinberg along in the hope of getting a contract for Ava and consequently finds the agent's every utterance irresistibly comic.

'And what can be seen after twelve o'clock, Mercury, apart from *Desert Flower* in the Rex?'

'*La Notte di San Lorenzo*, sir.'

'Fantastic film!' shouts Suzanna.

'I don't speak Italian.'

'The night of the falling stars, sir.'

'What's that? Is somebody finally talking about me?' asks Cindy, rubbing a wet finger over her gums.

'I don't want to hear that sort of talk, bevvy.'

Richard is looking at Cindy with such desperate love that even Ted, whose heart is not easily melted, begins to feel sorry for him.

'Then turn off your hearing aid!'

'Cindy! That's enough!' Suzanna tears the glass from Cindy's hand and pours the champagne out of the window.

'Falling stars! I want to see them too!' shouts Ava, overly high-spirited.

'Forget the falling stars! You're staying in the car! I don't want to start a riot!' Ted shuts the window. 'Just imagine! If they recognise her!'

Just before she disappears behind the dark window, Mercury catches a glimpse of Ava. Their eyes meet for a moment, just long enough for him to understand that she wants to get out of the car, that she, probably a little lightheaded, wants to gaze at the heavens with him, overwhelmed by the power they radiate, whilst he, holding his breath, supports her with his arm around the small of her back, so fragile, so close and yet so out of reach.

The door of the limousine suddenly flies open and Ava springs lithely from the car. Like Rita Hayworth out of a Studebaker, thinks Mercury. He jumps to his feet, but his knees lock, his legs turn to lead, his soles stick to the melting asphalt. 'Ava, come back!' he hears Vangenechte shout before she slams the door with a bang.

'Has it already started, Mercury?'

'Not yet, madame. And we're not in the perfect place. The lights of the motorway and the air pollution above the airport won't help. But you never know.'

'I've never seen a falling star.'

Mercury is moved by the perfect innocence of that little sentence. Her voice sounds pure and natural, the way it does when she is larking around in the swimming pool after lunch with a girlfriend.

'I heard on the radio that they're expecting a real meteor shower. A curtain of light. It's a rare phenomenon, a magical event. Just like fireworks. I hope madame will be able to see it.'

Ava turns around, stretching her neck to gaze at the sky.

'It's making me go all dizzy!'

She totters. Mercury sometimes frightens himself: he knew this was going to happen. Ava stumbles against him and for a moment it is unclear which of the two is supporting the other.

'You're the only star in the sky tonight, madame.' A lock of her hair sticks to his lips.

'That's sweet of you, Mercury!'

'With her charisma, madame shouldn't act in films such as *Desert Flower*,' he mumbles to himself, intoxicated by the thousand perfumes he is inhaling. 'It's dangerous. It's asking for trouble,' he hears the other who lives inside him whisper.

'There, look!' Ava exclaims, pulling away from Mercury's hesitant grip and pointing with outstretched finger at a speck of light that is moving through the darkness.

'That is an Airbus A-310, madame . . .'

Below them, as if by agreement, all the cars begin to toot their horns simultaneously and an endless procession of glowworms slowly sets itself in motion.

'I think madame had better get back in,' says Mercury, recovering his composure. He opens the door for her.

'La Notte de San Firenze, my arse!' If you really have to see lights dancing in the sky, all you have to do is to watch the fireworks I've arranged for the party!'

When Ava had been introduced to Ted, he had been rather ashamed, charming, almost enchanting. He had taken her under his wing like a father, with the greatest delicacy and the necessary humour, and had showered her with roses and pearls and, despite his blotchy complexion, had been able to persuade her, with the most unexpected promises, to follow him for a time to Antwerp, where she would be bathed in luxury, like a diva, whilst he was promoting her career. She had been far away from home for many years and thought she had nothing to lose. Since then, he has had his grey hair dyed and has put on fourteen kilos. He wears golden signet rings and trousers that are too short. He sweats more than he used to, sleeps with his socks on and has started to behave like the most ignorant pig on his farm, first in private, but now also in the company of others. Looking at the dandruff on his shoulders, Ava realises with horror that she has lost everything.

'Ted, darling, you'll never cease to amaze me,' she says.

'I know that,' he answers. 'Why do you think they call me "The Magician"?'

18

In the Rex, the screening of *Desert Flower* is being watched by a disappointed audience in the greatest silence. The film, which had been announced as 'the most erotic cinematographic experience of the past decade', and which, according to the press release, made 'Madonna look like Soeur Sourire and *In the Realm of the Senses* like *Mary Poppins*', has not lived up to the high expectations of the invitees. *Desert Flower* has turned out to be yet another tedious, pretentious, tired, pseudo-exotic literary porn film. Neither its cinemascope format, nor its overwhelming Dolby-stereo soundtrack could rectify that.

Patrick de Busschère, who has so far been yawningly watching the uninspired spectacle from the projection room, is beginning to wonder whether it might not be better if Ava Palomba and Ted Harlow do not appear on the stage this evening. He is worried that a triumphant curtain call from Ted might be embarrassing for an audience that has so far remained in its seats out of courtesy. He can only hope that this one mistake will not have fatal consequences for Ava's future career. He fosters hopes of directing. He has just added the finishing touches to the script of a not unappealing Hitchcockesque psychological thriller and would like to cast her in this debut film.

Next to him, however, Colonel Cornelis is gazing spellbound through the control window at Ava, who is wrestling through the umpteenth dreary seduction scene on the screen below. Cornelis is not only a member of the same lodge as Vangenechte; they also did their military service together with the paracommandos in Leopoldsburg. And such double brotherhood forges a lifelong bond.

'What presence!' Cornelis exclaims, loudly gulping down the saliva that has built up behind his teeth during the previous scene.

'It would indeed be a great loss to our national film industry if anything unfortunate should happen to her,' de Busschère sighs hypocritically.

'With the girdle of security I've had put in place here this evening, nothing could possibly happen to her.'

'M is exceptionally cunning.'

'So am I,' answers Cornelis, without taking his eyes off the screen. 'God in heaven, what an arse!' With his left hand, he crushes a mosquito on the window in front of him and carries on watching through the smear of blood.

While he walks from the projection room to his office, de Busschère searches his diary for the number of Harlow's mobile phone. If he wants to salvage his reputation as a film promoter and avoid wrecking his own film ambitions, then he will have to come up with some convincing lie that will persuade Ted not to turn up at this evening's premiere. And Cornelis is beyond talking to.

In the limousine, which is now jammed amongst the other cars shuffling off the viaduct, Mercury picks up the telephone.

'Harlow Productions, good evening . . . Certainly . . . Just one moment, I'll put you through to Mr Harlow.'

'Ted Harlow speaking . . . Who? . . . Ah, Patrick! Any problems? How's the screening going? . . . A triumph? Just as I expected.' Ted covers the receiver with his hand and elbows the ribs of Richard, who, without his hearing aid, is completely cut off from the world and starts awake from a dozing sleep. 'De Busschère on the phone. It's already beyond all doubt: *Desert Flower* is going to be a cult film! And mark my words, those fairies can smell a hit a mile off! The audience is applauding every scene! Ava, pigeon, you see the Magician is never wrong!'

'Ted?' De Busschère has still not managed to utter a single useful word and now the connection seems to have been broken, perhaps because they are driving through a tunnel, which would mean that they are very close and that he would no longer be able to stop them.

'Ted?'

'Yes, yes! Don't panic! I was just telling Ava the good news!'

'Are you still in that jam?' Hopefully, in a voice that trembles and then cracks.

'It's starting to move, don't worry. You can expect us within fifteen minutes. Better late than never!' To the others, whispering: 'He's in a right old state, the luvvie!'

'Have you been listening to the news?'

'Yes, and?'

'Lova Spencer.'

'That cock-sucking jellyfish? She was begging for it, believe me!'

'I was thinking . . .'

'Leave the thinking to me.'

'I was thinking . . . it might be wiser if you didn't turn up this evening, Ted. M might use the crowd to get close to Ava without being noticed. After all, he might well be hidden amongst the guests and . . .'

'Out of the question! I have the fullest confidence in Cornelis and his troops. And we'll enter discreetly through the side door. Tell him to close off the alley and to wait for us there. Or did you expect me to throw away a million and a half on a party for a pack of jealous profiteers without turning up to enjoy their envious looks?'

'Personally I think it is inadvisable.'

'Scaredy cat! Brace yourself, it's going to be a long, hot night! La notte di San Fernando!' Roaring with laughter, Ted hangs up.

'Is anything wrong?' asks Suzanna.

'Of course not! Success makes fairies nervous. That's common knowledge!'

'And that jellyfish you mentioned, I suppose you meant me?' Cindy sobs in her corner.

'They weren't talking about you, bevvy.'

'They never do.'

19

From his office, on the eleventh floor of the Oudaan, Antwerp police headquarters, Van Laken enjoys a panoramic view of the old city centre, the quays, the River Scheldt, the housing blocks of the left bank, and further, around the bend in the river, the petrol refineries, and even further in clear weather, so he claims, of the Netherlands, where all M's victims have so far originated. And at night, when he is sitting behind his desk like a guardian angel surveying his dark domain, he sometimes plays with the thought that M may have the same view from his hiding place and be patiently watching from afar as his prey approaches, so that he can swoop down silently like a bird of prey, preferably on a moonless night, like this one.

The vague silhouettes of the five detectives who have been solely occupied with the M case for months are mirrored in the tall windows. They are sitting amid a cloud of smoke on either side of the long metal table at which Van Laken usually chairs his emergency meetings.

The five are:

Somers, a bachelor, thirty years on the force. Nicknamed 'the Whore-hopper', because he primarily concentrates his investigations on the neighbourhood around the St-Paulus-plein and is on more than friendly terms with the ladies. Always suffering from a cold but never absent. Has limped since he was hit in the knee by a bullet during a classic café brawl on the Vrijdagmarkt. Is known for his flamboyant Antwerp accent, coarse language and scatological jokes, which he tells at the most inappropriate moments. Within the framework of the investigation into M, he is primarily occupied with the Lilly von Strass case.

Palmans, the oldest, a widower. Nicknamed 'the Congolese', because before independence he was a military instructor in Leopoldville, a period of his life about which he never tires of talking. It left him with both a pathological need for discipline and a preference for African women. Van Laken has therefore put him in charge of the Zsa Zsa Morgan case. Zsa Zsa Morgan is the only black, and therefore the only unconfirmed victim of M.

Feyaerts, a newcomer, good connections in the underworld and the Chinese ghetto, thanks to his stormy past. Nicknamed 'the Gambler'. Divorced from his wife because of his addiction to mah-jong, the eastern domino game, which, according to departmental rumour, has earned him a fortune in shares of the Sun-Wah supermarkets. In charge of the Peggy 'Sue' Laenen case.

Vandenbos, nicknamed 'VDB', not only because those are his initials, but also and primarily because, with his hooked nose, bushy eyebrows and high, bald forehead, he is the spitting image of that other VDB, Vandenboeynants, the former prime minister, a resemblance made even more striking by the ever-present pipe in the left corner of his mouth. Married. Catholic. Father of three daughters, one of them a cute little mongol, probably his favourite. Until recently, strictly a desk man, but because of staff shortages Van Laken has put him in charge of the Pussy de Bauvoir case, via which, stumbling from the one shock to the other and without any preparation, he has been confronted with the real world outside the four walls of his stuffy office.

De Mulder, nicknamed 'the Mole'. Author of a pioneering study of infiltration techniques. Of all Van Laken's men, he has been on the trail of M the longest. Discovered the body of Lolita Moore when he was working under cover in the livestock industry, trying to expose the trade in illegal hormones.

'Gentlemen.'

Van Laken breezes into his office a quarter of an hour late, followed by Courtois, who lays a paper bag, filled to the brim with rolls, in the centre of the table.

'From the Panaché,' says Courtois, 'my idea!'

'But Big Mac is paying!' Van Laken adds, surprisingly cheerfully. His voice sounds younger, less flat. He loves these late, rather secretive meetings, all comrades together, just him, Courtois and the lads, the core, the basis – without examining magistrates, public prosecutors, deputy public prosecutors, psychiatrists or police physicians, who each have a different, vague opinion – high above the city, which is sleeping under a purple dome, whilst in the distance the silence is only broken by the sirens of patrolling cars.

Van Laken sits down at the head of the table behind a slide projector and a telephone.

'Gentlemen, there is beer in the fridge. Don't be shy, this could take quite some time. Courtois, fetch the slides from the drawer, the one on the left in my desk.'

Feyaerts gets up and walks to the fridge.

'Beer everybody?'

'Make mine a fuckin' cold one, with a head as thick as a donkey's dick,' says Somers.

The others simply nod.

'Plain water,' says VDB, lighting his pipe.

'I assume we have all heard about the body in the zoo?'

General affirmative mumbling.

Van Laken picks up the telephone, dials an in-house number and waits.

'Van Laken here. Sorry to wake you. Are the photos ready? . . . From the zoo, yes . . . Wonderful . . . Okay. Have them sent up to my office . . . Yes, immediately.'

'Gentlemen,' Van Laken begins in a solemn tone, 'I know

this isn't the first time we have come together to exchange and compare information about the M case. The reason for this emergency meeting is that the frequency with which M strikes is constantly increasing. In the past, he struck only every two or three months, now it's every week. It is Wednesday, and I don't want to be confronted with a seventh macabre discovery on Monday. I'm giving myself precisely five days to catch him. If I don't, I'll hand in my resignation. I've had it up to here.' Van Laken waves his hand above his forehead.

When his wife left him, she had taken much more than some of the furniture. Since then, Van Laken has been a man without a past, without memories and above all without a future. A broken man who has become accustomed to despair.

'Come, come. It's not that bad!' shouts Feyaerts, head in the fridge, still young and brimming over with superficial confidence.

'And what do we do in the meantime? Fiddle with our dicks?' Somers moves his left leg with a loud click. The steel joint in his knee.

'We pretend,' says De Mulder, the Mole, the infiltrator.

'Right,' says Van Laken, 'we pretend we've come up with the solution tonight.'

'So how do we go about it? Usual method?' asks Palmans, rummaging through the bag of rolls. 'Anything spicy? A few martinos?'

'Yes, specially for you,' answers Courtois, as he lays five grey boxes of slides on the table.

'We go through all the murders again in chronological order. I can't shake the feeling that there must be some common factor hidden away somewhere, that we have so far overlooked and that ought to put us on the right track.'

'That we supposedly never noticed?' asks VDB, sipping his glass of tepid water. 'That would surprise me.'

'Goddamnit, VDB, stop drivelling! We're not in your

fuckin' archives now!' Somers interrupts. 'It's fuckin' late for everybody and I've got other things to do tonight.'

Van Laken loads the first tray of slides into the projector.

'Would you turn-off the light, Courtois? Mole, over to you. The rest of you make detailed notes – legibly, VDB. I'll be having your little essays typed up afterwards.'

The first photo appears on the screen: a glistening, carmine skull, skinless and with the left eye missing. Beneath the double cavity where the nose would normally be, grinning gums take the place of the missing lips. The mouth is open. The teeth appear longer than normal and are dripping with blood. The black tongue is hanging over the lower set of teeth like a slice of calf's liver.

'Anna Maria Zonhoven. Fourteen years old. Born in Groningen, Northern Netherlands, on 18 May 1978. Murdered on 7 January last. The photo was taken in a cold-room at . . .'

'We know that, get on with it.'

'At that time, she was working as a stripper in various Antwerp nightclubs, amongst them the Wall Street, the Crazy . . .'

'. . . and the Blue Moon,' interrupts Palmans, smacking his lips. 'These martinos are delicious! Just as good as in Bumba in '58! And that's saying something!'

'. . . under the name Lolita Moore.'

'Sounds like Lolite Amour to a French-speaker.'

'Thank you, VDB. She'd been living in Antwerp for two months, alone, in a furnished apartment behind St Paul's church, had no steady boyfriend and, according to the neighbours, with whom she had little contact, led a quiet, regular life. She went to jazz ballet classes twice a week and was following an open course in sociology at the university. No trace of drugs. Not seropositive. A trouble-free child. Oh yes, before she came to Belgium, she had appeared in two porn films.'

'Three.' Van Laken is unbeatable on this subject.

'Three. A Scrabble block with the letter M had been inserted into what remained of her vagina. That's it. For further details, I refer you to the photos, Old Stinky's report and the evidence preserved in formalin at the lab. A total of one thousand two hundred and sixteen identity checks have been carried out, both in the Netherlands and Belgium, leading to eighty-seven interrogations and eight arrests, all without result. Every video shop between Groningen and Antwerp has been investigated and all the clients who had rented her films have been questioned.'

'Except for me!' Van Laken chuckles.

'Your name did indeed appear in the client lists of several video shops, primarily in that of the Erotheque in Hulst.'

VDB pushes aside an untouched cheese roll and gazes at Van Laken open-mouthed.

'I examine everything, VDB. Within the framework of the investigation, naturally.'

The next slide is a full-length portrait of the skinned body of Anna Maria Zonhoven: a dripping hunk of meat, dangling from a meathook.

'We've no convincing theory about the Scrabble block,' says Courtois, 'but we have been wondering why only Lolita Moore was skinned by M.'

'Lolita Moore was a stripper,' answers Van Laken, opening a Stella.

'And not a fuckin' bad one either,' adds Somers. 'I've seen her at the Crazy. She always picked out some punter and then, when she was totally fuckin' starkers, she used to let him stick his nose in her cunt. Used to give me two stiff legs!'

'Somers! Save your filthy language for your lady friends, later!' At such moments, VDB longs to be back in the archives, where he can work his normal hours undisturbed, alone and in silence, far away from the violence, the decadence and above all from Somers' vulgarity.

'All M's little tableaux are highly symbolic,' Van Laken continues calmly, 'determined by the personality and the life of his victims. And Lolita was a stripper . . .'

'And so?' asks Courtois, opening his notebook and wetting the tip of his pencil with his tongue.

'Every evening she appeared naked on stage, in the spotlight, after having stripped off her clothes excruciatingly slowly, like some unapproachable automaton. Like a moth creeping out of its cocoon. Like a ripe chestnut bursting out of its shell. But without ever completely revealing her secrets. M went further. After having strangled her, he first removed her clothes and then her skin, as if he wanted to show her to the world more naked than naked, as if he wanted to bare not only her body but also her soul.'

'Nice theory,' says De Mulder, nodding at Van Laken admiringly.

'Who'd have thought it, our boss is a fuckin' poet.'

'A nice theory, but unfortunately, it doesn't bring us a single step closer,' Van Laken sighs, and changes the tray in the projector. 'We're listening, Somers.'

Somers picks up the metal pointer that is lying on the table in front of him, struggles to his feet with a dry click, limps to the screen and waits until the first photo appears.

A naked woman is lying prostrate, in a dark pool of blood, in the centre of a circular, pink-plush-covered bed. She is wearing an ash blonde wig. Her face is pressed into a green satin cushion, her arms are extended together above her head, the wrists bound together with shining handcuffs. She is kneeling, knees spread, her small breasts dangling beneath her arched torso like two flaccid cones. In the hollow of her back, the gold glitter which covers the whole of her body sparkles in a beam of purple light. Her full, rounded buttocks, raised and turned towards the camera, appear to hover like a gilded balloon in the centre of the small, mirror-covered room. At first sight, the photo looks like an average pose from a porn magazine.

Maartje kneeling over her hairdresser, thinks Van Laken.

'Okay. Off we go. Lilly von Strass. Twenty-six years old. Former clothes horse, that's a fashion model to the posh ones amongst you,' Somers begins in a deliberately monotonous voice, as if he is trying to counteract the erotic impact of the photo. 'Born in Eindhoven on 2 September '67, into a rather toffee-nosed family. Father a lawyer, mother a chemistry teacher. Two older brothers. Her real name was Shoeke van Mierloo. After a promising start as a photo-model, she went rapidly downhill: got less work and then no work at all. Drink, cocaine, nightlife. At that time, she was living in New York. The money flew out of the doors and windows and soon she was flat on her arse. Last year, she ended up totally broke in Antwerp, where she first posed butt-naked at the Academy and then worked the street behind the high school, before finally ending up waggling her naked arse every night until seven in the morning in the Peeping Tom, that peepshow in the Anneessenstraat, where she was found on Monday 4 February, still in a working pose, but as dead as a fuckin' doornail. You'll have to ask Van Laken whether she ever acted in smutty films.'

Van Laken shakes his head.

On the screen, right next to Somers' head, a greatly enlarged close-up of the dark, hairy zone between her spread buttocks appears: the lips of her vulva tightly shut together, a flawless, vertical, somewhat lighter strip, exactly in the centre of the photo. Somers taps his pointer, just above the hermetically closed vagina, on the relaxed anus from which a trickle of blood is flowing.

'They found both of her eyes stuck up her arse. Pretty eyes. Light blue.'

'The work of a surgeon,' Courtois remarks. 'Next photo, please.'

95

The next slide shows her face. With its garish make-up, smeared lipstick and, above all, empty eye sockets, it looks like a cheap carnival mask. Her throat has been slit from ear to ear, a bloodless gash. Long paste earrings are hanging from her ears. The letter M has been stamped on her forehead. She is smiling.

'That's all, folks.'

'Thank you, Somers,' says Van Laken, munching on a cold hot-dog with sauerkraut. 'In this case, M has once again improvised on a particular theme, namely voyeurism. He has, so to speak, reversed the roles. It's no longer the clients' eyes staring through their windows at Lilly's arse, but her eyes staring from her arse at the voyeurs. Our M is a moralist. Intriguing, isn't it?'

'If you look at it like that,' replies VDB.

'The question is: how did he manage to get in there to kill her?' says Feyaerts.

'The music is always very loud and besides, we're certain that she knew him and that, suspecting nothing, she therefore let him in through the corridor that connects with the Vegas, the disco in the cellar. The staff have naturally been questioned, even though all of them are women . . .'

'And?'

'Nothing, of course.'

'Somebody must at least have seen her last client,' De Mulder remarks rightly.

'Right,' answers Somers. 'I even managed to trace the bugger and question him. He was a regular client, a drooling old codger of eighty-two, who'd lost his false teeth during the war, couldn't see fuck, was as deaf as a post and shaky on his feet. He admitted that he'd been in the Peeping Tom that night. Turns out he'd sat there staring at her without ever realising he was staring at a stiff that was bleeding dry on a rotating mattress. Completely fuckin' gaga.'

'No fingerprints?'

'No. Not a spot, not a smear, not a thread. No footprints, no hair, fuck all. If you ask me it's the work of a fuckin' robot.'

'No weapon? No razor, for instance?' asks VDB.

'What do you fuckin' think!'

'7 January . . . 4 February. Exactly four weeks.' Courtois jots it down pro forma in his notebook.

There is a knock on the door.

'Enter!'

A young uniformed officer comes in and hands Van Laken a manila envelope.

'The photos you asked for, commissaris. The slides will only be ready tomorrow.'

'Thank you.' Van Laken tears open the envelope and deals out the photos like playing cards, one to each of them. 'Lova Spencer. Number six.'

'Art with a capital A,' says Palmans. 'When this is over, we ought to publish the series as an art book.'

'What's she got in her mouth?' asks VDB.

'A cheese butty!' shouts Somers, his raucous laughter shattering the businesslike atmosphere. VDB spits his last mouthful discreetly into the palm of his hand.

'A scorpion fish,' says Van Laken proudly.

Courtois leafs through his notebook.

'A clown wrasse.'

20

'Can't you get a goddamn move on, Mercury?' Ted bellows into the telephone. 'It's a quarter past one! There won't be anything left to drink soon!'

'Once we're past the site of the accident, our problems ought to be solved, sir,' Mercury answers calmly. About a hundred metres away, he can now see the charred carcass of a tipped over tanker lying diagonally across the road, illuminated by the blue glare of dozens of flashing lights. He replaces the receiver and changes the CD: Cello Concerto No. 2 in D, performed by Alexander Michejew and the English String Orchestra, conducted by William Boughton. A gem.

'I sometimes think he does it on purpose,' says Ted, grabbing Cindy's glass from her hands and gulping it empty with a grimace.

'What in God's name was that? Aftershave?' he shouts, spitting out the indefinable mixture.

'No idea,' replies Cindy, slurring her speech. She is barely capable of following even the most superficial conversation. Her eyes are misty and dazed, her jaw loose and her gestures uncertain. She looks like a broken Barbie doll with a nervous twitch.

'And the hard shoulder?' screams Ted through the telephone.

'That is free now, sir.'

'So what are you waiting for?'

'May I politely draw sir's attention to all the policemen a little further along and . . .'

'They'd kiss my arse if I asked them to!'

'If they were to pull us over, sir, we'd arrive . . .'

'Mercury, either drive on to the hard shoulder immediately, or I'll take the wheel myself and you can gaze at the stars while you walk home to pack your bags!' Ted slams down the receiver. 'Do your staff give you this much trouble, Rich?'

'I haven't had a chauffeur since '68.'

'What do you mean? Why ever not?'

'I find it somewhat . . . passé.'

'Just like white dinner jackets,' says Suzanna.

Mercury flicks on his right indicator, pulls over carefully and slowly begins to overtake the queue. Just as he feared, the limousine is stopped by a wildly waving policeman as it draws parallel to the wreckage. He puts on his Ray-Bans and sinks a little deeper into his seat. On the one hand, he wants no part in this lamentable incident; but on the other hand, he is smiling with something approaching relief, because he cares little about the premiere and this way he will be close to Ava a little bit longer.

'I suppose we can forget it now,' says Ava, gazing outside uneasily.

'I'd have done better to stay home with Arthur,' sighs Suzanna, 'cosily watching our latest videos together, whilst he . . .'

'Stop whining!' Ted interrupts. 'Firstly: nobody has ever stopped Ted Harlow from doing what he wanted. Nobody! Secondly: that teenager in uniform is not going to be the first one to do so. And thirdly: just watch the Magician in action!'

Ted gets out and walks up to the policeman, who towers a head and shoulders above him. He takes out his wallet, hands the policeman his visiting card, begins to wave his arms passionately, points to the limousine, then towards Brussels, then at his watch, then at the sky, folds his hands as if in prayer, holds his head, beats on his chest, stamps his feet angrily, points to his dinner jacket, lets the policeman feel the material, points to the car, takes out his wallet again, takes the policeman by the arm, shows him a photo of Ava and walks back with him to the open door.

'Jerry Lewis,' whispers Richard.

'Look!' pants Ted, pointing at Ava. 'There she is! Just like in the photo, only with her clothes on! Ted Harlow never lies!'

'Good evening, ladies, sir.'

'Well?' asks Ted.

The young policeman hesitates.

'What was your name again?' asks Ted.

'Snoeckx, Albert.'

'A fine name. Well, Snoeckx Albert, don't let this opportunity pass you by, man. I'll discuss your promotion with my good friend Cornelis this very night! What do you think of that! And I'll take full responsibility.'

Snoeckx hesitates a moment, then stands to attention.

'I'll inform my colleague, and then if you'd be so good as to follow us. As you so rightly remarked just now, this is a clear case of emergency, in which the law has to bow to common sense.'

Ted pats him conspiratorially on the shoulder and gets in. Snoeckx shuts the door and gives a brisk military salute.

'What did I tell you. He's learnt his lesson. I've got them eating out of my hand. Just like the other pigs!' Ted quivers with self-satisfaction.

'Given a little skin care, not too bad at all,' says Suzanna, 'For a policeman that is.'

'What did you promise the poor darling?' asks Ava.

'A night of torrid passion with Cindy in Capri,' says Richard, staring inertly into the distance.

'Dreams, my precious! Dreams and moonbeams. I'm not the biggest producer in Belgium for nothing!' He wipes away the sweat from his forehead and picks up the telephone. 'And now to put Chicken Little in the picture . . . Mercury? Would you be so kind as to follow those two motorcycle policemen?'

Mercury cringes at the thought of driving into Brussels

under police escort. When he decided to go under cover as Vangenechte's chauffeur, it was not only to be closer to Ava.

Ted pours himself a Chivas, rummages in the fridge for ice cubes, tries to relax, takes a deep breath and shuts his eyes.

'Out of my hands . . .'

21

The willowy, naked body of a white woman is lying on the sagging, mouldy back seat of the rusting wreck of a Cadillac Eldorado '58, surrounded by lilies, torn books, blood-smeared candles and costume jewellery which is sparkling in the moonlight. Her head is leaning on a large, lace-edged white silk cushion, which contrasts sharply with her black Louise Brooks hair-style. Her staring eyes are light grey and, oddly enough, still clear. Her eyelids have been darkened, as have the heavy, horizontal eyebrows above her horn-rimmed glasses. Anybody who looked only at her head would think she was daydreaming: of Sunset Boulevard, of patios filled with palm trees, of Panavision, Technicolor and barbecues in Malibu. Her neck, wrists and ankles are adorned with strings of pearls. Her nails are of the same purplish red as her nipples and her lips. Her long, slender arms and legs are spread. Her left knee is grazed and her black nylon stocking is torn at the place of the wound. She is wearing shiny black stilettos. In these respects, the photo resembles a still life.

Her belly has been slit open just below the navel and eviscerated. Her intestines, which are still attached to her stomach, have been carefully unrolled from the gaping wound and the black snake disappears outside, over her left shoulder, through the rear window of the wreck.

VDB is standing with his back to the screen. Unlike his colleagues, he has never been able to look at the abhorrent pictures, time after time, with so-called 'cool professionalism'. He curses the new assignment Van Laken has given him. Normally, he would now be sleeping peacefully between his wife and her poodle in his furnished flat on the seafront in Blankenberge, with the children, grains of sand in the corners of their eyes, fast asleep on the sofas in the living room, tired out from the wind and cycling through the foam of the ebbing waves.

Through the open window he would be able to hear the familiar, intergalactic violence of the funfair below and further, vaguely, the breaking of the waves and the whispering of the dunes. He is reading from his notes, but speaking so softly that the others can barely hear him.

'Magda Serneels . . .'

'Louder!'

'Magda Serneels-Van Schalken. Twenty-four years old. Born in Amsterdam. Actress and author of the controversial first novel *The Corruption of Pussy de Bauvoir*, an erotic autobiographical text hailed by the Dutch newspaper NRC as "the *Histoire d'O* of the Nineties". Cohabited with the father of her three-year-old son, the Antwerp fashion journalist Tony Serneels. Murdered by strangulation on 22 April. Her body was discovered the following day in a car wrecker's yard near Wommelgem. On 22 April, her partner was in Milan, interviewing the Belgian designer Van Beirendonck. The beauty spot above her lip later turned out to be fake . . . uh . . . the ripped books around the body were copies of her own novel . . . Her execution was undoubtedly the work of M . . . uh . . .'

Van Laken presses the remote control.

An exterior shot of the Cadillac, the wheels of which are sinking into a red sludge. Struggling to overcome his disgust, VDB follows the intestine, with the point of his pencil, from the rear window out onto the dented roof of the wrecked car.

'What you can see here, trailing out through the window, is the caecum, the blind-ended pouch at the junction of the large and small intestines. The clearly legible M on the roof has been formed from the caecum, the colon and the rectum. Could we possibly open the window?'

'It's naturally a question of taste, but personally I find this the most impressive of his *tableaux vivants*,' Palmans remarks drily.

'The most literary,' Courtois corrects.

'And naturally you've read the book?' Van Laken asks VDB.

'Which book?'

'*The Corruption of Pussy de Bauvoir.*'

'Naturally.' Without conviction. Short of breath. Bored.

'So tell us how it ends.'

'I don't remember exactly.'

'So you haven't read it?'

'Yes, but quickly and long ago. My wife read it too. Actually, we didn't think very much of it.' VDB feels as if he is back at school. Why did Van Laken take such delight in humiliating him in front of his colleagues?

'Well I'm afraid you didn't read it as thoroughly as M. Sit down, VDB. The book ends like this: the famous psychiatrist and high-class call girl Pussy de Bauvoir, a sort of modern courtesan, who specialises in the portrayal of her patients' most diverse and bizarre fantasies, is strangled by one of her wealthy clients – an impotent Lebanese diplomat, if I'm not mistaken – in Bornes-les-Mimosas, on the back seat of his Cadillac Eldorado. That's why Serneels' corpse was found in a wrecker's yard, VDB, because M searched for the appropriate car and finally found it in on a scrapheap near Wommelgem. That's also why it took him the almost three months between 4 February and 22 April to prepare his *mise en scène*. But it was worth the effort and the wait: apart from the intestines, everything, down to the tiniest details, matches the last chapter of her book, which thanks to his gruesome intervention has unfortunately become totally autobiographical.'

'And has topped the book charts for weeks,' says De Mulder.

'Her publisher couldn't have dreamt of a better publicity stunt,' Feyaerts admits.

Van Laken turns to VDB, who is standing at an open window breathing in deeply.

'Nothing else unusual, Vandenbos?'

'Either I'm overtired and dreaming, or I've just had a vision,' answers VDB, staring at the sky, 'but I could swear I just saw four falling stars.'

'That's nothing fuckin' new, him seeing stars.'

'You are dreaming,' answers Van Laken. 'And you've just had a vision.'

22

Since that sunny Monday afternoon when he had fallen into a cesspit during a childhood summer holiday at the country cottage of a distant aunt – an accident that had almost cost him his life, had long traumatised him and which had left him with both his obsession with tidiness and his pathological aversion for everything that was dirty and stank – Mercury has never felt as claustrophobic as he does tonight. He is sitting, sweating in his uniform behind the wheel of a ridiculous Hollywood-esque limo, slaloming through the crawling traffic at great speed in the wake of two motorcycle policemen, with, in the back of the car, a whooping pig farmer, a deaf mummy, a snivelling whore, a fancy-dressed fashion designer and Ava, Ava Palomba, his Ava, who seems to be totally unaware of the danger surrounding her, and is allowing herself to be tossed from side to side at every turn, squealing as if she is at the funfair and hasn't a care in the world.

Mercury wrenches open his shirt collar, loosens the knot of his tie and blinks his eyes to remove the stinging beads of sweat. He longs for a cigarette. His hands are clammy, as if his gloves were made of rubber. The lights of the oncoming traffic blind him. He presses the windscreen washer and turns on the wipers, but it doesn't help. Everything is still blurred, as if he is driving through drizzle. His legs are trembling. He presses a finger to his midriff, where the cramps are the most severe, as if the sludge from the cesspit was once again seething inside him, or a biting acid was gradually corroding his insides, blistering his intestines and eating away his stomach. His face contracts with pain. He opens the side window. His mouth fills with bile, but it is again the excrement of his aunt that he tastes. The cello of Alexander Michejew is still resounding from the loudspeakers, but now he is playing Joseph Haydn's Concerto in D Opus 101, recorded in 1985, during a concert in the Great Hall of the University of Birmingham. He swallows, closes his eyes for a moment, sees Ava, naked and blindfolded, crawling over a sand dune on her hands and knees, a burning candle stuck in her arse. He looks in the mirror and does not recognise himself: there is shit in his hair, his teeth are ochre, urine is flowing from his nose and his ears, his eyes are bloodshot and he thinks: The end is nigh. Tonight or never.

23

'Okay, Palmans, your turn.'

'Ah, our Watusi and her black dick!' shouts Somers.

'Our Surinamese,' Palmans corrects him, 'that's not the same.'

'They're all the fuckin' same in the dark. You ought to know that!'

Palmans gets up and walks self-confidently to the screen. The first slide appears.

She is hanging in a graveyard, nailed to a wooden cross like a chocolate Christ, like the bats people used to nail to barn doors to avert evil, behind a grey granite tombstone overgrown with clematis. Around her neck glitters a gold chain, from which a severed black penis is dangling like a shapeless, fleshy jewel in the nebulous valley between her nippleless breasts. Her open-spread cape of gleaming leather, fastened at her wrists with little straps, makes her look even more like a crucified vampire. Apart from that, she is naked, just like all the other victims. Her skull has been shaved almost bald. A slimy thread of saliva, mixed with blood, is hanging from her mouth. She is wearing Oliver People sunglasses with interchangeable lenses, as if she shuns the light even after death. Steel nails have been driven through her pale palms, her ankles have been bound to the post with rope just above the gravestone. On the granite, between the flowers, there is a clumsily chalked M.

'Louisa Morgan. About twenty-two years old. Born in Paramaribo. Better known on the street under the pet name "Zsa Zsa Morgan". Prostitute. Usually sat in the window at number 7 Burchtgracht. When that hovel was demolished, she moved in with her Dutch pimp, a certain Tony van Doorn, a known linchpin of the international traffic in women, currently being held on remand. She was found as you see her in the photo, next to her mother's grave in Schoonselhof cemetery, two weeks ago. To be precise, on Monday 5 August. I found no evidence that she had been involved in porn films.'

'She featured in *Black Dracula and the Seven Virgins* in '92,' Van Laken interjects flatly.

VDB puts on his glasses.

'What's that shiny, bright pink little worm between her legs. That's the first time I've noticed it.'

'Don't tell me you've never slept with a negress?' Palmans exclaims, appalled.

'No, never.'

'You don't know what you've been missing,' laughs Palmans. 'You have to admit, my woman is much prettier than yours.'

'We are all familiar with your aberrations, Palmans.'

'Oh really? Which aberrations?'

'Your Congolese ways!'

'I don't understand.'

'You understand well enough.'

'Van Laken, shut that bald bastard up, before I chuck him through the fuckin' window.'

'Gentlemen, gentlemen! In God's name! We've come here to work!'

'Exactly,' says VDB, 'and to take note of every new detail.'

'And this is simply an anatomical detail,' Palmans quickly snaps, like a child determined to have the last word.

'Okay, let's be serious now. I wouldn't rule out this Tony van Doorn.' Van Laken struggles to his feet, rubbing the small of his back with both hands to ease the pain. He leans over the table. 'The more I think about it, the more I'm convinced that this is not the work of M. What do you think, Palmans?'

'As far as I can see, everything fits: the victim has the right profile, the murder is signed, the staging refers to a film scene, Zsa Zsa was murdered on a Monday . . .'

'But she isn't white,' Courtois interrupts.

'Whatever the case, she was quite a babe,' Somers adds dreamily.

'According to our graphologists, the letter M on the gravestone was not written by the same hand. It's less elegant. Less . . . feminine. Besides, I sense a difference in atmosphere, there's a sloppiness here that we're not used to from M. And neither the choice of her mother's grave nor the lopped-off dick between her breasts makes any sense at all. No, this is a clumsy copy, carried out by a man without taste, without style, without imagination, without a sense of harmony, without humour – I know this all sounds odd – in short a man without talent. I want to talk to that Dutch pimp myself tomorrow, face to face.'

At such moments, Van Laken sounds as if he harbours a genuine admiration for M. As if he wants to protect him against vulgar imitators, who shamelessly misuse his oeuvre in an attempt to cover up their own dirty deeds, as if he respects the man who has been defying him for months and who remains elusive. As if he has begun to identify with the monster.

'Watch out for the Stockholm syndrome!' De Mulder jokes.

'That point is still a long way off. But you have to admit, there is a difference. M is so refined, I sometimes think he can't be Belgian.'

'Much less a fuckin' Dutchman!' says Somers.

'Now I know why you asked if that black man in the skip had been emasculated.' Courtois gazes at his boss in admiration.

'That penis had to have come from somewhere,' Van Laken

answers laconically, stubbing out his cigarette butt in an overfull ashtray, his yellow nails disappearing in the ash.

'Which black man?' asks Feyaerts, as always indignant because he had not been informed of everything immediately.

'We'll know more about that tomorrow. A job for you, Somers! And Feyaerts, in the meantime, tell us all you've found out about Miss Laenen. There are still plenty of rolls for those who are still hungry.'

Feyaerts takes a ham and gherkin roll, bites into it greedily and walks to the screen. Through the window he too has now clearly seen a star streaking through the sky above Antwerp's only skyscraper, the 'Peasants' Tower'.

'Peggy "Sue" Laenen!' he shouts, spraying breadcrumbs, as if he is announcing the performance of a singer.

The walls of the marble bathroom of the Presidential Suite, on the top floor of the Pullman Hotel, look like a Jackson Pollock canvas. Every square centimetre has been spattered with blood. The pool of blood on the floor has oozed to the four corners, filling the room like a slippery, red linoleum, dotted with saturated towels. The wash basin, bath and white melamine furniture are daubed with brown smears. Pieces of her body are spread throughout the room: her chopped-off hands are lying on the floor next to the toilet, out of which her pelvis and her legs protrude. On the left ankle, a fine, gold chain. Her armless torso is floating in the bath, which is half filled with pink-foam-covered water. Her head has been twisted off – yet more evidence of the murderer's exceptional strength – and displayed, amongst the perfume bottles on the dressing table, next to the framed nude photo which was published in Penthouse and made her famous. Her Nivea-covered face is turned towards the mirror.

'Her arms were found in the minibar in the bedroom, along with a reprint of Lode Zielens' *Mother, why are we alive?* The M of Mother had been circled with a red pen.' Feyaerts stuffs the butt of his roll into his mouth and licks his fingers. 'Peggy

Laenen was twenty-six and came from Utrecht. She was already well known as an actress. She lived in Amsterdam, but had been staying in Antwerp since the previous week, for the shooting of her new film, the title of which now escapes me.' Feyaerts automatically turns to Van Laken.

'*Blood, Sweat and Tears II*, according to what I've read, a sequel even more violent than the first film. Amongst other places, it was set in the fort at Breendonk during the Occupation.'

'Thank you. On Monday 12 August, the day of the murder, the hotel receptionist says three people called at her room between seven and nine p.m. A waiter, who brought her a Waldorf salad and an apple juice; Simon Maarschalk, her director; and a certain Mr Harlow, a film producer, who came to show her a film scenario, a copy of which we found on her writing desk, together with his visiting card.'

'Ted Harlow?' Van Laken exclaims, surprised. 'Are you sure of that?'

'Our Ted Harlow?' asks Courtois. 'Vangenechte?'

'Have you questioned him? As a witness?'

'The man is totally unreachable, but that seems to be normal for a film producer. And besides, he's as pure as snow. He announced his arrival at reception, didn't spend more than ten minutes with Peggy, according to witnesses, and then went down to the bar for a quiet cognac, which, incidentally, he forgot to pay for. His clothes didn't show the slightest trace of blood. Bloodstains were however found on the stairs of the emergency exit.'

'So how did M get to her?'

'He must already have been in her suite when she returned from the set, at around six-thirty. Both the waiter and the director say they had the impression there was somebody in the bedroom while they were talking with Peggy.'

'So she knew her murderer?'

'Very probably. It must have been somebody she trusted.'

'Her lover?'

'She had several. Three to be precise. But all three were in Amsterdam on the Monday in question. According to Maarschalk, she didn't want any distractions while she was filming.'

'So she didn't let him in herself?'

'Not necessarily. He probably had the magnetic card that opened the door of her suite.'

'Any idea about the murder weapon? Or better said, the murder weapons?'

'Not a trace. M took all his tools with him when he left.'

'Just like a fuckin' plumber,' Somers remarks.

'But surely she was under surveillance?'

'I think I need a cup of coffee.'

'In the corridor, De Mulder. The machine.'

'For me too, milk and sugar!' shouts VDB.

'Of course she was under surveillance.'

'Feyaerts?'

'Nothing to do with me! Ask the two officers who were on duty. They didn't see a thing. No, what I'm wondering is why he hacked the poor creature to pieces.'

'Because in '90, she'd played the lead in *Bloody Mary*, a free adaptation of the Suchnam Singh Sandhu murder. You must remember . . .'

'No.'

'But of course you know that case! It was in all the papers. The torso of a nineteen-year-old Indian girl, Sarajit Kaur, found in a green Spartan suitcase in Wolverhampton on 5 April 1968!'

'I'll never fuckin' forget it,' says Somers. 'They found both her legs in another fuckin' suitcase, floating in the River Roding, under a bridge in Ilford, a suburb of London.'

'Right. And her head was discovered by accident, in a sports bag, by a cyclist . . .'

'A certain Bill Sallis.'

'Well done, Somers!' Van Laken is beaming. He loves conversations in which he can measure his knowledge against somebody else's. 'And do you still remember when?'

Somers thinks deeply, moves his leg.

'About a month later.'

'On 8 May, Somers. And do you also remember where?'

'Right next to Winstead Flats. Your turn!'

'And did Scotland Yard ever apprehend the culprit?' asks Palmans.

'Oh yes! It was the victim's father. He made a complete confession on 13 May and was sentenced to life imprisonment on 11 November.'

'If, like me, you haven't seen the film,' says VDB, excusing himself, 'you can hardly be aware of all the details. We seldom go out, my wife and I. Once a month to the Chinese on the corner, and even then . . .'

'How's her rash?'

'None too good. None too good . . . thank you.'

'Your wife's a redhead, isn't she?'

'Yes. Why?'

'People with red hair and a pale complexion are often more susceptible to skin complaints.'

'And they've also got a very distinctive body odour.'

'Yeah, specially when it rains!'

'Aren't we digressing?' De Mulder walks in with two beakers of steaming coffee. 'Here, VDB, milk and sugar.'

'We were waiting for you,' says Van Laken. 'Courtois is just dying to tell us all about the Lova Spencer case, isn't that right, Pol?'

This was the second time Van Laken had called Courtois by his Christian name. And what's more, he had now done it in the presence of all of his colleagues.

24

'I've got toothache,' Cindy whimpers.

'You've always got toothache!' Richard sneers.

Suzanna is wondering what could possibly prompt a refined and cultured man like Richard Weinberg to get married to such insufferable creatures time after time. Cindy is a curse. Suzanna's gaze must be extremely telling, because Richard gives her the answer without her even asking.

'To get married you have to relish solitude.'

'I'd sooner pay my monthly six hundred thousand francs alimony than enjoy your sort of solitude!' says Ted, waving the cassette of *Desert Flower*. 'If you like, I'll show you the end, the scene in which Ava discovers that the priest she has seduced is not a real priest at all, but John Drake, her very own brother . . . Nobody?'

'Don't bother, Ted. We're almost there.'

'You never told me you'd been married,' Ava says, surprised.

'You never asked me, pigeon! Are we really not going to watch the end? It's pure magic!'

'Ted, let's play that game again,' says Ava, who doesn't feel like watching herself yet again on video, 'you know, the one where everybody takes turns to give a clue about their favourite film and the others have to guess the title.'

'Not now surely!' Ted protests.

'Exactly now! As a diversion. It'll relieve the stage fright.' Ava kneels down and lays her head on Suzanna's knees. 'I'll begin: My angel! Let me look at you one final time! I'm with you. And I'm staying with you! For eternity!'

Nobody reacts.

'Well?'

'No idea.'

'You have to give more details.'

'Name names.'

'Or a year.'

'Is it a Flemish film?'

'Okay. They're Anna von Geschwitz's last words to Louise Brooks in . . .?'

'*Lulu* by Pabst,' says Richard calmly.

'We have a winner!' Ava shouts, and returns to her seat. 'Your turn, Rich!'

'This isn't so easy.' He thinks a moment. 'It's the sound of the waves, breaking against the rock on which Liz Taylor and Richard Burton are living.'

'*Boom!*' squeals Suzanna.

'What's wrong?' Ted exclaims, coughing and spluttering out his whisky.

'*Boom!* That's the title! A Joseph Losey film, isn't it?'

'Very good,' says Richard. 'My compliments.'

'What a ridiculous game!' growls Ted.

'Your turn, Suzy!' Ava is getting excited, like a child, as if she has forgotten all about the journalists, photographers and fans she'll be thrown to at the party.

'Let me think. The only film in which the leading character, who normally walks around half-naked, wears a double-breasted, pinstripe woollen suit.'

'Is it a Flemish film?' asks Ted for the second time.

'No, no, they don't count.'

'Am I in it?' asks Cindy.

'That's all I'm saying.'

Everybody is sunk in thought. At last there is some silence in the limousine; they hear Debussy's Sonata for piano and cello, performed by Rostropovich and Benjamin Britten, resounding from the driver's cabin.

'*Rolande met de Bles*!' shouts Ted in triumph. 'The only film in which Jan Decleir wears a suit!'

'It's not a Flemish film, Ted!' Ava repeats. 'And it has to be her favourite film!'

'Toothache!' Cindy howls.

'Is it a film by Richard Thorpe?' asks Richard.

'Yes.'

'Produced for MGM by Frederick Stephani?'

'I don't know who produced it.'

'You're supposed to know what you're talking about.'

'Hush, Ted.'

'Was the original title *Tarzan against the World*?'

'Possibly . . .'

'*Tarzan's New York Adventure*, with Johnny Weissmuller, Maureen O'Sullivan, Charles Bickford, Chill Wills and Paul Kelly.'

'He's won again!' Suzanna and Ava clap their hands.

'This game is rigged. I'm not playing anymore,' mumbles Ted, gazing at his reflection in the window and combing his orange hair. 'For the photo, later.'

And then to Ava, sharply: 'You ought to tidy yourself up a bit too. You're a mess! And on your opening night!'

'Come on, Ted, don't be so childish. It's only a game! You have a go. Come on, we'll guess. You must have a favourite film?'

'Of course I do. Everybody does.'

'Well then?'

'You can keep your hat on.'

'I haven't got a hat on!' says Ava, playing along. She already knows the answer. Ted always comes up with the same film.

'That's my clue, idiot. You can keep your hat on!'

'Has anybody got anything to stop toothache?'

Richard and Suzanna have also guessed the title: $9\frac{1}{2}$ *Weeks*, by Adrian Lyne, in which Joe Cocker sings Randy Newman's

'You can leave your hat on', whilst Kim Basinger performs her historic striptease for Mickey Rourke.

'It's not an easy one,' sighs Richard, winking at Suzanna.

'Can't you tell us a little more?' she asks.

'You didn't help me either.'

'*Lassie*?' asks Ava.

'Wrong!'

'*Gone with the Wind*?' says Suzanna, hiding behind her veil.

'Wrong again! You'll never guess it!'

'And it's your favourite film?'

'Definitely!'

'*Desert Flower*!' shouts Richard.

'No!'

'Then I give up, Ted. You're too good for me.'

'Ava?'

'Beats me.'

'Cindy?'

'I'm not playing. I've got toothache.'

'Suzanna?'

Suzanna shakes her head, barely able to suppress her laughter.

'So, shall I tell you?'

'Yes, you've won.'

'*$8\frac{1}{2}$ Weeks*!'

Except for Cindy, who is rubbing white powder on her gums with her index finger and then running the curled tip of her tongue back and forth across them, they all burst into tension-breaking laughter. Ted takes it to be a token of admiration.

'If this goes on much longer, I'm jumping out of the car and dragging myself to the very first dentist I can find!' Cindy shrieks, immediately stopping the laughter.

Despite its foolishness, the game has temporarily distracted them. Nobody has noticed that Mercury carried on driving straight ahead when the two policemen on their leaning motorcycles had left the ring via the exit Centre. The limousine is not now driving along wide boulevards between empty office blocks, but through the age-old oaks of the forest to the south of Brussels.

25

On the Rex's gigantic screen: a luxurious hotel room. A sultry breeze is drifting through its open windows. The white net curtains, which filter the bright sunlight, are fluttering gently to and fro. The floor is wooden: broad, dark, polished planks. Palms, yuccas and laurel bushes are growing in earthenware pots. Ava is lying naked on her back in the middle of a rumpled, three-metre-wide bed, toying with a bunch of grapes. The scene is shot from above, through the slowly rotating blades of a ceiling fan. Overprint: 'Acapulco – Three months later'.

The seats creak and a muffled shuffling murmurs through the auditorium like a wave of relief, as if all those present were heaving an embarrassed but hopeful sigh. The comforting overprint. 'Acapulco – Three months later' might well be announcing the long-awaited epilogue.

'Perhaps you'd better wait for them downstairs yourself,' de Busschère says to Colonel Cornelis, who is still sitting mesmerised, with his nose against the window, watching the final scene of *Desert Flower*. 'They might arrive at any moment.'

When de Busschère reflects that soon he will have to brave the audience at the cocktail party, many of them friends who had had every confidence in him until this evening, he feels so ashamed he wishes the ground would open up and swallow him. If he had not been so strapped for cash, he would never have blindly accepted Vangenechte's more than attractive offer. Vangenechte could envisage the premiere only in this film temple. To the cunning pig farmer, the choice of the Rex meant a cultural seal of approval and the sum he was willing to pay for a single night meant temporary financial salvation for Knopff and de Busschère.

'The Rex is renowned for its cineaste programming,' they had protested initially. 'This production is not in keeping with the courageous philosophy at the basis of our project.'

'I've got nothing against art,' Ted had answered, 'but cinema is also about making money. Hard cash. One hundred and fifty thousand?'

'We're in the middle of an Ozu retrospective,' Knopff had said, 'I fear that . . .'

'Ozu can wait. What I'm offering you is not exactly a load of philistine balls either. Do you realise who I got in to write the scenario?'

'Yes, of course.'

Desert Flower was a very free adaptation of *It's Raining Buttercups*, the first scenario by the now blind experimental poet Marcel Verbeke, who had been awarded the city of Dendermonde's Gwij Paelinckx Prize for Poetry in '58 for his anthology *Lex.Icon, Dia.Metraal*, but this was certainly not an argument that would sway dc Busschère.

'To be honest, we'd rather not.'

'After the screening, Ava Palomba could sing a song. The theme song, for instance. Free of charge.'

'There are dozens of other prestigious cinemas in Brussels.'

'Five hundred thousand. Half a million!'

At midnight, worn down by the nagging, and after one *sabayon* and two *pousse-cafés* in the Villa Lorraine, de Busschère and Knopff had finally agreed, resolving that such decisions should be avoided in future if they wanted to maintain the good name of the Rex.

'Commander!'

'Colonel. Okay, I'm on my way.' Cornelis sticks his glasses in his jacket pocket, walks to the steel door of the projection room and turns around.

'You can tell me how it ends later. I want to hear every single detail.'

'You can hear it from Miss Palomba herself,' de Busschère answers. 'Unless you ignore her, that is!'

'That would be fantastic! But why not? Is she really so . . .?'

'Even better!' says de Busschère, pushing him into the corridor. 'I'll talk to you later at the party!'

26

'What strikes me is that he is becoming more and more daring.'

'That's true: his last two victims were fairly well-known actresses, difficult to get close to.'

'Especially Peggy Laenen.'

'He's taking more and more risks.'

'And striking ever more frequently.'

'But if he continues to choose Monday above the other days of the week, he fortunately can't step up his rhythm. One murder per week will remain the maximum.'

'If only we could figure out the symbolism that lies behind the choice of that particular day.'

'It would bring us a great deal closer.'

'That remains to be seen.'

'It's not as if there are that many Dutch prostitutes or porn actresses.'

'You'd be fuckin' surprised!'

'I mean, we ought to be able to draw up a complete list of potential victims and have the ladies shadowed.'

'And catch him red-handed.'

'Forget it. He's too clever for that.'

'We haven't got enough men to keep an eye on all the Dutch tarts in Antwerp. I know I'm a fuckin' superhero, but I can't do it all on my lonesome.'

'We could bring out a fake video and lure him into a trap that way.'

'Featuring Josiane from the juvenile squad in the leading role!'

'Josiane, together with VDB!'

'That would take too long.'

'Right! I've heard it takes our Josey quite a while to build up steam!'

'Oh really? I've been told exactly the opposite,' says Palmans, suddenly out of sorts.

'Sorry, only fuckin' joking!'

'Of course, we mustn't forget that the man basically wants to be caught.'

'Why would he want to be caught?'

'So it will all be over.'

'So why doesn't he simply stop?'

'Because he can't stop anymore, you morons! Because he's driven by an irresistible urge!'

'Well if he wants to be caught, he could leave a few hints, a couple of clues, couldn't he?'

'Perhaps he already has. But perhaps he also enjoys tormenting us. It mustn't be too easy. It's up to us to decipher his clues. It's a game, pure and simple.'

'A gruesome game, that has cost the lives of six women.'

'Not to mention the five missing boys we haven't found a trace of yet. Courtois, hand me that file there, on my desk, the blue cover.'

'Didn't the examining judge transfer that case?'

'So?'

Courtois walks to the desk, which is practically buried under files.

'There! On top of the second pile. On the left! De Mulder, fetch us some more coffee.'

'At least I haven't come here for nothing,' laughs the Mole. 'Coffee everybody?'

'Coffee for everybody.' Van Laken removes the elastic band from the bursting file. A flood of various sized photos, with cards attached, spills out over the table. He spreads the photos in front of him and picks out five.

'This ought to be them: all of them escort boys, pretty boys who either prostitute themselves around Central Station and in City Park, or entertain clients at home. Two of them are trained masseurs.'

'So what has this all got to do with M?'

'It's a hunch, that's all.'

Unflagging, Van Laken shows the photos to his yawning colleagues. Since Maartje's departure, he only returns to his apartment to sleep for a few hours on his mattress, to feed the cat or to take a bath. Any excuse is enough to have him out and about day and night, hanging around at headquarters or in bars, sometimes for his work, sometimes not. This is one of the reasons why he has called this unnecessary meeting, so that he will not have to be at home alone and be confronted by his old ghosts. His colleagues, who know that the miracle will not take place tonight and that the solution will not be found, are playing along with him, staying more to support him in his pitiful loneliness than because they think it will bring any real progress in the M investigation.

'Karel Verbiest. Twenty-one. Worked as a waiter at Le Monsieur. Missing. Baudouin Bongo. Twenty-two. Zairean student. Picked up three times for soliciting in City Park. Missing. José Martinez. Twenty-six. Entertained men at home by appointment. Posed as a Spaniard, because of his flamenco striptease act in the Lord. Real name: Jos Maartens. Missing.'

'Surely no relation of Maartens from logistics?'

'His son.' Van Laken continues, imperturbable. 'Beverly Hills. Twenty-four. Transsexual. Performed at the Flamingo as Mae West and worked as a high-class prostitute in the bars of various hotels in the city centre. Real name: Ludo Meirmans. Missing. And finally: Nguen Van Tang. Seventeen. Vietnamese refugee. Specialised in Oriental massage. Missing. They disappeared respectively on Monday 11 and Monday 18 February, on Monday 4 March, Monday 20 May and Monday 10 June.'

'Are those his real tits?' asks Somers, carefully studying the photo of Beverly Hills. 'He's got a fuck of a sight more than our Josey's mosquito bites!'

'And hopefully he still has them,' Van Laken continues coolly. 'In my opinion, these five disappearances offer us a very real chance to ensnare M. Either he has already killed them, in which case he'll make his first mistake by doing everything he can to let us discover the bodies – even if it's only for the sake of sticking to the rules of the game, or for the recognition he thinks his little artistic tableaux deserve – or they are still alive and then sooner or later we'll find them. What we know for certain is that, for reasons so far unknown, he always kills his victims on a Monday, but that some of his victims have actually disappeared on other days.'

Courtois reads aloud from his notebook: 'Magda Serneels-Van Schalken on 18 April, a Thursday. And Lolita Moore on Sunday 30 December last year. The former was murdered four days later, the latter one week later.'

'Which could mean that he keeps the women locked up somewhere until all of the prerequisites for the final ritual have been fulfilled.'

'This is a new element, lads!' Feyaerts sounds genuinely elated.

De Mulder comes in carrying a tray on which seven cups of coffee are quivering.

'Did I miss anything?' he asks without conviction.

'Yeah, this!' Somers shows him the photo of Beverly Hills. 'Tasty little bugger, isn't he?'

27

Cornelis looks at the imitation Rolex he wears on the inside of his wrist: it is a quarter to one, and whilst he is pacing up and down like some sergeant at the side entrance to the Rex, he is missing the end of *Desert Flower*, already his favourite film of the year. He is nervous, because he realises that within just a few minutes he will be helping Ava out of her limousine, the same Ava he has just seen writhing shamelessly across the screen. He dries his clammy hands with his handkerchief. Not only will she be the first film actress he has ever seen in real life, she will also be the first woman whose every anatomical detail he knew before he had even met her. This flusters him enormously. He knows that soon – stark naked in his imagination – she will be holding out her hand to him, the hand he must not forget to kiss, because that was how one greeted film stars, he had learnt that from Roland Lommé's film programme on the television.

De Busschère appears in the doorway and looks questioningly at the tall gendarme-colonel, who is keeping an uneasy watch in the poorly lit alley.

'Still nobody?' he calls out nervously. 'It's all over inside!'

'I didn't hear anything!' answers Cornelis.

'The applause was rather discreet. That's often the case at premieres.'

'And people have no taste.' Cornelis folds his handkerchief into a stiff triangle and sticks it into the breast pocket of his dinner jacket.

'I think I'd better wait here with you,' says de Busschère, who cannot summon up the courage to show his face at the party, defenceless and alone, and, feeling increasingly breath-less, is eagerly using the situation to enjoy the sultry evening air for a moment. A plump rat is meanwhile gnawing at one of the plastic bin-bags which are piled up against the rear wall of the Tropical Snackbar. Through the brick wall above the gleaming pile, a rusty ventilation pipe protrudes, from which white steam, strongly smelling of mussels, is rising. It is an odour which – at that time still indefinable – had penetrated the projection room and which Cornelis from now on will always associate with the naked, writhing body of Ava Palomba.

'There's something wrong,' says de Busschère. 'I can feel it.'

'Another one of those wretched people who operate solely on their emotions,' thinks Cornelis, as he looks at the frail figure silhouetted in the light of the corridor. 'But that nancy boy might just be right.'

'I'll phone Vangenechte's car at once.'

'I'll come with you.'

'You stay here!' It sounds like a military command. Even Cornelis is startled by the tone of his voice, by its hollow echo between the high walls of the alley. 'Or rather, you telephone and I'll wait for them. That's probably safer.'

This sudden change of strategy has little to do with security. Above all, Cornelis does not want to miss the arrival of Ava, that stolen moment of absolute intimacy he has so been longing for. He automatically takes his handkerchief back out of his pocket, this time to wipe away the dry white saliva from the corners of his mouth. For the kiss on the hand that is soon to come.

28

The limousine is gliding along the E411, in the direction of Luxembourg, as if on a cushion of air. Mercury turns down the volume of the *Sonata da Chiesa Op.* 3 No. 5 by Arcangelo Corelli, performed by the London Baroque Ensemble, conducted by Charles Medlam, extinguishes his cigarette in the ashtray and picks up the telephone.

'Ted!' screeches a shrill little voice, like that of a child who has been caught red-handed.

'This is his chauffeur speaking.'

'May I speak to Mr Harlow?'

'Vangenechte, you mean? I'm afraid not.' Mercury could never have imagined the intense pleasure he gets from this simple answer. He has hijacked the limousine, one of the many plans he has been toying with for weeks, just like a terrorist diverting a plane. He is in charge now and suddenly it is up to him to decide whether or not Vangenechte is available. He had taken off his gloves, his cap, his jacket and his tie and rolled up the sleeves of his shirt immediately after implementing his plan, whilst still driving. He is a free man again, a man without a uniform.

'What has happened?' he hears de Busschère blubbering desperately through the telephone. 'You should have been here ages ago! The screening is over. And I've no idea what I'm supposed to tell the audience!'

'The truth,' Mercury replies calmly. 'Tell them the truth. Tell your guests that Miss Palomba will not be attending the party, that she is ashamed of the film and is afraid of possible reprisals from M.'

'But that's absurd!'

'I thought that's what you wanted.'

Mercury looks at Ava's anxious face in the mirror. She finally seems to have realised that the limousine is driving away from Brussels.

'Believe me, Mr de Busschère, Miss Ava is terrified.'

'But there's no need for her to be afraid!' de Busschère shrieks. 'The Rex is better guarded this evening than Fort Knox! Let me talk to her!'

'Madame does not wish to talk to anyone at present.'

'This is the worst night of my life!'

'Don't worry. She's in good hands.'

Mercury replaces the receiver and turns up the volume of the music.

'Hello? Hello?' De Busschère cannot understand what Mercury means and even less why he has hung up so brutally. He rushes down the stairs in panic, to the emergency exit where Cornelis is still standing gazing at the sky.

'You'll never believe it,' he mumbles. 'You'll never believe it.'

'What's the matter now?' asks Cornelis, gazing in shock at the trembling, breathless man who is spluttering out almost incomprehensible gibberish with tears in his eyes. He is almost sobbing as he searches for his words, grabbing Cornelis by the arm and desperately clinging to it to stop himself from collapsing.

'For heaven's sake, Mr de Busschère, get a grip on yourself!'

Taking deep breaths, de Busschère signals with his free hand to be patient a moment, while he recovers his composure. Cornelis pats him paternally on the shoulder and hands him his damp handkerchief to dry his tears.

'So. Now tell me calmly what the problem is.'

'She's in good hands,' blubbers de Busschère.

'I don't understand.'

'The chauffeur. He says she's in good hands.'

'Who?'

'Ava!'

'I still don't understand. Where are they?'

'God only knows! I think I'm going to faint!'

'Come on, de Busschère, what exactly did their chauffeur say?'

'That they're not coming, that Ava is ashamed, that she's afraid, that I had to believe him, that we needn't worry, that she didn't want to talk to anybody and that she was in good hands.'

'Not forgotten anything?'

'No, I don't think so.'

'And then?'

'Nothing. The brute hung up on me! Poor Sylvain, this will be the death of him!'

Cornelis ponders a moment, takes back his handkerchief and walks inside, dragging de Busschère – who refuses to let him go – along behind him like a doll. As they enter the cluttered office next to the projection room, the telephone begins to ring. Cornelis answers it.

'Colonel Cornelis speaking.'

De Busschère collapses in a heap in a corner and gazes at the Colonel like a beaten dog. Cornelis, nodding affirmatively, is standing as stiff as a rod, listening to an endless loud monologue, with the receiver held at a safe distance from his right ear. When Cornelis hangs up, pale and with clenched teeth, and stares tensely at an invisible spot on the wall, de Busschère writhes with misery. His eyes mist up and the room begins to spin, its walls slanting like in *The Trial* by Orson Welles. In the foyer, the orchestra begins to play a slow version of the Rolling Stones' 'Back to Zero', one of the theme songs of *Desert Flower*. Normally, Ava should now be dancing the opening dance with the Flemish Minister of Sport, Leisure, Environment, Tourism, Folklore and Culture, a personal friend of Ted's. A totally overwrought Sylvain Knopff appears in the narrow doorway, sees his friend hunched on the floor like a pile of rubbish, and casts a malevolent look at Cornelis.

'Good heavens, titch! Did he hit you?'

With a feeble wave of his hand, de Busschère signals no. Sylvain helps him to his feet.

'Gentlemen,' says Cornelis, his forehead deeply furrowed in thought, articulating carefully in a voice that sounds even more dramatic than usual, 'I have bad news. I have just been talking on the phone to the commander of our traffic control centre at the Reyers Tunnel. Two motorcycle policemen who were escorting Ted Vangenechte's limousine have just reported the sudden disappearance of said vehicle.' He pauses. 'Gentlemen, I fear Ava Palomba does indeed not wish to attend the premiere.' Frowning and with quivering nostrils he adds: 'And I would be lying if I said I did not feel personally distressed by this.'

De Busschère and Knopff curse the day they had let Vangenechte's cheque persuade them to screen *Desert Flower* in their cinema. Patrick bursts into tears and begs for a glass of water.

'Here, blow your nose,' says Sylvain, handing his drivelling friend a Kleenex. 'And then we'll go and explain La Palomba's sudden caprice to our guests.'

'I'm driving home and crawling into bed with two valiums,' grizzles de Busschère, 'Don't bother about me. You two go off and dance and enjoy yourselves. And, Sylvain, please don't wake me up when you come home.'

'It's your choice, titch. But I do think it's rather impolite.'

'But Syl, I'm in no state to mix with people.'

'Okay. Captain?' Knopff invites Cornelis to follow him to the foyer.

'Colonel,' answers Cornelis. 'You go ahead. For me, it's duty before pleasure. First I have to regroup my men and send them back to their base.'

An orchestral version of 'Lonely Without You' is now resounding from the foyer.

29

When Ted came to the staggering realisation that Mercury has taken an unforeseen route, and that the limousine was not driving through Brussels as anticipated, but along some deserted motorway, he had become hysterical. Ava had had to give him tranquillisers, and at least a dozen spoonfuls of honey to soothe his convulsive coughing and save him from inevitable death by choking. To make matters worse, the phone seemed to be out of order, and when he had tried to lower the glass partition that separated him from Mercury, so that he could grab the hijacker by the throat and force him to turn back, that mechanism also appeared to be defective. Ted had ranted and raved like a man possessed, hammering with clenched fists on the glass until his knuckles were bleeding, threatening Mercury with life imprisonment and hard labour, after he had broken his arms and legs and ripped off his balls with his bare hands.

Ava is now lying trembling in the arms of Suzanna, who is stroking Ava's head with her strong hands and trying, as far as possible, to reassure her.

'You know, such a kidnapping might do wonders for your career, sweetie. What a publicity stunt! I can just imagine tomorrow's headlines: "La Palomba kidnapped just before her premiere!", "The mysterious disappearance of the Desert Flower". "Night of the falling stars also fateful for film star". Fantastic publicity for the film!'

'And for my comeback!' mumbles Cindy. 'We have to drink to that!'

'Publicity or not, one thing is certain,' screams Ted, 'if your little stunt man is after my money, he can forget it! He's not getting a franc out of me! Nothing! Nada! Rien du tout!'

'Don't be so miserly, Ted,' Cindy laughs. 'And besides, perhaps his brakes have simply gone.'

'I have a rich and exciting life behind me,' Richard whispers almost inaudibly, in a voice like glass, as if he is talking to himself. 'I've met the most elegant women on the planet, buried the dearest of friends, drunk the best wines. I've seen the landing on the moon and collected thousands of sunsets. I've heard La Callas sing and seen Nureyev dance. I have a Memling hanging in my library and a safe that smells of lipstick, filled with paper tissues with the lip-prints of the most beautiful mouths in the history of film. But now I think it is late, I am cold and I am sated . . .' Then he dozes off, his mouth open, his chin resting on his neck-brace.

'Follow Richard's example,' Suzanna says to Ted. 'He's not letting it bother him nearly as much!'

'He won't have to pay nearly as much ransom money!' Ted snaps, casting a sidelong glance at Cindy.

'You never know,' she slurs. 'Mercury looks to me like a boy with taste.'

'I'll have him hung, drawn and quartered! Publicly broken on the market square in Leopoldsburg!' Ted screams. 'After he's paid back every last cent of the money I've blown on this evening's party.'

'You all know very well what's really going on,' Ava says quietly, scared that Mercury will overhear her.

'Of course I know what's going on! That bastard's after my money! Well he can whistle for it!'

'No, Ted, he doesn't give a damn about your money.'

'Oh really? Then he must be the first one!'

'He's not a bit like I'd imagined him,' says Cindy, mumbling her way back into the conversation and seemingly cured of her toothache.

'Shut the fuck up, you stupid tart!' Suzanna shouts with unaccustomed vulgarity and kicks Cindy in the shins.

'I am what I am!' roars Ted. 'And that's what's got me where I am today!'

'Cindy wasn't talking about you,' says Ava.

'So who was she talking about?'

'About . . . M,' she mouths silently.

'About M. With the M of Mercury,' Cindy whispers into Ted's ear.

He turns to stone. Deathly pale, he reaches for the nearest decanter and gulps down a couple of large mouthfuls of neat vodka. These bitches are simply trying to pull his leg. It is impossible: he had interviewed Mercury himself, vetted and engaged him. They had come to a clear understanding. And he was never wrong.

'What's his day off again?' Suzanna asks.

The answer sticks in Ted's mouth.

'Monday,' replies Ava, her head still resting in Suzanna's lap. 'As if that means anything!'

'Maybe the telephone is working now,' says Cindy, snorting a line. 'Perhaps we'd do better to phone the police, rather than just sit here scaring each other to death.'

'I'll call the Rex and alert Cornelis!'

'I wouldn't do that right now,' whispers Suzanna. 'Who knows how Mercury will react if he's eavesdropping. Let me have a discreet word with Arthur. He'll understand me and take the necessary steps.' She presses the numbers one by one with her blue-varnished nails, then waits tensely, clasping the receiver tightly with her two hands.

'Panther? It's me, Suzy.'

'Good evening, Mrs Rizzoni.'

Suzanna recognises Mercury's sensual, genteel voice and turns around. He smiles and waves the receiver at his hostages. Ted tears the telephone from Suzanna's hands.

'Mercury, I'm giving you one last chance!'

'Shut up, Vangenechte, from now on, it's you who has to listen to me. I don't think you fully appreciate the situation. Firstly, shouting won't help. That will only distress your guests and, what's more, prevent me from listening peacefully to the music. Nobody outside can hear your bawling. Just like in *Alien*: "In space, nobody hears you screaming." Secondly, I have everything under my control. And by everything, I mean the doors, the windows, the sun-roof, the telephone, the radio, the television, the video, the air conditioning, everything. I've had three weeks to convert the car to meet my new requirements. Thirdly, you needn't bother to threaten me with dismissal, or anything else, since I no longer consider myself to be in your service. I'll contact you again in half an hour. In the meantime, I suggest you relax and listen along to Glenn Gould's unsurpassed interpretation of a couple of Brahms' *Ballades*. A technically very pure Japanese recording by CBS/Sony, Tokyo. It's never too late to learn something new.'

Ted is speechless with anger. He presses all the buttons at once, breaks his nails on the windows, pounds the television screen and the loudspeakers, tears at the door handles, all to no avail. Mercury is not bluffing. He controls everything from his cabin and they are indeed totally at the mercy of his whims. Ted slumps back helpless and covers his face with his hands.

Ava tries to remain calm and to hide her panic as much as possible.

'I always felt there was something wrong with that boy,' she sobs. 'He was too genteel, too intelligent, too well-read, too well-bred to simply be a chauffeur. I'm almost certain he only took that stupid job as a cover . . .'

'Under an assumed name.'

'Perhaps he had debts?'

'Or a broken heart,' Cindy suggests dreamily, 'and was running away to forget a woman and wanted to start a new life . . .'

'Something along those lines, yes. Do you know his real name, Ted?'

'Ask Richard, our champion, he seems to know everybody!' Ted hisses from behind his hands. 'And by the way, I think it's pretty low falling asleep like some lily-livered wimp, when his friends are in the process of being kidnapped!'

Cindy strokes Richard's hollow cheek, a gesture so tender it surprises everybody, blows softly in his ear, kisses his closed eyes.

'He's cold. Hey, you old rascal! Wake up!'

'He should have become an actor himself,' says Ted.

'Wait! I know something he can't resist!' Cindy pulls her T-shirt over her head, takes her full left breast and rubs the nipple over Richard's dry lower lip. But the old man shows no sign of life.

'You're wasting your time, Cindy,' says Suzanna drily, as she strokes Ava's hair. 'You're wasting your time. Your husband is dead.'

30

'Come on, lads, one final effort and then I'll let you all go home.' Van Laken struggles to his feet and makes his way slowly – with his back hunched, as if he is walking though the rain – to the yellowed street plan of Antwerp that is fastened to the wall with drawing pins. Somers rests his chin on his arms and watches Van Laken through a forest of empty beer bottles. Feyaerts and De Mulder are leaning back in their chairs, resting their crossed legs on the table. VDB already has his raincoat on and is playing with the lock of his thin briefcase. Palmans is gazing through the open window at the orange glow surrounding the tall flame of the oil refinery, just around the bend of the River Scheldt. Courtois is sharpening his pencil. It is twenty past two.

Van Laken waves a card on which something is written in green ink.

'The addresses of the five missing boys. Now listen carefully.'

He takes a thick felt-tip pen from his inside pocket and points without hesitation at a particular place on the map.

'The Van Putlei. The first disappearance. 11 February.' Van Laken takes a pin and fastens the photo of Karel Verbiest to the place he has just indicated. 'Then 18 February, Baudouin Bongo: the Falconrui.' Again he pins up the corresponding photo. 'Then, 4 March, City Park: José Martinez, our flamenco dancer.' Photo. 'On 20 May, the Schijnpoortweg, at the corner with the Pothoekstraat: Beverly Hills, alias Ludo Meirmans.' Photo. 'And finally, 10 June, the Bilmeyerstraat in Borgerhout: Nguen Van Tang.' Photo. 'It may just be coincidence, but look what happens if I connect the five photos with each other chronologically.'

The felt-tip pen makes a squeaking noise on the plasticised map, like chalk on a school blackboard. VDB grimaces and sticks his fingers in his ears.

Joined together, the five points on the map form a clearly recognisable capital M, with long, vertical legs, the left one a little shorter, precisely the same letter as the psychopath's trademark.

'Conclusion?' asks Van Laken, not without some pride.

'Coincidence,' Feyaerts says hastily. As far as he is concerned, the meeting ended some time ago. He still has a date with his Chinese friends for a game of mah-jong in the scullery of the Wah-Khel at half past two.

'That fuckin' map should have been chucked out years ago,' adds Somers from behind his beer bottles.

'Suppose that letter on the map is a hint from M, then logically that would have to mean that he's come to the end.'

'Right!' shouts Van Laken, beaming like a school teacher in front of a cooperative class. 'Keep on supposing!'

Palmans turns around and looks questioningly at the others, hoping they will help him out of difficulty by also saying something, but they avoid his gaze and the ensuing silence is only broken by the exasperating sound of Courtois' pencil sharpener.

'I mean, he's come to the end of the kidnappings. He's carried on murdering since 10 June.'

'And therefore?'

Shaking his head, Palmans turns back to the window and gazes wearily at the streaks of light in the sky.

'There's a storm brewing,' says Courtois.

'And therefore the disappearances have nothing to do with the murders,' Van Laken continues. 'But if we assume that they are the work of one and the same person, a person governed by two different ritual obsessions, then we find ourselves making progress. He has completed the first ritual, because the letter M does indeed consist of five points and four lines. But I'm afraid the other is not yet over. He has other plans for those five youths we assume he has kidnapped. The fact that he has not yet ostentatiously served us up with their bodies, even leads me to presume that they are still alive. And five young lads can't simply be shut away without anybody noticing, no matter how weak they are, unless one has a suitable hiding place.'

'You took the words right out of my mouth,' says Courtois. 'Perhaps some of us ought to continue our investigations in that direction?'

Van Laken winks proudly at his protégé. No doubt about it, one day this lad will succeed him splendidly.

'Good thinking, Pol.'

'So what are we looking for from now on?' asks Feyaerts.

'From tomorrow morning on,' VDB corrects him.

'From tomorrow morning, right.'

'For any large, isolated, deserted, locked-up property in and around Antwerp, in which five screaming youths could be discreetly imprisoned for months on end without the slightest hope of escape: cellars, garages, storage sheds, warehouses, dry docks, ruins, containers, ships, God only knows . . .'

'I have an appointment with the dermatologist tomorrow,' says VDB. 'It could well be contagious.'

'Now that's what I call a fuckin' rash decision!' Somers guffaws. 'Is that it, lads? I'm off for a couple of jars, my hinges need a bit of grease. But I'll give it my full fuckin' attention tomorrow!'

'Me too,' says Feyaerts.

'Rendezvous in my office at eight-thirty?' De Mulder suggests.

'I think that's just about manageable,' says Palmans, and closes the window.

31

At the Mexican buffet, where sweating cooks in sombreros and ponchos are frying tacos, a long line of seemingly ravenous guests are queuing up, paper plate under one arm, paper napkin and plastic cutlery in their left hand, glass of tequila in their right hand. Practical it is not. But it is so much part of the *couleur locale* that nobody even thinks of asking for table service. And besides, a little spillage is only to be expected at such a lavish reception. The smokers are holding their cigarettes clamped between their lips. Shaking each other's hand is a hopeless task. There is a lot of kissing, which is normal in the film world, and a lot of shouting because of the nearby live orchestra. A party is not a party without feigned exuberance. Since it is always the same people who attend Belgian premieres, everybody already knows everybody else, which does not detract from the apparent total amazement and surprise when two guests bump into each other, whether by accident or by design.

Desert Flower is almost unanimously considered to be the flop of the year and so the film is being discussed with great enthusiasm. After a successful screening, the atmosphere is usually much more subdued, because a premiere audience is less generous with compliments than it is with criticism.

Colonel Cornelis, whose lamé dinner jacket has only become really noticeable now it is catching the spotlights, appears at the top of the stairs that lead from the auditorium to the foyer, pushes his way through the crush to the stage, jumps up onto the rostrum, signals to the orchestra to stop a moment and raps his nails against the microphone. The clamour in the foyer slowly subsides.

'Honourable Minister, Madame Alderman for Culture, eminent ladies and gentlemen, dear film enthusiasts, as Colonel of the security and criminal investigation brigades of the Belgian gendarmerie, entrusted this evening with coordinating the security of our beloved artistes, and in the name of the directors of this magnificent complex, Messrs Knopff and de Busschère, whose efforts have made all of this possible, may I please have your attention for a brief, but unfortunately disappointing announcement. I have just received the sad news that Miss Ava Palomba, exhausted by the great exertion of recent months, will not be attending this evening's celebration. She has asked me to extend her heartfelt apologies and hopes that all of you – and I know I did – have enjoyed the film. Furthermore, she wishes all her friends and fans a pleasant, wild and carefree night despite her absence. The show must go on! I thank you for your attention. Music!'

The orchestra strikes up an insipid version of 'El condor paso'. Cornelis makes his way to the VIP lounge, where the director and his entourage, hidden behind potted azaleas, far from the roaring crowd, are chewing with little appetite on cold tacos. Along the way, every time Cornelis overhears guests making hostile comments, it takes all of his self-control for him not to lose his temper.

'Put on weight? Ava? She's twice the size she was in her last film . . . I forget the title . . .'

'And of course she's still too young to rely on body-doubles for the nude scenes!'

'She loves them too much herself! Can't get enough of them!'

'Exhibitionism often disguises a lack of talent. It's sad, but it's true.'

'I didn't have cellulite when I was twenty-four, not an

atom, I swear it, but I still didn't go parading around stark naked!'

'And she's no Madonna!'

'Mind you, I've nothing against nudity, not if it's artistically justified, not if it furthers the plot.'

'I'm sorry, Monseigneur, but first there has to be a plot.'

'And at the very least it ought to be erotic. Unerotic nudity is like spoiled meat! Be honest: were you aroused for a single second?'

'Less than if I'd been watching a documentary about people picking lily-of-the-valley in the Black Forest.'

'Perhaps that's going a little too far. That scene with the burning candle . . .'

'Vulgar! But not arousing.'

'And when she came, when the leader of the terrorists was licking the honey from between her legs?'

'*Déjà vu* and poorly acted. Like an epileptic drinking vinegar!'

'And where on earth did John Drake ever buy that pot of honey in the middle of the desert!'

'At the supermarket, of course!'

'The script was full of holes . . . No bad pun intended!'

'Or some sweeping cuts were made afterwards, that's also possible.'

'The plot was totally unbelievable.'

'I don't see Vangenechte, excuse me, Ted Harlow, being raised to the peerage just yet!'

'You can buy such titles nowadays.'

'Yes, but not with the profits from *Desert Flower!*'

'Ted Baron Harlow, it doesn't sound right.'

'Don't get me wrong, but there are genres we Flemings should leave well alone. Leave eroticism to the Japanese!'

'*In the Realm of the Senses!*'

'For instance! Now that's what I call erotic!'

'Or the Italians! They have a tradition.'

'*La comedia dell'arte!*'

'Right. What we're good at is historical films.'

'Absolutely. Costume films. Not films without costumes!'

Seething with rage at such ignorant nonsense, Cornelis enters the VIP lounge and walks up to Steve Mendeiros, who is hiding behind his lank hair and dark glasses.

'Cornelis, gendarmerie, criminal investigation brigade.'

'Well you didn't waste any time!' sniggers the director. 'Have you come to arrest me already?'

'Quite the contrary! I've come to congratulate you!' Cornelis shouts enthusiastically, shaking Mendeiros's hand and not releasing it. 'This is not the colonel who is speaking to you now, but the deeply moved, sincere admirer. This is a great day for our national film industry! Congratulations, Steve! Or better said: thank you!'

Mendeiros, the son of Portuguese immigrants, curses the day he graduated from film school and pulls himself free from the clammy grasp.

'I'm very flattered.'

'I mean it, straight from the heart. And if Ava Palomba had been present, I would have congratulated her in exactly the same words.'

'To be frank, I'm extremely disappointed by her and Ted's attitude,' sighs Mendeiros, as he hands Cornelis a glass of Moët et Chandon, 'I feel very let down.'

'I'm sure that wasn't her intention. I know her well. She panicked. Quite understandable, given the tension and the atmosphere of terror which has surrounded the poor child these past weeks.'

'M?'

Cornelis nods cryptically. He has always avoided uttering the fatal letter in public.

'Bullshit! As if he'd have dared to strike here, this evening, in front of all these people! And on a Tuesday too.'

'The chance was small, but very real. Perhaps he was sitting in the auditorium just now enjoying himself and is now dancing with one or the other unsuspecting starlet.'

'Ava could at least have informed me.'

'All stars get temperamental sometimes, believe me. And Ava is a star, a true one, a great one. I even think you ought to phone her at home, in half an hour or so, to put her at ease, to describe her triumph. "A kind word can work wonders", that's what we always say at the gendarmerie.'

'I wouldn't exactly call it a triumph.'

'I loved the film. Even though I missed the end. If I was you, I wouldn't let myself be influenced, much less disheartened, by the bullshit of a handful of stuck-up intellectuals. If need be, I'll call her myself.'

Cornelis does not realise he is drying his hands on his trousers as he says this.

32

All attempts to inform Mercury that they have a corpse in the back have failed. He is listening to Gould's mathematical rendition of Brahms on his headphones with a blissful smile on his lips, and when he occasionally glances in the mirror it is only to try to catch Ava's eye, or to admire the curves in her dress, which sheathes her body so tightly that the dim twilight makes her appear to be naked.

'If this goes on much longer, it'll be my turn soon,' says Ted, teeth-chattering, belching, wet, trembling.

The stink in the back of the car is almost unbearable. When it had finally got through to Cindy that Richard had died in his sleep, she had vomited all over him and a part of the back seat and she now lay trembling on the floor, groaning in her bile. Immediately after the lugubrious discovery, Suzanna had covered Richard's head with Cindy's besmeared T-shirt, not just any old how, but artistically folded, almost like a turban. She had laid his hands one over the other and threaded the golden chain and crucifix she wore under her dress through his fingers.

'That's hardly appropriate,' Ava had said. 'Richard was Jewish.'

'Weinberg! Of course! I'm totally shaken.'

'To make it in show biz like he did, you either have to be Jewish or homosexual, or both,' Ted had added with his usual delicacy, 'or have feeling and work hard, like me.'

Ava empties her atomiser over Richard, but the mixture of the various scents – smoke, alcohol, vomit, urine and sweat – with Chanel No.5 is even more disgusting. Ted cannot fight it off any longer, his mouth fills with saliva, then with gastric acid. He clenches his teeth, but the pressure on his bulging cheeks becomes too great and he too vomits, like a volcano spewing out magma, a dark brown jet which spatters over Cindy's breasts, over her belly, over Ava's Kilian shoes.

'You goddamn pig!' Ava screams, climbing up on the seat. 'Why the hell did you have to drink so much?!'

'That had nothing to do with drink!' screams Ted, deathly pale and sweating again profusely. 'Nor with the stink, I'm used to that from the farm! And what's more, I'd like to point out that I may drink more than this hero here next to me, but at least I'm still alive!'

'Barely,' Suzanna observes matter-of-factly from behind her fan. 'And for how much longer?'

'I'm planning to become very old, madame. If possible even older than you. But of course, you won't be around to see that.'

'Shut up, Ted!' Ava screams. 'For Christ's sake, I beg you . . .' She bursts into tears again. Then, softer: 'Please shut up.'

'You lot make me sick! Life makes me sick! People make me sick! People who want a lift in my car, want to stay for dinner, want to stay the night, work together, become friends, the people who are stealing my air, standing in my light and in my way! The whole damn world makes me sick! I already used to break out in boils when somebody forced me to listen to piano music as a child! But most of all, I'm sick of withered, over-dressed fashion designers of Italian origin, of Jewish geniuses who come and die in my car and of pathetic unemployed actresses, who lose control at the slightest setback and piss all over my upholstery!'

'What I was trying to say' – Suzanna is a mistress of self-control – 'is that if Mercury is indeed the man we suspect he is . . .'

'Mercury, or whatever he's called, is a petty, a very petty, moronic, pretentious extortioner!'

'I said if,' Suzanna continues without losing her composure. 'If Mercury is indeed the man we suspect he is, then he'll have to kill us all, you included, Mr Vangenechte, before he can carry out what he has planned for Ava ... or for Cindy.'

'Shut up! Stop saying such dreadful things!' Ava has assumed the foetal position, arms around her ankles, and is hiding her head behind her bended knees. In a flash, she sees Lova floating amongst the goldfish, Peggy's torn-off head displayed on a marble slab between the perfume bottles and herself burnt alive, rolling down a sand dune, with an extinguished candle stuffed down her throat.

'I can't think what he'd want with me!' she sobs, trying to talk some courage into herself. Her voice sounds girlish. Shaking, she gasps for breath.

'I've been wondering that for quite a while.'

'Drop dead, Ted.' Suzanna gives it up.

Cindy pulls herself up with her elbows, looks imploringly at Ava and does not even notice Ted's vomit slithering over her breasts.

33

On the deserted parking lot in front of the Oudaan, Van Laken takes his leave of his detectives. De Mulder offers to drop him at his house; he has an appointment in the Van Wesenbeke-straat and can drive along the Breyidelstraat. But Van Laken would prefer to walk; the night is warm and it is still too early for him to lie on his mattress staring at the pale rectangle on the wall, where Bernard Buffet's clowns used to hang, a picture now brightening up the hairdresser's salon of Maartje's lover. Courtois calls jokingly from his car that he had better not hang around anywhere if he wants to get home before the storm.

'A good shower might clear my head!' Van Laken calls back with a tired smile.

Naturally, he does not go straight to the dingy flat above the Café Brabançonne, where only a hungry miaowing cat is waiting for him amongst the cobwebs, where the plants have wilted, the mouldy plates are piling up in the kitchen and the sheets have not been changed since the love of his life had betrayed him in the most heartbreaking way. He would rather doze off over a cup of cold coffee in the first café he comes to that is still open.

Somers and De Mulder watch the long, hunched silhouette as it disappears into the Everdijstraat like a shadow skimming over the façades.

'Funny old bugger,' says Somers. 'Did you see how happy he was that we all turned up to look at his smutty photos?'

'The man is simply exhausted, Somers. If we don't keep on giving him our moral support, I wouldn't be surprised if he chucked the whole lot in.'

'Balls, Gerard! All he needs is some young bit of skirt, to put a bit of lead back in his pencil.' Somers makes a circle with his right thumb and index finger and penetrates it with his left index finger. 'All them smutty films, that's not healthy!'

As he is walking through the empty shopping arcade, the iron shutters of which, to his great surprise, have not been lowered, Van Laken listens to his own footsteps, which are echoing, the way they did this evening in the aquarium at the zoo. He stops in front of the lingerie shop where he occasionally used to buy a frivolous gift for his wife, and studies his hazy reflection in the window, a gaunt and groggy ghost, a hologram amongst the bustiers, baby-dolls and knickers, and he thinks of Maartje who is now lying on her side asleep in the perfumed arms of her hairdresser, her clammy behind pressed against his hollowed stomach. He wishes he could be attacked, right now, by a desperate junkie, who would steal his automatic pistol and fatally wound him with a clumsy shot in the gut. He would not resist, but sink down slowly with a grateful smile and bleed to death peacefully in a spreading dark pool before daybreak. But at this late hour nobody dares to wander the deserted area so Van Laken shrugs his shoulders and walks on through, out into the Huidevetterstraat, on his way to Video Take-out on the St-Paulusplein. For the third time today, he lights a last cigarette and swears, as usual, that he will give up smoking the day Maartje appears in the doorway with tears in her eyes. He looks at his watch: if he hurries he will get there just in time. The night shop never closes before three o'clock. Perhaps he should have got Somers to give him a lift. By now, Somers would already be around the corner, somewhere in Senegal, joints creaking, spilling champagne over his corpulent girlfriend.

Van Laken has now been up and about for more than thirty-six hours, but he would clutch at any excuse to put off that dreaded moment when he rolls himself up alone in his musty sheets.

There is nobody about, not on the St-Katelijnevest, nor on the Minderbroedersrui. There does not seem to be a living soul on the street; the city is dead. He remembers the wild night life of the Sixties, when cars were still allowed to drive anywhere they wanted, most bars stayed open until dawn, he had not yet joined the police, a beer cost six francs, Maartje was a redhead and used to party with him until the small hours, and he had lots of friends and few cares.

As he arrives at the St-Paulusplein, it suddenly begins to rain, very hard, like in a film, a curtain of plump, tepid thunder drops. A light is still shining in the shop and he hurries across the square to escape the downpour. Drying his face with his handkerchief, he walks through the first room, straight to the adult section, in the little room to the left past the counter. Four sleepy customers are still studying the photos on the empty boxes in the racks, silently and avoiding each other's gaze. He knows the whole selection by heart, immediately sees which films are missing, which are the new additions, and curses when he discovers that *Twenty Thousand Virgins Under the Sea* is out on loan, the film he wanted to fall asleep with tonight, dreaming that Lova Spencer was giving him a blow job with her generous mouth, in a Jacuzzi in the hills above Palm Beach, while she masturbated with a bottle of Dom Pérignon. Even if it was only to sublimate the macabre memories from the zoo and the morgue. Annoyed, he walks up to the counter, where a pale girl, with lank, black-dyed hair, and a ruby in her left nostril, is smoking and staring into the distance.

'Still out and about, commissaris?'

'Check your files to see who's taken out number XX-410/01.'

'*Twenty Thousand Virgins*? Just a moment . . . By the way, the correct translation is "Twenty Thousand Rods", in other words, twenty thousand cocks.' She says this with such natural innocence that van Laken starts to blush.

The salesgirl slides lithely from her bar stool, types the necessary data into the computer and waits. The light from the screen turns her pallid skin light green.

'XX-410/01 ... Friday 16 August ... Should have been back long ago.'

'Name and address?'

'A certain M. Koeberghs, Antwerp Tower. Strange, that's all it says.'

'Could you describe the man to me?'

'I do nights. It says here he came in Friday afternoon, when I was fast asleep.'

'No telephone number?'

'No.'

Van Laken jots down the name on a crumpled pink receipt that is lying on the counter.

'Two packs of Gauloises non-filter. Two cans of Coke ... And a bottle of J&B.' He strolls yawning to the large deepfreeze at the front of the shop and has to delve down into it to pull out a pack of frozen hamburgers. When he straightens up again, Maartje is standing in front of him, in a soaking summer frock that is sticking to her skin.

'You look terrible,' she mutters. 'Ashen.' She means it well, because her voice sounds warm and tender, and as she is saying it, she runs her tiny hand over his unshaven cheek, as if it was a piece of tree-bark.

Recovering his composure, Van Laken gibbers: 'Hey! Maartje! What are you doing here at this hour?' He tries to sound as natural as possible, as if there had never been any problems between them.

'It's this lousy weather, I can't sleep and ...'

'Me neither.'

'... and then I'd rather be watching an exciting film than staring at the ceiling!'

'What a coincidence, eh?'

'You can say that again!'

'Did you see the stars?'

'Stars?' Van Laken thinks of Lova Spencer, Ava Palomba, Peggy 'Sue' Laenen.

'The falling stars! It's the night of . . .'

'No. But I wasn't really looking.' He doesn't dare to ask her if there are any problems with her hairdresser. 'I love your hair. Short. Takes years off you.'

'Flatterer!'

'It's also lighter than it was, isn't it?'

'A rinse.'

'Why not . . . if you're close to the source.'

They look at each other in silence, moved by the scars, the scars of the pain they have caused each other.

'And . . . still happy?' he coughs, with a bitter taste in his mouth.

'So so.'

The hamburgers are defrosting in his hand.

'Well I hope you find something you like. I've heard the latest Jean-Claude van Damme is pretty amazing.'

Van Laken mumbles something incomprehensible.

'What did you say?'

'Nothing. Just talking to myself. A new habit.'

'Emiel . . .'

It has been months since anybody has called him by his Christian name.

'Nino and I have split up.' She cuddles up to him, wraps her arms around his waist. He had almost forgotten how dainty she was. She smells different too, of expensive cosmetics, but perhaps that's just the rinse and the rain. He feels the ground opening under his feet, sits on the cold rim of the freezer and gazes deep into her eyes. She wants to say something else, but he presses two yellowed fingers to her mouth, caresses her trembling lips, kisses her on the tip of her nose, where a drop of water is hanging, that tastes salty, not like rainwater.

'Don't say anything,' he whispers, 'everything will be all right.'

She nods. Smiles shyly. Wipes away a new tear.

'What do we do now?'

'It's up to you.'

'You decide.'

'Champagne, at Paula and Aphrodite's, on the other side of the street, in the Madonna. My treat.'

'Why not . . . Tell me, how are you doing?'

'Me? Great!' He is dying for a Gauloise.

'No big news?'

'No. Well yes, actually! I've given up smoking.'

He throws the hamburgers and his Zippo lighter into the fridge.

34

As he changes the CD with one hand and the 'Laudate pueri Dominum' from the *Laudate Pueri* (Psalm 112) by Georg Friederich Handel, performed by the Deller Consort, replaces Glenn Gould in the loudspeakers, Mercury gazes into the mirror, watching Ava pull her shimmering dress up above her hips, drop her knickers to her ankles and squat on the leather back seat to urinate into an empty crystal decanter. He adjusts the mirror and sees the powerful jet fill the bottle with foaming yellow liquid. Her pubic hair is trimmed short and shaved in the shape of a heart.

'Madeline Chambers in *Behind the Green Door*,' Mercury says aloud, picks up the receiver and presses a red button in his armrest.

Ted grabs the telephone.

'Ted Harlow here. I'm being kidnapped. My numberplate is EVG007, call the police and my lawyer at number . . .'

'May I speak to madame?'

'Who am I talking to?'

'To your ex-chauffeur.'

This answer throws Ted into such confusion that he speechlessly, almost meekly, hands the receiver to Ava with a weak flick of his wrist.

'Who is it?' she asks, as she wipes the last drops from between her legs with the neck of the decanter.

'Your bodyguard.'

'Who?'

'The pleb behind the wheel!'

Ava looks at Mercury and catches his penetrating gaze in the mirror.

'Here, hold this a moment.' She hands the full decanter to Ted, wriggles her tight dress back down over her legs and takes the receiver. Her voice is quivering with fear, but also with excitement at the thought that Mercury had been spying on her just now when necessity had forced her to spread her legs.

'Mercury?'

'I found it very beautiful, Ava. Beautiful, touching, obscene, shameless, arousing, disarming, frivolous, diabolic, subtle, preposterous and poignant.'

She is deeply embarrassed, but also flattered. Ted has never spoken to her like that, not even in the beginning, when he was still doing his utmost to seduce her.

'I simply couldn't wait any longer,' she says with lowered eyes, almost coquettishly, not understanding what has prompted her to apologise. After all, it was the fault of that freaky flatterer that she had had to relieve herself in front of everybody.

Mercury sees Ted creeping closer to her, trying to eavesdrop and trying to tear the telephone from her hand.

'And tell your bleached-blond pig farmer he needn't worry about his money, that as far as I'm concerned, he can stuff it up his arse . . .'

'Have you two been on first-name terms for long?' Ted asks, totally shaken.

'. . . and that I'd appreciate it very much if he didn't interrupt our conversation.'

'Now listen here, laddie!' Ted shouts through the telephone, so close to Ava that her face is sprayed with disgusting drops of spittle, 'In my richly filled life, I've had to live through far worse experiences than you lot put together, things you don't even have words for, things beyond your imagination, so don't kid yourself that this evening has impressed me for a second! You don't realise who you're dealing with! Whatever your half-baked plans may be! You'll soon come crawling to me on your hands and knees through your own shit, begging me to put you out of your misery! And as far as my hair is concerned, it is not bleached, understood? It's simply changed colour because of the hole in the ozone layer! A natural process!'

Mercury turns up the volume of the CD player.

'Ava?'

'Yes?'

'Do you like Handel?'

'Mercury, we have a problem . . . Mr Weinberg has died.'

'How dreadful . . . I'd noticed he hadn't moved for a while.'

'He hasn't moved for years,' sobs Cindy.

'The good always die young . . . Heart attack?'

'Mercury, for the love of God, we've got a corpse back here!'

'What do you suggest, sweetheart?'

'Keep him talking,' whispers Suzanna.

'What do I suggest? That we drive home as if nothing has happened, that we simply forget all about it! I swear on my father's life that I won't press charges . . . Chapter closed, agreed?'

'That doesn't sound very realistic.'

Ava no longer knows what to say, covers the receiver with one hand and looks at her friend imploringly.

'Stay friendly and natural. Use your talent, play the great seduction scene. He's confused, sooner or later he'll make a fatal mistake . . . and then we'll pounce!'

'He called me sweetheart!' says Ava, as if she has only now realised.

'What?' gasps Ted, his cough reviving.

'Shut up, Ted!'

'The honey! Give me the pot of honey!'

'Cindy's lying on it.'

'Mercury?'

'Yes, Ava?'

'Whisper where you're taking us. The others aren't listening.'

'I fear that would be a little premature.'

'Darling, whoever you are and whatever your plans may be, you know this can't succeed . . .'

'Trust me. And you can drop the darling for the time being.'

'Is it me you want?'

Their eyes meet.

'You know, it's an interesting experiment, studying how the cream of society behave when you shut them up in a confined space. Rats have got nothing on them!'

'It stinks like a pigsty back here! I can't bear it with this corpse any longer. He's already starting to go stiff!'

'Do you want to throw him out? Okay by me. I'll release the locks. But at 140 kilometres per hour, I wouldn't advise you to jump out after him!'

'He suggests we throw Richard out of the car.'

'Do it!' shouts Ted.

'But without stopping. Without slowing down.'

'So?'

'Have you all gone completely mad?' screams Cindy, in a brief moment of clarity. 'You can't just leave Richard behind on the motorway, like some run-over dog!'

'Why not?'

'Don't you dare, Ted. If you do I'll jump out too!'

'Even better! We could use the space!'

Mercury notices in the mirror that Ava's black lace knickers are still hanging around her ankles. The sturdy ankles of the other Ava, on the beach in *The Night of the Iguana*, he thinks. His heart melts.

'Ava?'

She signals to the others to stop their hateful bickering.

'I have a proposal.'

Suzanna, Ted and Cindy gaze tensely at Ava, who is listening to Mercury open-mouthed.

'And?' asks Suzanna impatiently.

'He's willing to leave Richard behind on a bench at one of the next rest areas we pass.'

'What did I tell you? That's his first mistake!'

'But he wants something in return.'

'May I inquire what?' Ted snaps irritably. 'Or is it none of my business again?'

Ava can barely suppress a nervous laugh.

'You'll never guess!'

'A rise!' shouts Ted.

Ava sticks her legs in the air.

'My knickers!'

35

At the Rex, the festive floodlights have been turned off earlier than planned. After the screening of *Desert Flower* the drowsy, stupefied audience did not have the energy to party the night away. The various buffets had been quickly plundered. But when it turned out that the drinks at the bar had to be paid for after two o'clock, the foyer slowly began to empty, whilst outside, amongst the palm trees, the fireworks were let off unwatched.

Cornelis and his chauffeur, a sentimental adjutant who had never before come into contact with people from the film world and is deeply moved by this unexpected honour, are still sitting in the VIP lounge, together with Steve Mendeiros, who is staring unkempt and watery-eyed at an overflowing ashtray; a nitpicking newspaper journalist, who is famous for his mustard coloured teeth and his staying power and is very keen to discuss the film; three young women with bags under their eyes, who nobody knows and who giggle nervously at just about anything; Marcel Verbeke, the blind poet, who is still under the illusion that his script has been faithfully filmed; the exhausted Minister of Sport, Leisure, Environment, Tourism, Folklore and Culture, who is plagued by nervous tics; and the film's make-up mistress, who this evening is in love with Mendeiros.

During the party, nobody had summoned up the courage to exchange a friendly word with Steve, with the result that the depressed director had thrown himself wholeheartedly into nicotine and drink.

'They're overawed by his greatness,' Cornelis had concluded, as he waved to distant, familiar, rapidly disappearing faces from his privileged position. 'That and intellectual vacuity. Two ailments we fortunately seldom encounter at the gendarmerie.'

It is now half past three and, according to his calculations, Ava should have arrived at the villa in Brasschaat long ago. He suggests to Steve that it is now time to make that phone call – even if only out of courtesy, he adds cuttingly – but the humiliated director is barely capable of holding up his head, let alone of uttering an articulate sound. This is precisely what Cornelis has been counting on. This way, he can phone her himself and whisper purringly in her ear the extravagant sentence he has been perfecting all evening. Perhaps she is already in bed, lying on her belly like she did in the film. As he dials Vangenechte's number, he imagines her writhing again like a wildcat, on the satin sheets, in Acapulco, three months later.

'I'll let it ring ten times, that's all,' he says aloud, as a voice test, and clears his throat.

He is just about to hang up, when a sleepy, female voice answers.

'Ghallo?' With a throaty H and a long, drawn-out O. Cornelis feels his stomach churn and the blood pound in his temples.

'I realise that even a star like you disappears from the firmament in a cloud of gold and glitter during the night of the falling stars, but . . .'

'Hallo?' The voice on the phone now sounds louder and clearer. Cornelis interrupts the monologue he has so carefully practised.

'Who am I talking to?'

'To Conchita.'

'Shit!'

'No, señor, Con-chi-ta, the maid.'

'This is Colonel Cornelis, of the gendarmerie. A friend of the family. May I speak to your mistress a moment? Privately.'

'The master and mistress are not yet home. It is the great premiere in Brussels this evening, it could be very late . . .'

'Thank you, Conchita.'

Cornelis hangs up, rubs his chin and then waves to his blushing chauffeur. There is still no reason for him to worry. To save the evening, Vangenechte, who is a man of the world, will have taken Ava and her friends to some fancy restaurant, and then they'll have gone for drinks in the bar of the Conrad, perhaps Ava will have wanted to go dancing afterwards, who knows, they might even spend the night in Brussels. After all, there is no obvious reason for them to go straight home. This is of course what Cornelis had been hoping for. Subconsciously, he fears that Ava is now enjoying herself in a nightclub with her entourage, whilst he is stuck with a blind-drunk director of Portuguese origin and a journalist with yellow teeth.

Disappointed that he has not been able to chat with his new idol, he decides to slip away unnoticed without saying goodbye to anyone. The main thing was that he loved the film and that Ava was still alive, so that later today, after lunch, he could call her up on some pretext or other. Now it is time for him to go home and creep stealthily into bed without waking his snoring wife and to fall asleep, smiling, thinking of Ava's beguiling body.

36

Halfway between Namur and motorway exit 16, for Wierde, the limousine slows down and pulls into a deserted rest area, shielded from the motorway by a clump of pine trees. Mercury stops the car in front of a concrete bench, which he lights up with the yellow beam of his fog lights. He turns off the engine, takes the key from the ignition, takes the 6.35 automatic pistol from the glove compartment and gets out. The rest area is deserted for as far as he can see.

In the back of the car, the hostages are sitting stock-still waiting for Mercury to open the door. If they react quickly and together, they should be able to overpower him and bring an end to this grotesque nightmare.

They have agreed that Ted will blind him with Ava's urine and then crack him on the head with the empty decanter, that Cindy, who is again wearing her stinking T-shirt, will pin him down while he is still surprised, at least in as far as she is still capable, that Ava will then claw him with her sharp nails and that Suzanna will strangle him, scratch out his eyes, tear out his hair and cut his throat and wrists with pieces of the broken decanter, after which Ted will courageously relieve him of the keys and start the car. It is a daring plan, conceived and pushed through by Ted as ex-paracommando, but it has the advantage that Richard's body will not be left behind. They can hear each other's hearts pounding.

Mercury cautiously turns the key in the lock. The smoked glass windows are so filthy and covered in condensation that there is no way he can see what is waiting for him inside. He throws open the door and aims his pistol blindly at the passengers, none of whom move a muscle, except for Ted, who sticks his hands in the air, so that the contents of the decanter gush out over his head.

'The first one to move is a goner!' Mercury has lowered his voice, trying to approximate the forceful, calm determination of Lee Marvin in *Point Blank*. He sticks his head inside, but the stink is so revolting that he has to cover his nose and mouth with his hand to stop himself becoming nauseous. He notices that Ava is clasping her knickers in her trembling fist and signals to her that she should slide them over the barrel of the pistol.

'Vangenechte, push Mr Weinberg out!'

'Why me?' Ted protests in a last, pathetic attempt to establish his authority.

'I'm giving you five seconds.'

Ted tries to push Richard out, but cannot budge him.

'He's much too heavy,' he moans, 'I'll never do it on my own!'

'Help him.'

With the help of Suzanna, whose unexpected strength impresses everybody, Ted manages to wrestle Richard's body out through the door. The old man's head hits the asphalt with a loud crack, but his left foot remains wedged between the seat and the hinge of the door.

'Richard!' Cindy tries to jump out of the car and throw herself on to her husband's corpse, screaming wildly that she wants to die with him, that life has no meaning without him, but Suzanna grabs her by the throat with one hand and pushes her back into her seat.

'The foot!' Mercury keeps the pistol trained on Vangenechte. 'Free it!'

'But that's my gun,' Ted mumbles.

'Right.'

Ted carries out the order slowly and mechanically, as if in a dream, not comprehending what is happening to him and so humiliated that he can no longer summon up the strength to resist.

Mercury slams the door shut. Cindy rummages frantically in her Fendi handbag for the envelope of white powder.

'Cindy, get a hold of yourself. It's the only realistic solution,' says Suzanna, as if reality still has any part to play in their situation. 'Soon, when they find him, they'll immediately know in which direction to search.'

'It's been quite some time since I've slaughtered a pig with my own two hands, but this swine is for me!' Ted rummages in the fridge. 'Is there anything left to drink here?' He finds a full bottle of Mandarine Napoléon, a bottle of Glenfiddich and half a bottle of Parfait Amour.

'Parfait Amour, delicious!' shouts Cindy.

'Did you see the way he was looking at me?' asks Ava.

'Lovingly! Can I have a little glass?'

'He was looking at you like a randy dog, like a mangy, randy dog!'

'I think that boy is definitely disturbed, but not really dangerous.'

'Bullshit!' shouts Ted, waving the bottle of liqueur. 'He's already hacked half a dozen women to pieces, and madame still thinks he's charming! But, of course, it's easy for Mrs Rizzoni to talk! She's got nothing to fear, since M only falls for young, sensual women! Dame Edna Average is not exactly his type!'

'You had much less to say for yourself just now,' says Ava.

'I wasn't about to go getting myself shot in the head for a dead man! And with my own pistol! Better clever and alive than . . .' He wipes the flat of his hand over the misty window and sees Mercury dragging Richard's body to the bench. 'Bloody hell, he's going to sit him on that damned bench!'

'As he said he would,' says Ava.

'Luckily,' sobs Cindy, 'at least that still has a little dignity.'

'Dignity! I didn't know Cindy even knew the word!' Ted guffaws out his mouthful of Parfait Amour.

With a raw, animal cry, Cindy throws herself on Ted, knees him between the legs, claws open his cheeks, spits in his face, tears at his hair, tries to rip open his throat with her teeth, grabs the empty champagne bottle by the neck, smashes it to bits against the bulletproof window and tremblingly holds the jagged remains in front of Ted's staring eyes. It takes all Suzanna's strength to pull her away from the thrashing Vangenechte, to disarm her and restrain her in a powerful stranglehold.

'I'll murder him,' she pants, foaming at the mouth, 'I mean it. If he says one more word, I'll murder him.'

Suzanna holds Cindy securely in her arms and whispers soothingly in her ear that she has to calm down, that that is the only way to get through this, that Ted is not worth getting upset about, that they will have to combine forces, pool their strength, if they want to get out of this alive. And when she feels that Cindy is beginning to relax, she adds loud enough for everybody to hear: 'Come on, give each other a hand.'

But Cindy hisses: 'Over my dead body.' Hoarsely. Hatefully.

The whimpering Ted meanwhile slithers back upright, feels the deep, heavily bleeding gashes in his face, wipes his hands on his drenched shirt, and wants to say something, but Ava nestles up to him, retching, and smooths down his orange-yellow hair, the way somebody who hates dogs would soothe a poodle.

'Hush . . . Calm down . . . Do as Suzy says. Hold your tongue. Cindy is upset, we all are . . . calm down . . . it's not so bad . . .'

'Not so bad? I'm goddamned blind!'

Outside, in the rest area, Mercury has lifted Richard's corpse on to the bench, laid one arm casually across the backrest and crossed his legs over each other. With his head, kept upright by the hidden neck-brace, his relaxed pose and above all his evening clothes and the white carnation in his buttonhole, he looks like an old uncle who has been left behind after a wedding feast and is waiting stoically until his relations come to pick him up. Mercury straightens Richard's bow tie, combs his silvery hair, sticks a lighted cigarette between the fingers which had once caressed the legs of Betty Grable, and takes a few steps backwards to admire his still life, as if it were a wax dummy in a mysterious tableau in the Musée Grévin, and to take a final look at the man who knew everything and had known everybody.

'And to think that they won't even recognise him,' he mumbles a little sadly, as he walks back to the limousine without turning around. 'A man who called Myrna Loy by her Christian name!'

Part Two

37

When he is finally awoken from a restless sleep, Van Laken has
no idea how long the telephone has been ringing amongst the
clutter on the floor next to his mattress. It must have been for
quite some time, however, because the incessant ringing had
become part of a ghastly nightmare, a shrill alarm from which
he was fleeing, running through a narrow, flooded passage,
between aquariums full of gaping whores, with Peggy 'Sue'
Laenen's twisted-off head in his blood-smeared arms. Without
opening his eyes, he stretches out his left arm to grope along
the cable and pull the phone towards him and realises he is not
lying in his usual spot. Instead of rummaging amongst empty
beer cans, full ashtrays, old newspapers, breadcrumbs, video
cassettes and dirty plates, his hand bumps against the warm, soft
buttocks of Maartje, who is lying next to him, fast asleep, in
the foetal position – the way she always used to lie – as if she
has never been away. He freezes, not daring to move his hand
in case he wakes her up.

Only then does he blink open his eyes, afraid that she is also
a part of his dream and will disappear just as suddenly as she has
reappeared. But then, from under his pillow, he sees her lying
there in a dusty ray of sun, breathing peacefully, with the cat in
her arms. So it was all true, it had really happened, the meeting
in the night shop during the storm, their hesitant whispering
next to the fridge, her tears at the bar of the Madonna, the
long walk through the empty rain-perfumed streets, the coffee,
downstairs in the Café Brabançonne, their first embrace in the
lift, their first touch between the musty sheets. And outside
the sun starts shining again.

The telephone stops ringing. Van Laken wriggles cautiously upright, automatically reaches for a cigarette, but remembers he has stopped. He looks at the green numbers of the digital alarm clock: it is a quarter to nine. Normally he would already have phoned the lab by now, or have been questioning Zsa Zsa Morgan's pimp with Courtois in the Begijnenstraat. But now that Maartje is again lying beside him in bed – feigning sleep, the way she used to so long ago, waiting for him to cuddle up against her back, touch her, caress her until she is dripping, while he swells between her thighs – he couldn't care less about M. He edges his cramped body closer, until he is curled around her, and with his left hand, he caresses her small, slack breasts, her soft tensing belly, he sticks his tongue in her ear, licks her throat, kisses the downy hairs on her neck. She smells different; the cat is purring. She moans and pushes her surging pelvis back against his abdomen. He knows the gaping wound that separates them will never heal completely and that from now on, no matter how hard they try, they will neither be able to live with or without each other. He realises that this fumbling morning embrace is rather pathetic, both theatrical and fleeting, and his searching fingers come to a halt. Somewhere in the room, the telephone starts to ring again. Van Laken pushes himself away from Maartje, crawls on his hands and knees through the clutter and picks up the receiver. It is Courtois, naturally it is Courtois. He sounds agitated, perplexed, almost reproachful.

'The lab report has arrived.'

'Which lab report?'

'The man in the skip.'

'And?'

'I think you'd better come down here.'

'Is it urgent?'

'It could well be important, yes.'

'Okay. I'll meet you in the Quick hamburger restaurant in twenty minutes. I could do with a hearty breakfast today.'

'Which Quick?'

'Opposite de Fouquet's. That way you can wave to your little friends across the street.'

Van Laken turns around feeling guilty. Maartje is sitting upright, leaning against the bare wall behind the mattress. She is stroking the cat. Her mascara has run, she looks pale, her face is swollen.

'You can see he still loves you.' He is talking about the cat, but he means himself.

Maartje lights a cigarette and gazes with malicious delight at the gaunt, naked man who is standing in front of her, hanging his head like a child who has been caught misbehaving and for whom, light years ago, she used to cycle to Antwerp three times a week in the winter.

'I have to go to the office for a while,' he mumbles.

'So no coffee in bed, then?'

'Well . . .'

'Goodbye, Miel.'

'Goodbye, darling. I'll be back before twelve. If you like, we could go out for a bite to eat. You can choose the restaurant. Okay?' Van Laken disappears into the bathroom.

She listens to the wheezing splash of the shower and smiles. She knows this film by heart. She has already played this scene a thousand times. Nothing has changed. She knows that later, at around half past eleven, he will ring to say that something has come up, that she will spend the whole day tidying up the apartment, taking a brief break to wander around the shops making unnecessary purchases, that this evening she will sit waiting for him watching *Wheel of Fortune*, with a burnt joint in the oven, until he returns home exhausted and flops down on the bed, waiting for the next telephone call from Courtois.

The familiar hum of the electric razor stops. Gazing at the photo of Lolita Moore's flayed body in the corner of the mirror, Van Laken calls from the bathroom:

'I promise I'll pack it all in as soon as I've caught M! And then we'll go and live in the caravan at the lake! Just you and me! In the country! And we'll buy a dog!'

'Fantastic!' she shouts back. But she does not want a dog and she hates the lake. She has always dreamt of living a life that would seem like several lives all rolled into one, a life full of surprises and adventure, not a life where she is stuck in some caravan, a life Emiel will never be able to give her, even if he takes early retirement.

Suddenly she shudders at the thought that he might see her naked body in the daylight, a body even thinner and paler than it used to be, and she pulls the sheet up over her flaccid, limp-nippled breasts to her chin. She feels as if she is with someone she does not know, some anonymous one-night stand. Emiel has become a stranger to her and it is as if all those years they had shared have never existed.

'Fantastic!' she shouts again, softer, with a lump in her throat, knowing that later, when he returns home, she will have left the apartment for ever.

38

Courtois, who would rather starve on the street than go into a fast-food restaurant alone, is waiting on the corner of the Quellinstraat, leaning against the red and white striped traffic lights and listening to the latest Springsteen on his Discman headphones. The violent storm of the previous night has lowered the temperature and the ominous clouds that are building up over the city could well give rise to a new downpour. He counts the aluminium beer vats that are disappearing into the cellar of de Fouquet's. If Melinda Mercouri and Gene Hackman had had a son together, then he would probably look like the gigantic picture of Schwarzenegger which is staring down at him, with its two-metre chin and clenched teeth, from the façade of the Calypso Cinema.

'*Last Action Hero*,' Courtois says aloud, when he sees Van Laken crossing the De Keyserlei, whistling, clean-shaven, wearing fresh clothes and looking ten years younger, waving exuberantly from the distance and apparently in an exceptionally good mood.

'Well, brother, scared to go in alone?' he laughs, patting Courtois on the back with exaggerated heartiness.

Van Laken takes his assistant paternally by the arm and leads him across the street through the heavy traffic. Courtois can hardly recognise his boss: he is talking articulately, his voice is clear, almost cheerful, he smells of aftershave and he has overslept. A new man. Either he has made a major break-through, or he managed to pull somebody in the Madonna last night, or he . . .

'Why are you staring at me?' asks Van Laken, as he sits

down at a table on the terrace of de Fouquet's. 'Order whatever you like. I'll have the same. You only live once.'

Courtois can't believe his eyes and ears and gazes uncomfortably at the waiter, who wipes their table with a damp cloth and sets a crystal ashtray in front of them.

'Morning, Angelo.'

'Good morning, Monsieur Pol. Not too cold on the terrace?'

Van Laken answers in his place.

'If we can't eat outside in August, when can we?'

'Quite right, sir. And what would the gentlemen like to drink?'

'To eat and drink,' Van Laken corrects him.

'For me, the usual: a mimosa, then smoked salmon with toast and a coffee.'

'Twice!' adds Van Laken. He gazes pensively at the waiter, who is on his way back to the kitchen, and then bends towards Courtois. 'What's that fellow called?'

'Angelo. A Sicilian.'

'Across the street, you are not served by mafiosi. That's the difference. So what's a mimosa?' As if he has never known.

'Champagne and orange juice. It's right back in fashion. Everybody's drinking it.'

'Of course.' He waits until the ambulance that is racing past with blaring sirens has disappeared into the Appelmansstraat. 'So, Pol, what were you in such a hurry to tell me?'

Courtois takes out his Gauloises and automatically offers one to Van Laken, but Van Laken waves away the cigarettes resolutely.

'No thanks. I've given up.'

Courtois begins to wonder whether some candid camera is filming him talking to a poorly informed Van Laken lookalike. He sticks a cigarette pensively between his lips and reaches for his Dupont lighter, but then he pauses: 'You don't mind if I smoke?'

'You know me, Pol. When I've made up my mind . . . But you go ahead, they're your lungs!'

Sunk in thought, Courtois lights his cigarette and inhales deeply, understanding less and less what could be behind Van Laken's bizarre attitude.

'So?'

'Well, Old Stinky didn't let the grass grow. The autopsy report on the black man in the skip was already on your desk this morning.'

'And?'

'To summarise: the poor bugger had already been dead for more than three weeks. Cause of death: a shot in the back of the neck. The bullet, which was found in the left lobe of his brain, came from a 6.35 automatic pistol. Various contusions and minor injuries over the whole body lead Old Stinky to suspect that the body was brought to the skip after the murder to confuse the investigation. Seems at first sight to be a routine case of gangland score-settling.'

'Is this what you phoned me out of bed for?' Van Laken gazes in horror at the luxurious, pastel coloured breakfast that is being laid before him with an elegant flourish by Angelo.

'We also know his identity.'

Enjoying the suspense he has been able to build up in his report, but disappointed that Van Laken is reacting less patiently than usual, Courtois stubs out his cigarette, sips his mimosa and gazes at the tanned legs of a young woman who is walking past, swaying her hips, in a short summer frock.

'Get to the point, Pol, get to the point.'

'Not hungry? I thought you wanted a hearty breakfast?'

'I do. It looks wonderful. Elegant. Sumptuous . . .'

Courtois bites into his toast greedily, but with a delicacy which will always amaze Van Laken. He then wipes the corners of his mouth with his linen napkin.

'Thanks to the label in his trousers – special cut, expensive material, made to measure by a tailor in the Hoogstraat who specialises in uniforms and workclothes – we have been able to ascertain that the man in the skip . . .' He pushes the last morsel of toast into his mouth with his index finger, closes his eyes, chews slowly and blissfully. 'Divine! You ought to try some. Where was I?'

Van Laken knows Courtois is doing this deliberately, but today nothing can irritate him. In his mind, he is still with Maartje, who is now lying in his bed, where he was lying, in his smell, playing with the cat in the beaming sun.

'Oh yes, his name is Dieudonné Mwembu Bomboko. Born sixty-four years ago in Coquilhatville, Congo. Worked there as the provincial governor's boy. Followed his boss to Belgium in '60. And, listen carefully, he had been employed for quite some time as the private chauffeur of Vangenechte, the pig farmer, alias Ted Harlow, the film producer. Went missing on 20 June . . .'

'What?' Van Laken reaches for the pack of Gauloises, nervously winkles out a cigarette, but keeps it clenched between his fingers, until it breaks and the tobacco scatters out over his smoked salmon. 'This is it, Pol.'

'I knew you'd be pleased.'

'We've got him!'

'Who?'

'M of course! I'm as good as certain. Who is one of M's next potential victims?'

'There are several likely candidates.'

'Think. For whom did we drive to Brussels yesterday?'

Courtois drinks down his mimosa, pours three drops of milk into his coffee and begins to stir it with a pensive frown.

'Ava Palomba? But I thought she was under twenty-four-hour surveillance.'

'Beside the point.' Van Laken sits on the edge of his chair and pushes his plate aside. 'And with whom is this tasty morsel currently living?'

'With Ted Harlow, her producer.'

'Right. And does Mr Vangenechte drive his limousine himself?'

'Probably not.'

'Of course not! And so? Think, Pol, think!'

'He must have a new chauffeur?'

'One I want to know everything about. That's it!'

Courtois slowly shakes his head and stares incredulously into the distance. 'And that new chauffeur supposedly did away with the old man, so he could take his place and thus force his way into Ava's private life? That seems a bit far-fetched.'

'There's no such thing as coincidence, Pol. Are you parked nearby?'

'On the square. In front of the Hong Kong. Illegally.'

'As usual.' Van Laken glances at the bill, gulps and slides a thousand franc note under the sugar bowl.

'You haven't eaten anything!'

'Some other time. Waiting whets the appetite.' He gets up, signals to Angelo that the money is on the table and, rubbing his hands together and without looking around, crosses the street, followed by Courtois.

'Before we interrogate the man, we'll phone Cornelis!' shouts Van Laken. 'He must have spoken to Dieudonné Whatsisname's replacement yesterday.'

'Are you sure Vangenechte was travelling by limousine?'

'Certain, yes!'

'I've often wondered why film people feel the need to be driven around in such unparkable battleships,' says Courtois, panting along behind Van Laken, embarrassed because his boss has paid the bill at de Fouquet's.

'Because you can't buy train tickets on credit, Pol!'

39

'Where are we?' Ava opens her eyes and sees a hand with swollen veins and blue nails fiddling with a satin rose just in front of her mouth.

'Nowhere,' she hears Suzanna answer sombrely.

Ava has slept like a baby in her friend's lap and has dreamt about her parents. Her father was standing on a red ladder in the orchard picking pears, a wide-brimmed straw hat on his head. He passed the fragrant fruit one by one to a girl, who laid them in a wicker basket, carefully, so they did not get bruised. It was summer and it was snowing. In the buzzing meadow behind the vegetable garden, her mother was standing amongst the beehives, her face hidden behind a gauze mask. She was waving slowly to her daughter, which was impossible, because she had already died of bone cancer by the time Ava went to live with her father on the farm.

'What time is it?' Ava stretches, turns onto her back and looks up at Suzanna, her comfort, her guardian angel.

'Quarter past eleven. You've been asleep for ages.'

'How long?'

'About six hours.'

'I've been dreaming about papa. And about mama. They both looked like you.'

'That happens to me too. Nightmares.'

'Are your parents still alive?'

'Not for ages! They both died on the same day. In 1950.'

'How dreadful. An accident?'

'My mother was murdered in her sleep. With a butcher's knife. A bloodbath. It was in all the papers. And when my father discovered her, he killed himself. They say it was with the same knife. Probably out of love.'

'And did they ever catch the murderer?'

'Never. Who knows, perhaps they killed each other.'

'How old were you then?'

'Fourteen.'

'Poor Suzy . . . And how did you feel?'

'I was relieved.'

'Relieved?'

'Yes. It's a long story. Is your father still alive?'

'Oh yes! He's a gentle, unworldly man. A bit old-fashioned. I miss him terribly.'

'Don't you see him anymore?'

'He stopped speaking to me when my photos were published in *Playboy*.'

'That's much worse.'

'Maybe . . .' Ava sits up and looks around drowsily. Ted is lying blind drunk on the floor, with his head resting against an empty bottle of Parfait Amour, and Cindy is fast asleep on the back seat, with her thumb in her mouth. Through the dirty windows, Ava can just make out a shadowy, dusty scene that looks like a ghost town. Blackened, brick houses with walled-up windows and boarded-up doors, pavements overgrown with weeds, dead, petrified trees, hoardings covered with ragged election posters. In front of the abandoned café on the corner of the street stands the wheelless wreck of a colourless Simca. In the distance, above the collapsed roofs, two conical, black mountains and an iron tower with gigantic, paralysed wheels stand out against the sky.

'It looks like an abandoned mining town. Do you have such things in Belgium?' asks Ava.

'Of course. My father used to work in the coal-mine, like many Italian immigrants . . . until the poor wretch met my mother and they moved to Charleroi . . . after his accident.'

Suzanna crushes the rose in her clenched fist. 'But who says we are still in Belgium?'

Ava gazes through the glass partition at Mercury, who is still lying peacefully asleep. She finds him almost attractive.

'He looks like an angel.'

'*Il angelo della morte.*'

The stink in the car is now even more nauseating than it was before. During the endless nocturnal journey, everybody had pissed into empty bottles or simply on the floor and before he had fallen into a snoring sleep, Ted had vomited his purple liqueur profusely over his shirt.

Ava clasps Suzanna's hand tightly, brings it to her lips and kisses it.

'You have such graceful, strong hands,' she says, 'and such long fingers.'

'All the better to strangle you with, my dear,' laughs Suzanna.

'Don't be so gruesome. What do we do now?' Ava realises how desperate her question sounds.

'Wait to see what Mercury decides when he wakes up. We've little choice. But don't be afraid, sweetie, no matter what happens, you can count on me.'

'I'm going to wake him up. I've got to get some fresh air. I can't take it in here with Ted any longer. It's coming out of every orifice! Can't you smell it?'

'You get used to everything.'

'I don't! I'd rather kill myself here and now than spend another second locked up with that convulsing moron!'

'What's all the row about!' Cindy takes her thumb from her mouth, tries to swallow the fur on her tongue, clears her throat and tries to sit up.

'Watch out, Cindy, mind you don't step in the shit!'

'Where?'

'The magician . . . on the floor.'

Ted has indeed become little more than a festively wrapped

pile of excrement, a fermenting heap, a gas-filled sack. While the others were sleeping, or pretending to, he had frantically drained all the bottles to the last drop and, if his guts had not been making gurgling noises, he could easily have passed for dead.

'So where are we now? In East Berlin?' Cindy asks, as she tries to look out of the window at the lifeless, carbonised landscape. She takes a magnifying make-up mirror from her Fendi handbag, looks at herself and starts. 'God, whatever do I look like?!' She begins to smear her face with green cream.

'Shall I wake him up or not?'

'Up to you, sweetie, but be careful, do it gently, tenderly. You don't want to rouse the beast in him.' Suzanna caresses Ava's cheek, bends over her, kisses her forehead, her eyes, her nose, her trembling, parched lips and Ava lets her. Suzanna is like a mother to her.

40

'Cornelis residence.'

'Good morning, Mrs Cornelis. Commissaris Van Laken here. May I speak to the colonel, please?'

'My husband is ill, Mr Van Laken.'

'Yes, I've already been informed, most unfortunate. That's why I'm being so forward as to bother him at home. I hope it's not serious?'

'He feels depressed. We are waiting for the doctor.'

'Stress?'

'Nerves. Eddy is so sensitive. He was deeply touched by that film yesterday. He spent the whole night staring at the ceiling and now he's sitting in the sofa on the veranda with the poodle, sighing and moaning to himself. He says he wants to have his arms tattooed.'

'That doesn't sound too good. Forgive me if I insist, Mrs Cornelis, but it is of the greatest importance that I talk to him.'

'In that case . . . Stay on the line a moment.'

'A hangover,' says Courtois, who has been listening in to the conversation. 'Our hero must have overdone it a bit at the party.'

Van Laken raps his long nails nervously on the metal desktop, the receiver wedged between his chin and his shoulder. After a seemingly endless minute's silence, he hears bumping, a dog yapping and a man swearing.

'Cornelis speaking.'

'Sorry to bother you, colonel. Van Laken here, Antwerp CID. I'm calling about . . .'

'Ava Palomba.'

'More or less . . .'

'Exquisite woman! What presence! What charisma! Ava . . . Ava Palomba . . . "Hot stuff!" as we always say at the gendarmerie . . .'

'Did you talk to her chauffeur last night?'

'To her chauffeur? No. And not to her either as it happens. Haven't you been informed?'

'Apparently not, no.'

'You know she didn't attend the premiere?'

'What?'

'I'm not sure exactly why, but I can't say I blame her. She had every reason to stay away from that pack of pretentious snobs. As a matter of fact, I have to call her in a moment to congratulate her.'

'The man is off his head,' Van Laken whispers to Courtois. 'So, colonel, thank you for the helpful information. I won't keep you any longer and I wish you a speedy recovery.'

'Oh, it's not all that bad. I simply have too much imagination to work for the gendarmerie.'

'Why don't you write a book? Everybody's writing books these days. They say it helps.'

'Perhaps . . . My memoirs . . .'

'For example. Until next time, colonel.'

'Yes . . .'

Van Laken slams down the receiver. 'Mad as a hatter!'

'I think it's time we paid a visit to Ted Harlow,' says Courtois. 'The man can't be reached by telephone.'

'I'll have to inform Maartje first,' says Van Laken, trying to sound as relaxed as possible.

Courtois stops in the doorway. Has he heard correctly, or has his boss totally lost it and begun taking his dreams for reality? At first, he doesn't dare to turn around, but when he hears Van Laken actually talking to his wife, stumbling over his words, apologising, promising heaven and earth, swearing he will be home before eight o'clock, that they will go to the cinema together, that she can choose the film, that they will spend the weekend at the lake, he understands the breakfast at de Fouquet's . . .

'Bravo!' shouts Courtois when Van Laken hangs up: the first words that spring to his lips.

'What for, Courtois?'

'I understand that Mrs Van Laken has returned?'

'Who said she'd ever gone away?'

41

Richard Weinberg, the great Richard Weinberg, the friend of Humphrey Bogart, Liz Taylor and Monty Cliff, the wise man who had beheld the gods, the world's greatest collector of lip-prints, the owner of a Memling, three Renoirs and a Mondrian, is sitting peacefully on the concrete bench beneath the sodium-vapour lamp smoking a cigarette when a gigantic woman looms up out of the mist that surrounds him. Her wide hips are squeezed into a tight-fitting short skirt. She is wearing a crimson belt around her slender waist and a pink angora sweater with a plunging V-neck, out of which her pale bosom is bulging. She is walking with tiny steps because her skirt is too tight and her stilettos too high. She sits down next to Richard, runs her hand over his head and, in the yellow glare of the streetlight, Mercury thinks he recognises her as Jayne Mansfield. She leans over Richard and presses his face between her enormous breasts. Intoxicated by her sickly perfume, Richard begins to thrash about, stamping on the tarmac with both his feet, but the sound is not that of shoes on asphalt. The poor man is suffocating, thinks Mercury, and yet he does nothing to rescue his helpless hero but simply lets the giantess carry on. Perhaps this was the voluptuous death Richard had always dreamed of. The woman turns around, she is no longer Mansfield, but a cross between Cindy Beaver and Bette Midler. She gazes greedily at the camera, sticks out her fluorescent tongue and whispers: 'Mae West, home is best.'

Ava has already been pounding on the glass partition for more than five minutes before Mercury finally awakens from his dream and gazes around in wide-eyed bewilderment at the sooty landscape that stretches out in front of him. He had spent the whole night in these hills, aimlessly driving along deserted country roads, until finally, at six o'clock, he had arrived in this ghost town and decided to park the car behind the carcass of a tumble-down factory and rest for a few hours.

He turns around with difficulty – his back is stiff and his neck muscles knotted – and finds himself eye to eye with Ava, who is looking at him imploringly. Her face is not more than ten centimetres from his, and despite her parched lips, her smeared make-up, the tangled locks of hair sticking to her forehead, and the dark rings beneath her bloodshot eyes, he finds her more beautiful than ever. It is the first time they have woken up together and he feels like kissing her. His lips move closer to the glass, which steams up, shrouding her face behind a misty haze. He wipes the glass clean with her lace knickers and realises she wants to speak to him on the telephone.

'Good morning, Ava. Did you sleep well?'

'Mercury, this has to stop.' This is all she dares to say, all she is capable of saying. It is becoming obvious that Mercury has no idea where he is heading and is only now beginning to realise the ramifications of his rash behaviour.

'Have you any reasonable requests?'

'Reasonable!' Ava is dumbstruck. She feels Suzanna's reassuring hand on her neck. 'You might at least open the window a little. It's suffocating in here. Ted has . . .' She can't bring herself to say it. 'Please . . .'

'And tell him I've got toothache,' groans Cindy.

'I'm sure that will upset him terribly.'

'Suzanna, you're the most heartless creature I've ever come across. I hate you. And stop laughing!'

The windows open a few centimetres, just enough to let through the fingers of Ava, who gulps down the fresh air.

Mercury gets out. The tail of his shirt is hanging over his trousers. He raises both arms in the air, fists clenched, and stretches, looks around, takes a bottle of Evian from under his seat, drinks a couple of tepid mouthfuls.

Then he crosses the road and urinates against the wreck of the Simca, which turns out to be blue under its coating of grey dust. Families used to live here, striving for an embryonic form of happiness, making plans for the future. Children used to play in the dust of these streets. When the sun was shining, as it is today, sheets were hung out to dry in the wind, in gardens where potatoes and cabbages and rhubarb grew. On Sundays, men with coal-blackened pores and eyelids used to sit and play cards in the café on the corner. Even with ruined lungs, they could joke about their fate. To lighten their despair they drank themselves into oblivion, until it grew as dark outside as it was down below, in the pit. While Mercury is buttoning up his flies, heroic scenes from the films of Joris Ivens are projected on his retina. Nothing is important. Everything perishes. Everything crumbles. There is no future and the past consists of ruins. Those who wish to be truly alive today must let themselves be led by passion alone, all-consuming, devastating, burning passion, the merciless passion which melts the brain. The rest is lies. Delusion. Washing powder. Happiness does not exist. Happily. Ava is happiness. Ava does not exist. Ava is a photo. The glossy photo of woman as a beast of prey, stalking around the edge of a swimming pool, in which the word 'Hollywood' is reflected and the sun is sinking with a sizzle.

Dizzy with hunger and fatigue, Mercury looks over his shoulder at the limousine. Unrecognisable beneath the dust and the dried mud, it seems to be a part of the scenery. It is as if, in the chaos which followed the mine closure, the mine director had been chased away by enraged townspeople and had left behind even his most precious symbol.

'Careful, sweetie. Don't forget he's armed,' Suzanna says to Ava, who is waving desperately to Mercury from behind the misty glass.

Pistol in hand, Mercury walks towards the car – the way

Kirk Douglas walks towards his horse Whisky through the empty streets of Duke City in the exciting final scene of *Lonely Are the Brave* – and opens the door on Ava's side. The stench which escapes from the car is revolting, the same unforgettable stench as that of Aunt Jeanne's cesspit. Mercury sees himself again appearing out of the brown sludge, gasping for breath, spitting out sodden toilet paper and calling for help, clawing for the circle of blue summer sky above his head, and to suppress his mounting rage, he clenches his fists so violently that his gun goes off and slams a bullet, with an invisible thud, into the black dust between his feet.

Ava kicks her foot against the shapeless heap on the floor.

'Get him outside, Mercury, this is inhuman.'

'Tell him he can get out.'

'He can't get out, he's no longer capable.'

'Empty the magazine into Ted,' Mercury hears the voice inside him scream. 'Four bullets into his fermenting body, deflating him like a punctured tyre, and then the finishing shot, straight into his swollen, purple face, spattering it open like a rotten fig . . .'

'Mercury! Can you hear me?' The voice is Ava's. 'You have to help us. He's too heavy for me!'

'Let me do it, sweetie,' says Suzanna. 'I've shifted heavier loads. Just tell me where I have to put him, Mercury.'

Mercury does not know what to answer. But as long as he doesn't have to touch the stinking heap himself, he is willing to agree to any proposal.

'Okay, Mrs Rizzoni. Drag him out, if you can.'

Suzanna gets out, while Mercury keeps the gun trained on her from a safe distance. She grabs Ted by the wrists, drags him out of the limousine and lets him fall into the dust. Shit trickles out of his trouser legs onto his patent leather shoes.

'Shall I leave him here?'

'In the sun? Out of the question.' Mercury shuts the door. 'We have to hide him away.'

'Why?'

'For the flies. Besides, he doesn't deserve to see the sun.'

'But you left Richard on a bench at the side of the motorway.'

'Richard was dead and a man of the world. Doubly harmless.'

'So what does Ted deserve?'

'The worst.'

'How exciting! Tell me.'

'I haven't got the imagination for this sort of thing.'

'You? No imagination?' Suzanna says flatteringly.

'Drag him into one of those houses and throw him into the cellar.'

'You see!' Suzanna suddenly seems relaxed, reacts as if she finds the situation normal, like an actress who is enjoying the role she is playing and who has become totally immersed in her character. It is Mercury who seems to be troubled, disconcerted by the fact that Suzanna Rizzoni, the celebrated fashion designer, clad in a dress that had once belonged to the great Sarah Bernhardt, is dragging Ted Harlow to an empty miner's house like a sack of rubbish, to the accompaniment of Ennio Morricone on the synthesiser.

'My greatest dream was to become a film director,' he says, 'but I have no imagination . . .'

'Nothing's stopping you . . .'

'The thought that I'd be in the presence of those unapproachable film goddesses is already enough to paralyse me.'

'Don't be so childish,' Suzanna whispers in his ear in her deep voice, whereupon she grabs Ted by the collar and drags him through the swirling dust to the other side of the street, as if the excitement has doubled her strength. Without much effort, she batters open the worm-eaten door of the miner's house next to the café. Faded wedding photos are still hanging on the wall in the hallway. The flowered wallpaper is mouldy.

She drags Ted over the cement-tiled floor to the cellar stairs, opens the wooden hatch and gazes down into the dark hole from which the croaking of frogs echoes. Mercury can hear his heart pounding in his chest. He is breathing heavily, the way he does when he is spying on Ava from his studio. He is so amazed by the determination and cold-bloodedness of Mrs Rizzoni, whom he had assumed to be frivolous and superficial, that he forgets the drunken man who is lying groaning at his feet and becomes totally caught up in the exciting film in which he has landed.

The suffocating stench of stagnant water wafts up from the cellar. Mercury catches Suzanna's excited eyes and nods. She pushes Ted to the edge of the opening, until his head is dangling between the fungi above the darkness.

'I think he's trying to say something.' She leans over to listen to what Ted is mumbling. Saliva is dribbling from his slack, half-open mouth.

'So what has he still got to say?'

'Something about glamour . . . yes, that's what he's saying: glamour.'

'There are words that certain people shouldn't be allowed to say. Throw him in.'

'You do realise what you're doing?' she pants, unmistakably enjoying their complicity.

'Nobody really knows what he is doing.'

With her heel, Suzanna shoves Ted's cumbersome body into the cellar. It lands in the water with a loud splash. They hear him floundering, coughing, calling for Ava. And then even the frogs are quiet and silence fills the cellar. Suzanna is out of breath. She gazes at Mercury with bulging eyes.

'This wasn't your first *mise-en-scène*, was it?'

Mercury shudders. This woman is more dangerous than he thought.

'What are you going to call your film?'

'I don't know . . . *A Summer with Aunt Jeanne*?'

'Nice. A mysterious title. But a bit hermetic. Not very commercial. Who is Aunt Jeanne?'

'An aunty. When I was little, I had to call all my father's girlfriends aunt.'

'You're forgetting something.'

'What?'

'Your signature.'

Mercury hesitates. Shivers with pleasure. He has always loved fiction more than reality, preferred cinema to real life.

'The honour is yours.' In close-up, he watches how Suzanna's blue nail scratches the letter M in the dust on the floor-tiles.

'Mercury, I think you and I are going to get on just fine.'

Mercury is on his guard. Mrs Rizzoni is a cunning woman. She is obviously trying to win his confidence with her flattery, trying to make him believe she is on his side. He refuses to be lured into this blatant trap.

'Enough of this game,' he snaps. 'First you'll close that hatch and then we'll slowly walk back to the car, where you'll get back in and wait with your girlfriends until the evening falls. All girls together.' With the barrel of the 6.35, he signals to her to walk in front of him.

'You can put that thing away,' she says, pointing to the automatic pistol, 'I'm not planning on running away. I promised Ava I wouldn't desert her. I'll stay with her until the end, until this masquerade is over.'

The sun is now shining straight down on the silent ruins. In its bright light, they look even more like an abandoned film set. Mercury blinks his eyes, like Charles Bronson in *Soleil Rouge*. It seems not to have rained here for years.

'Your left sleeve is torn,' he remarks, as he watches the elegant woman who is crossing the street bolt upright in front of him.

'I know that, darling. That's the reason Sarah gave this frock to her dresser.'

42

The rest area beside the E411 has been closed to traffic by the gendarmes. This morning, at around nine o'clock, a lorry driver from Bruges who was having engine trouble had noticed Richard sitting on the bench under the streetlight and, although he was surprised to see the elegant old man sitting there in his evening clothes apparently relaxed, he had initially paid him no further attention. The men of Bruges are reserved by nature, almost wary, and faithfully respect the privacy of others. Besides, the leak in his oil pump was of more pressing importance than the enigma of the old man sitting on the bench. What did strike the driver after a while, however, was the total immobility of the old man. He hadn't once looked around at the lorry, but just sat there, staring at the bright, rising sun without turning his head away or blinking his eyes. Only when the driver had gone to sit beside him to wait for the tow truck, engage him in conversation and offer him a cup of coffee, had he noticed the wound on the old man's left hand where the cigarette had burned his stiff fingers. He had gingerly touched the rigid man, who felt cold despite the sun shining down on his ashen face, and immediately notified the police via his CB radio.

Half an hour after his call a traffic patrol arrived, and, an hour later, a team from the Namur public prosecutor's office. There are now six police cars and an ambulance parked in the rest area, and some thirty people are swarming around, like ants from a shattered nest, in search of evidence, clues and fingerprints. Richard is being photographed from every angle, as he had been in the old days, on the terrace of the Majestic during the Cannes film festival. A police physician had poked and prodded him with expert surgical-gloved hands and had concluded without hesitation that the body must have been sitting there in the same position for at least ten hours. He provisionally determined the cause of death to be a heart attack. But that did not solve the mystery. Quite the contrary. Richard was carrying no official documents, all he had in his pockets was a provocative nude photo of a young blonde woman on which the words 'To Rich, with all my love, Cindy' were written in purple ink, a considerable sum in crumpled banknotes and a creased invitation from a certain Za Su Pitts to attend a performance by Roberta Sherwood in the Château Marmont on 16 December 1962. The label 'Pierre's Taylors – 216 Rodeo Drive, Hollywood – L.A.' was sewn to the lining of his jacket. The questions were: how and why this rich American had ended up in the rest area of a Belgian motorway, and whether he had really died of a heart attack. But the latter would be revealed by an autopsy. The first task was to identify him and the examining judge had immediately proposed that they make inquiries in the Brussels underworld. The dinner jacket and the photo of the vulgar blonde seemed to him to point in that direction.

'We'll never get him in a bodybag like that,' a sweating gendarme complains to one of the team from the Namur public prosecutor's office. 'Can't we transport him sitting up?' he asks, pointing to the two stretcher-bearers waiting beside the ambulance.

'No. I don't know what they teach you at the gendarmerie, but the law stipulates that the body must be transported to the morgue in Namur in a regulation black-plastic body bag. And as far as the public prosecutor's office is concerned, the law is the law.'

'So what do we do then?'

'His neck has already been broken, right?'

'It looks that way.'

'Then simply break the rest.'

43

An invisible hand opens the cast iron gate at the entrance to *Harlow Land*, Vangenechte's estate, and a pack of dogs immediately begin to bark in the distance. Courtois drives cautiously through the tall gateway, the gravel crunching beneath the wheels of his Opel.

'Follow the main drive as far as the house,' a woman with a Spanish accent had shouted to him over the intercom, 'I'll be waiting for you on the steps.'

'Not a bad little place he's got, our Teddy. I think I'll go into film production too.'

'Films have got nothing to do with it, Courtois. It's the pigs that made him rich.'

'They fattened him up in return.'

The grounds are so impressive that Van Laken and Courtois are whispering to each other. After a final, gentle bend to the left, the monumental villa appears from behind a forest of purple rhododendrons. Conchita, in a blue and white striped uniform, is standing waiting for them on the steps between the marble pillars.

'Jesus! It looks like the White House!'

'Stop at the bottom of the steps, Pol.'

The two men get out simultaneously and climb the wide steps. Van Laken shows the maid his police I.D.

'Commissaris Van Laken, Antwerp C.I.D. My assistant, Detective Chief Sergeant Courtois.'

'Madame.'

'*Madre de dios*! Nothing bad has happened?' Conchita presses her right hand to her heart.

'What do you mean?' asks Van Laken.

'Well, Señor Harlow and Señora Ava left for their party in Brussels yesterday and I haven't seen them since. At first I thought, well, they're probably spending the night there in some fancy hotel, but then I thought, well, if that's the case, then why they haven't informed me. Señor Harlow usually phones home for even the most trivial of reasons. Sometimes as much as ten times a day. And Señor Arthur is also worried. He just phoned and . . .'

'Who is Señor Arthur?'

'Señora Rizzoni's friend, of course.'

'And who is Señora Rizzoni?'

'Señora Ava's best friend.'

'The fashion designer. The queen of the zip,' says Courtois.

'Yes. They had to pick her up. Señor Arthur too. But he told me he was staying at home, because he had too much work. With his poems. And then they had to pick up some other friends at a hotel in Antwerp.'

'Do you remember which hotel?'

'The Rosary . . . The Rosy, something like that.'

'De Rosier?' asks Courtois, who is jotting down everything in his notebook.

'Yes, that was it. De Rosier.'

'Something smells funny here, Pol. May we use the telephone?'

Conchita shows Courtois into the study, points to the telephone, a copper reproduction of an antique telephone, and then hurries anxiously back to Van Laken, who is now standing beneath the crystal chandelier in the circular hall staring restlessly at a copy of the Venus de Milo.

'I assume they went by car?'

'Yes. The long one. With so many people . . .'

'You mean the limousine?'

'The limousine, yes.'

'And who was driving?'

'Mercury, of course!'

'Who is Mercury?'

'The new chauffeur.'

'Mercury with an M? Is that his real name?'

'Well that's what Señor Harlow calls him . . .'

'And did you know Dieudonné?'

'Dieudonné?' She blushes.

'Mr Vangenechte's previous chauffeur.'

'You mean Uncle Bens? A lovely man. Whenever he had a moment free, he used to come into the kitchen and sit with me and tell me stories about Africa. But he let us down badly a month ago and we haven't heard from him since.'

'Do you happen to know where Mercury lives?'

'Of course I know where Mercury lives!'

Conchita is amazed that Van Laken has the nerve to ask such stupid questions. 'He lives in the studio, above the garage, out there in the grounds! Where Uncle Bens used to live!'

Courtois bounces in on his rubber soles, leafing through his notebook.

'And?'

'I talked to the owner. He didn't want to tell me anything at first. And certainly not over the telephone. The privacy of De Rosier's guests is sacrosanct. But after a lot of hot air he finally admitted that Ted Harlow had come to pick up two hotel guests yesterday: a certain Richard Weinberg, a Dutch Jew who emigrated to America in the Thirties and had a successful career there as a theatrical agent, and his wife, better known under the name of Cindy Beaver, an actress. "Of the dubious variety", that's literally how he put it.'

'You can say that again. She acted in *Draculanus*. And if I'm not mistaken, also in *Penetrator II*. American productions.'

Conchita makes the sign of the cross.

'Fodder for psychopaths.'

'So why didn't you talk to those people yourself?' Van

Laken already knows the answer, but he wants to hear it from Courtois' lips, to confirm his suspicions.

'Because they weren't in their suite. The owner hasn't seen them since they left there yesterday.' Courtois takes a deep breath. His eyes are sparkling.

'By the way, guess the name of the lord of the manor's new chauffeur? . . . Mercury!' Van Laken emphasises the first letter.

'That's a type of car,' says Courtois, jotting the name in his notebook, without the slightest sign of surprise.

'A type of car that just happens to begin with M.'

'Like Mercedes, Maserati, Mitsubishi, MG, Mazda, Morgan, Matra . . .'

'Stop trying to be funny, Pol! You just don't want to admit that the facts have proved me right again! What is your name, miss?'

'Conchita, señor.'

'Conchita, could you show us Mercury's room please?'

'I know nothing of cars, but I'll fetch the keys.' She hurries up the stairs, shaking her head. Van Laken flops triumphantly into a deep sofa.

'I think we ought to be careful,' says Courtois. 'We have no proof that . . .'

'Pol, my boy, how long have I been in this business? A long time. Too long, according to Maartje. And believe me, when I am on the point of cracking a case, I can feel it. Here.' He presses his midriff with his index finger. 'An alarm bell, a gnawing feeling, a burning lump, the signal that the solution is very close. And I can assure you, I've now got a lump as big as my fist.'

'I reckon the whole gang of them must have gone on somewhere in Brussels. A limousine doesn't simply vanish into thin air. Certainly not in Belgium.'

'If it's that simple, we'll find the car in no time. And starting tomorrow, I'll eat smoked salmon for breakfast every morning.'

Conchita comes running down the stairs, dangling a bunch of keys, and invites Van Laken and Courtois to follow her on foot to the garage. That way they will be able to see the garden, one of the most lovely in Brasschaat, and the swimming pool, which according to the excited Spanish maid is very impressive, especially in the evening when the illuminated fountains are playing, just like in America.

The garage is a long, low, yellow-brick building, with eight arched doors. On its right, a wooden staircase leads up to a studio with wide windows, the curtains of which are drawn. Van Laken has thrown his jacket over his shoulder and rolled up his shirt-sleeves. The short walk through the sun-baked grounds has exhausted him. It is indeed time for him to give up the Gauloises.

Conchita, who has liberally splashed herself with perfume while she has been fetching the keys, a fact duly noted by Courtois, has to try several different ones before she manages to get the door of the studio open. Van Laken can barely contain his impatience. He pushes past the others into the room, which is bathed in soft, filtered light.

'Shall I open the curtains?'

'Yes ... And Conchita, don't touch anything else, okay.'

'Have you been in here before?' asks Courtois.

'In the past, yes. When Uncle Bens used to live here. I sometimes brought him his ironed shirts, or tasty leftovers from the kitchen,' Conchita answers, as she tugs open the curtains and lets in the sunlight. 'But Mercury I didn't know well enough yet. And he never invited me up here. He was much more the quiet type. *Madre de dios*, I hope nothing has happened to Señora Ava! Such a lovely, sweet young girlfriend, Señor Harlow won't find another one like her.' She quickly crosses herself twice, folds her hands and gazes imploringly at the ceiling.

Van Laken is standing stock-still in the centre of the room. What strikes him first is the order and cleanliness of the monastic room. Highly suspicious for a bachelor, who, if his personal experience is anything to go by, would usually be obliged to live in a state of permanent chaos. The bed has been made up with military precision, the towels are folded, the clothes are hanging tidily on a row of wooden hangers, beneath which three pairs of polished shoes are gleaming in the sunlight. The electric cooker looks like new and the sparkling pots and pans are lined up neatly on the draining board. In front of one of the windows which look out over the grounds, stands a wooden Ikea trestle table, covered with neatly stacked piles of cardboard folders.

Van Laken begins to leaf through the files and turns deathly pale. His hands tremble, his lungs seize up. He drops his jacket on the floor, lowers himself slowly into the desk chair, without taking his eyes off the table top, pushes the ink bottle, the tube of glue, the ballpoint pen, the scissors and the stapler aside and calls to Courtois, who is checking the contents of the fridge, relieved that he has not found any severed hands, Tupperware pots of nipple paté, jars of pickled eyes, aluminium-wrapped labia or boiled and twisted-off female heads concealed amongst the vegetables and the sandwich fillings.

'Pol, look at this!'

Van Laken shows him the first folder, labelled LOLITA MOORE in black ink capital letters, and spreads the contents over the table: some fifty newspaper cuttings, chronologically ordered, all relating to M's first murder, complete documentation with handwritten comments and a list of sources.

'And there are ten more like that! Two for each murder! Look for yourself: Zsa Zsa Morgan, Peggy "Sue" Laenen, Lilly von Strass . . . That bastard's got better files than we have! And here, look, a file with dossiers on all the most infamous serial killers: the Rostov Ripper, Doctor Petiot, Thierry Paulin, Albert De Salvo, the Boston Strangler, Eugène Weidman, Ted Bundy, Peter Sutcliffe, Harvey Glatman, Jerry Brudos . . . and what is this?'

Van Laken takes a shoe box tied with string from beneath the table, sets it down in front of him and undoes the knots. Conchita turns away in terror, covering her face with her hands, afraid of what they might find.

'Photos . . . photos . . . and more photos . . . wait a moment . . . Jesus Christ!'

'Who are these women? They all look the same . . .'

'They are the same, genius! Ava! Ava Palomba! In the garden, on her balcony, in her bedroom, sunbathing, swimming, sleeping, playing with the dog . . . Look through the window, don't you recognise the background? These photos were taken from where you're standing! We've got him, Pol. I know enough! And you know what you have to do. Inform the public prosecutor. I want this studio sealed. Or better said: the whole building. And I want the estate under surveillance day and night. Inform the technical department. I want every square centimetre of this garage gone over with a fine-tooth comb. Today. And have an international arrest warrant made out against . . . Conchita, do you know Mercury's name?'

'Mercury, señor.'

'His full name.'

'No, señor, I don't know.'

'The numberplate! What's the numberplate of the limousine?'

'I don't know, señor.'

'Isn't there anybody in the house who does know something?'

'Señor Harlow's secretary? She knows everything. But she is on holiday.'

'Where?'

'In Tenerife. Ten Bel. Jesus Maria, what an adventure!'

'A telephone, quickly!'

'There, señor, on the wall, next to the fridge.'

'Pol, call the lads. I want everybody in my office at thirteen hundred hours. Emergency meeting. And have that limousine

traced. First in and around Brussels. And also have the borders
and the airports alerted, the petrol stations checked, roadblocks
set up on the motorways . . . And we also have to get a hold of
some sort of identification, anything, as long as his name is on
it. And . . .'

'Anything else?' Courtois breaks the point of his pencil.

'Conchita, have you got a photo of Mercury?'

She sits on the bed and bursts into tears. Courtois has taken
the binoculars from the wall and is looking out through the
window at the swimming pool and behind that at the rear of
the villa, at the large balustraded terrace, at Ava's bedroom
with its sliding glass doors.

'This Mercury is a peeping Tom,' he says quietly, almost
inaudibly.

'Conchita, do you have to burst into tears, just because I
asked for a photo of Mercury?'

'I hardly know the boy.'

'The boy? So how old is he then?'

'About thirty.'

'And you? How old are you?'

'Thirty-eight, señor.' She looks fifty.

'You look much younger.'

'Thank you . . .'

'Describe him to me.'

'Who?'

'Mercury.'

'He is . . . how do you say . . . a handsome man, a very
handsome man even. Tall, slim, well-groomed . . .' She bursts
into tears again.

'And did he ever behave strangely? Towards your mistress,
for instance?'

'Not that I know of.'

'Did he ever say dirty things?'

'You mean make indecent proposals?'

Van Laken nods.

'No. But I told you, he never spoke to anybody. He hardly ever came out of his garage. He had his hands full with Señor Harlow's eight cars.'

'Well, Courtois? What about those telephone calls?'

'There are quite a few. I think it would be wiser to go back to the office and get organised there. You could make a few of them from the car.'

'Me?'

'Unless you'd prefer to drive. Have you seen this?' Courtois points with the binoculars to the photo of Karlheinz Böhm on the wall.

'What is it?'

'A man with a camera, to which a bayonet has been mounted. A sort of weapon. It enables the murderer to capture the panic and the death throes of his victim on film.'

'Pol, I think we're in for a bundle of fun. Come on, let's get going.' Van Laken helps Conchita to her feet and wipes away her tears with his thumb. 'And, Conchita, remember not to touch anything. And don't let anybody in. Here's my card. If anything happens, phone me at this number. I'll send a patrol round to watch the house. Be careful.'

'Can't you tell me what's happened?'

'Nothing's happened, Conchita. Isn't that right, Courtois?'

'So far.'

'What should I do if Señora Ava comes home?'

'Courtois?'

'Yes?'

'Have you any more questions?'

'No.'

44

'Cindy, after my mother, you're the most vulgar, most repugnant, least interesting creature I've ever come across in the whole of my not uneventful life! You're unattractive and ungainly. You're arrogant and you stink. You're spoiled, stupid and superfluous. You get in the way. You poison the air around you. You've no talent, no charm, no humour and no self-respect. And you're too idle and vain to do anything about it. You're brimming over with pretension. You're a waste of space. And moreover, you were born in that provincial shit-hole Volendam and you've already waved your stupid arse around so much that it's a wonder you're still alive. M must have chosen to ignore you, just like everybody else does. But in his place, I wouldn't hesitate for a second. You're the perfect victim. Now that Richard has gone, there is nobody left to miss you. You'll finally make the front page of the tabloids and then be forgotten for ever. Nobody will mourn for you. No tears will be shed over your mutilated body, because the world will be a better place without you. So you can stop taking pity on Ava. You don't mean a word of it. And she is in less danger than you are.'

Although Suzanna was being driven to distraction by Cindy's ceaseless whining, Ava was nevertheless staggered by this vicious outburst. After all, the atmosphere had been becoming a little more relaxed. There was more room in the limo. The sunroof had been opened and was letting in fresh air. Mercury had even let the women get out one by one to stretch their legs. Ava had been allowed to freshen herself up at a pump from which rusty water gushed, whilst he kept his gun on her from a distance. Ted was no longer there to ruin the atmosphere. And the Glenn Miller Band was sounding almost cheerful. For a moment, it had even seemed as if Cindy and Ava were again getting on well together. (Perhaps this was when Suzanna had started to crack.) All they could do now was to wait until Mercury, who also seemed far from happy with the situation, came to a decision. There was little talking, as if each of them was sunk in thought, trying to imagine the possible outcome of their ordeal. As long as Mercury remained calm, the situation was bearable. Besides, it was as good as certain that Richard's body had meanwhile been discovered and that the search for them was already well under way. And surely Arthur was worried. Hadn't Suzanna promised to be home early?

'True. But Panther usually sleeps in the day. Especially when he's been writing the night before.'

'You're wearing your athlete out,' Cindy had remarked bitchily.

'Don't you worry. He's got inexhaustible staying power.'

'I think you two are perfectly matched,' Ava had comforted her.

'Despite the age difference!'

'There's less of a diffcrence than there is . . . was between you and Richard.'

'But I'm a woman, that's . . . was more normal.'

'What is normal . . .'

'I am. I'm normal. I don't need to go parading around in somebody else's clothes to be myself!'

'Perhaps that's what makes you so boring, Cindy.'

'Richard didn't find me boring.'

'The man was bored to death, literally, believe me.'

'That was your fault! He hated that incurable provincialism you exude from every pore. That so called avant-gardism, your superficial showiness, your schoolgirlish flirting. You know what Richard said about painted dummies like you?

"Paintings should be hung." That's what he said. He was a man of taste, who loved genuine antiques and who during the unfortunately brief period that I was able to make him happy was so seldom bored, Mrs Rizzoni, that he left me more than three million dollars, enough to keep a whole army of Arthurs for the rest of my life. In fact, I ought to thank you.'

It was at this point that Suzanna had finally exploded, crushing and unrelentingly abusing Cindy in her deep voice, making it crystal clear to her that she, Suzanna, is Ava's only friend and that nobody else should think for a moment that they have any right to try to win over the young film star. (Because this is what her fit of anger was really all about.)

Ava changes the subject, afraid the two women are going to scratch each other's eyes out.

'I wonder if Ted has slept it off yet.'

'He'll never wake up again.'

'You're not thinking of letting that mutant get back in?!'

'Come on, he wasn't that bad. You know he and his friends at the squash club have adopted two and a bit Bolivian children? Two point three if I'm not mistaken. It's a purely administrative adoption. We have photos. Two girls. Sometimes they send him drawings and he sends them chocolate or slippers. You can't just leave such a man behind. In a place that probably isn't even on the map!'

'And Rich then?'

'Rich was . . .'

'You ought to envy him, that festering pig of yours! Getting out of the car, that's what all three of us are dreaming of, isn't it? And besides, you're rid of him. Like I said, we ought to be grateful to Mrs Rizzoni . . .'

'You're talking as if Ted is dead too.'

'After what he guzzled down, that wouldn't surprise me! You're not going to try and tell us that you actually loved that moron? Or that you ever were in love with him!'

'In love? No. But still . . . I just don't think it's a very good idea to simply leave him behind in an abandoned house in the middle of nowhere.'

'But sweetie, we left behind every vestige of reality long ago. We are in another dimension, in a story . . .'

'In a film!' shouts Cindy. 'It's true, I'm not myself anymore. Sorry, Suzanna.'

'What's Mercury waiting for?'

'Perhaps until it gets dark.'

'Or until Monday. And he has to keep us hidden away from the world until then.'

'Or for a signal from M.'

'M is slumbering deep inside him,' Suzanna continues. 'Something specific has to happen to awaken the beast. Look at him closely: it's as if he himself doesn't understand how and why he has ended up here with us.'

'Yes. He is dreaming.'

'And what do you think might awaken the beast?'

'Cindy, I'm not looking for a row, but in your place I wouldn't draw too much attention to myself. Like I said, you're the perfect victim.'

'Why me? I look terrible!'

'If he'd been after Ava, which is what I feared at first, he could have got to her at any time, when he was alone with her. But you he could only have kidnapped last night. And that meant he had to kidnap the whole group. And now he clearly doesn't know what to do with us all.'

'I won't say another word.'

'I think that's wisest.'

'I'm hungry.' Ava sounds relieved. Suzanna's theory has given her courage.

'There's still some honey.' Cindy covers her mouth. She has just promised not to talk anymore.

'No, sweetie. Stay away from the honey. We might need it later. And it will only make you thirsty.' Suzanna strokes Ava's cheek.

'I feel so dry . . .'

'Precisely.'

45

Somers parks his grey Volkswagen on the narrow pavement
outside De Rosier. He had been just about to leave for the
land registry office, to collect a list of all the empty warehouses
and packing sheds in the Province of Antwerp, when Van
Laken had phoned him from the Opel. In a voice cracking
with emotion he had briefed him about the rapidly evolving
situation and had sent him to the hotel where a certain
Richard Weinberg and his wife had been picked up by Ted
Harlow the previous night.

'I'm afraid you can't park here, sir. These places are reserved
for our clientele,' says the elegant young man in the dark-grey,
three-button flannel suit in the doorway.

'I can park wherever I fuckin' like. Somers, Antwerp C.I.D.
Is your boss here?'

'Oh, excuse me, officer. I'll enquire whether Monsieur Bob
can receive you. We are not accustomed to visits from the
police in this establishment.'

'There's a first time for everything. You'll soon get used to
it.'

'If sir would be so kind as to follow me . . .'

Somers limps into a hall filled with antique sofas, cabinets of
porcelain and silver, old masters, flower arrangements and
curios, and gazes around in disbelief.

'It's like a flea market in here. Tell me, mate, how much
does a room here cost?'

'Per day, per week or per month, Mr Somers?'

'Per hour?'

'You'd better discuss that with Monsieur Bob. Would you

be so kind as to wait over there, in the purple salon. Can I get you some coffee?'

'Don't go to any trouble.'

Somers, sinks into a rust-coloured Chesterfield, crosses his legs with a metallic click, stares at the still life of bloody skates, pheasants, skinned hares, velvety peaches and wilted roses hanging above the mantelpiece and thinks that it wouldn't be unpleasant to come and have a romp here some night with Mimi La Togolaise, his current steady girlfriend.

'Powerful painting, isn't it? How can I help you, Mr Somers?'

Somers, who had not heard the hotel owner approaching, starts out of his daydream and struggles to his feet.

'Afternoon. I'm here about the disappearance of Mr Vangenechte's car. I believe he came here yesterday evening to pick up two of your guests?'

'Yes, that's correct. Mr and Mrs Weinberg. A very elegant gentleman, Mr Weinberg, a lot of class. Would you care for some coffee?'

'Your waiter already offered. No thanks.'

'As you wish.' Monsieur Bob steps back a few paces and looks Somers up and down. 'Don't I know you from somewhere?'

'I doubt it.'

'I'm almost certain we've met before. At the sauna?'

'No way!'

'Do you play golf?'

'Do I look like a fuckin' golfer?'

'Perhaps not. Anyway. You say another car has been stolen, officer? It's becoming a real plague.'

'This time a car has disappeared with everyone in it. That's the fuckin' difference! And we've every reason to suspect foul play. Did you happen to catch a glimpse of the driver yesterday?'

'Eh . . . yes . . . a good looking chap as it happens.'

'What did he look like?'

'Tall, a metre eighty, eighty-five ... well-built ... black hair slicked down with gel ... Rudolph Valentino style ... very personable, polite, stylish ...'

'Talked posh?'

'Very refined.'

'And who else was in the car when the Weinbergs got in?'

'Three people, if I'm not mistaken, but ...'

'Ted Harlow, Ava Palomba and Suzanna Rizzoni, the fashion designer!'

Blinded by the light of a flashbulb, reflected off the back of the fish in the painting, Somers turns around to face the dwarf in a Hawaiian shirt covered in green parrots, who suddenly appears from behind a Ming vase and, without warning, takes another photo of him.

'Who the fuck is that?'

'Monsieur Jean, our house photographer. We get so many celebrities coming in here: maestros, princes, film stars, sheiks, divas, politicians, you name it ... and I like to be photographed with them all! It sounds childish, I know, but that's just the way I am. Anyway. This gentleman's from the police, Jean.'

'So Johnny, did you take any photos yesterday?'

'But of course, of the limousine. What a car! And of Richard Weinberg, who could barely get in with his injured neck. And of Cindy Beaver. And of Ava Palomba in the car. But unfortunately, they weren't much good, rather blurred. Take a look.' He extracts a couple of black and white photos from his shoulder bag and hands them to Somers.

'Isn't their chauffeur in any of them?'

'Yes, here.' The dwarf points his stubby, nail-bitten finger at Mercury, who is holding the door open for Cindy with his back to the camera. 'He kept turning his head away. As if he was scared to be photographed. Has he done something wrong?'

'Done something wrong! That's a fuckin' good one! Ever heard of M? Our very own Flemish serial killer?'

'Tell me it's not true! Not in my establishment!'

The photographer rummages through his bag, takes out a contact print and examines the minuscule photos with his magnifying glass.

'You can see his face in this one, look.'

Somers studies the photo.

'Handsome fellow, isn't he?' says Monsieur Bob. 'Broad shoulders, narrow hips. Not at all your criminal type.'

'Have you still got the negatives of these, Johnny?'

'At home, in my darkroom.'

'Well hurry home and get them and bring them down to police headquarters, in the Oudaan. In an envelope, a clean envelope, addressed to Mr Somers, that's me, or to Commissaris Van Laken.' Why Somers keeps talking to the dwarf as if he were a little boy is a mystery even to himself.

'Excuse me, I may not be Miss Marple, but I was wondering . . . how can an eight-metre-long limousine with five passengers simply disappear into the countryside . . . Forgive me for asking . . .'

'Who says they're in the countryside? Don't you worry, we'll find it eventually. We only have to hope we're not too fuckin' late. By the way, how much do you charge for a room here?'

'For you, I'm sure we could arrange an attractive price.'

'If we catch him, I'll drop in here on Sunday evening, to celebrate with our Mimi. I bet she'd love to come in one of these auction rooms . . . eh . . . she's black by the way . . . and . . . she loves to shout.'

'No problem at all, Mr Somers. Last week, we had Miss Grace Jones staying with us!'

'No problem then.'

'It will be a pleasure to count you among our guests.'

'So that's agreed. But only if we catch him before Monday.'

'Whatever.'

Somers prepares to leave, rummages through his trouser pocket and takes out a crumpled tram ticket on which he scribbles a telephone number with a blunt pencil.

'Here, at this number you can always get through to somebody at Antwerp C.I.D. You never know . . . if the Weinbergs should return . . .'

'Their luggage is still in their room . . . that is to say, in their suite, so . . .'

'Okay then, hopefully until Sunday!'

'You can say that again.'

46

When Van Laken enters his office at around one o'clock, it is
filled with an unusual hustle and bustle. To an outsider, it
might seem like total chaos, but actually it is highly organised.
At such moments, he calls his office 'the Innovation', because
it resembles that department store during the sales period. He
loves the electric atmosphere. It makes him feel like an
indispensable general at the head of his troops. Dozens of
memos and handwritten notes cover his desk. All the
telephones are ringing at once. De Mulder, Palmans and
Feyaerts are standing in front of the street plan of Antwerp,
deep in discussion.

'There's a fax in from a certain Baudouin, an examining
judge from Namur. And Cornelis has already phoned three
times.'

'God give me strength! First the important news.'

'Apart from that odd fellow they found beside the E411 this
morning, there isn't any.'

'Which odd fellow? Nobody's told me about this!'

'It's all in the fax.'

'Has Somers gone?'

'To De Rosier.'

'And VDB?'

'Off sick.'

'Right.'

Van Laken goes through the fax, which is written in broken
Francophone-Dutch, three times, silently sucking on a soggy
pencil that has to substitute for his cigarette.

'Do you think there could be any connection with . . .'

'Feyaerts! A limousine full of dressed-up film people, on their way to a premiere in Brussels, disappears and the next morning the corpse of an old man in evening dress is found sitting on a bench in a motorway rest area, sixty kilometres to the south of the capital . . . You might find that the most normal thing in the world, but to me . . .'

'Ted Harlow?'

'No. Vangenechte is ginger, short and fat as a pig. And according to the description, this man was tall and grey and had a plaster collar around his neck and a hearing aid in his left ear . . .'

'And his name is Weinberg. Richard fuckin' Weinberg!' shouts Somers, who has been listening to the conversation from the doorway. 'He won't be paying his bill at De Rosier in a hurry!'

'What makes you so sure of that, Somers?' Courtois asks with a tinge of jealousy in his voice.

'Do you know many deaf buggers, with a broken neck and wearing evening dress, who disappeared last night? He was seen getting into the car in front of De Rosier! And here, I've got another fuckin' present for you!'

Somers tosses the photo of Mercury onto the cluttered desk.

'Who's that supposed to be?' asks De Mulder.

'According to the boss's theory, nobody less than M.'

Van Laken has been waiting for this moment for more than six months: his first sight of a picture of M, the moment when the phantom would finally get a face, an identity, the moment when the enemy became recognisable, was no longer an elusive abstraction, when the indefinable evil he had been impotently pursuing suddenly took on human form, enabling him to combat it with normal weapons. At first he doesn't dare to look at the photo, afraid he will be disappointed, afraid he will recognise himself or somebody he knows, afraid the man will not fit in with his own rather vague imaginings. He looks at the glowing tip of Courtois' cigarette, puts on his half-moon reading glasses and picks up the photo with a trembling hand.

'It only shows his back!'

'Wait! Better ones are on the way. De Rosier's house photographer is bringing over the negatives. A dwarf, with a shirt covered in parrots, you can't fuckin' miss him.'

Disappointed, Van Laken hands the photo to his colleagues, who are crowding around him.

'Just as I had imagined him,' says Courtois.

'Bluffer!'

'Not at all! Ask Van Laken! Tall, around thirty years old, well-groomed. At first sight, totally harmless . . .'

'Very true, Pol. Gentlemen, let's go and sit around the table next door and review the situation calmly. It's much too hectic in here. I'll be along in a moment. One more telephone call.'

The Congolese, the Mole, the Gambler, the Whore-hopper and Courtois (still too young for a nickname) leave the office and move to the more spacious, adjoining conference room, which still reeks of the previous night's cigarette smoke. Van Laken dials his home number and waits.

'Maartje?'

'Yes.'

'It's me, lamb-chop.'

'Yes, I can hear that.'

'Kiss.'

'Kiss.'

'What are you up to?'

'I'm writing you a letter.'

'A love letter, I hope.'

'But of course.'

'Romantic?'

'Yes.'

'About our meal . . .'

'No problem.'

'Can we postpone it until this evening?'

'Fine.'

'I think that would be more intimate.'

'Me too.'

'It's terribly exciting here. We're on the point of . . .'

'Don't worry about it.'

'You're an angel. If all goes well, we'll be in the caravan by Sunday, just the two of us.'

'Don't go promising too much.'

'Right. Are you happy?'

'You know I am. Can't you hear it?'

'Since you've been back, everything's been going wonderfully here.'

'Come, come . . .'

'It's true! Anyway, see you later. You wouldn't believe how . . . how happy I am. I missed you so much, all that time . . .'

'See you soon.'

Rubbing his hands, Van Laken enters the brightly lit room, where his colleagues are sitting chatting at the long table. He notices that they have automatically taken the same places as the night before.

'Still got a chair for the old man?'

'At the head of the table, where you belong,' says Courtois.

'Thank you. Right, Pol, you take notes. Okay, what are we a hundred per cent certain of? That Edward Vangenechte, alias Ted Harlow, film producer and sugar daddy of Ava Palomba, hired a mysterious young man, provisionally known as Mercury, to replace his previous chauffeur, who unbeknown to him has been murdered. That this Mercury lives on the estate, spies on Ava, prefers not to show his face in photos and has an impressive fact-file about M. That this Mercury absconded with Vangenechte's limousine and its five passengers at around ten o'clock last night on the way to the premiere of *Desert Flower* in Brussels. The passengers being: Vangenechte himself, Ava Palomba, Mrs Suzanna Rizzoni –

according to those in the know, a leading fashion designer – Richard Weinberg . . .'

'. . . an agent. A show biz agent that is, not a fuckin' insurance salesman.'

'. . . and his wife, Cindy Beaver, a former porn star. Weinberg was found dead this morning, in a rest area on the E411, direction Luxembourg, just before the turn-off for Namur, which may indicate that M is travelling southwards. Those are the facts.'

'So they've been on the road for more than twelve hours already,' says Palmans, 'and if they've kept on driving, there's little chance that they're still in Belgium. They could be anywhere: the South of France, Switzerland, Austria, Northern Italy, Germany . . .'

'And they would have been stopped at some border crossing long ago. No. I think they are still very close.' As he says this, Van Laken gazes outside through the window.

'An eight-metre-long car, that weighs three tons . . .'

'. . . doesn't simply vanish into thin air. That's fuckin' obvious.'

'. . . mustn't be that difficult to find!'

'Dozens of cars are stolen every week. And they're never found again. And not all of them are little grey Renaults.'

'I wouldn't worry too much about the car. The gendarmes are taking the necessary steps to trace it. If need be, they'll call in the army. What I think might help us is a logical analysis of all the details that don't fit in with the hypothesis that this Mercury is actually the man we are looking for.'

'Could you repeat that?' asks De Mulder, who has spent a sleepless night in the scullery of the Wah-Khel and is on the verge of dozing off.

'Suppose this Mercury is indeed M. What doesn't fit?' Van Laken repeats calmly.

'Fuckin' tonnes!' Somers guffaws.

'For example?'

'It's Wednesday.'

'He's operating outside Antwerp.'

'He probably doesn't know where he's going.'

'He's stuck with punters he has no use for.'

'He's leaving behind a trail.'

'He's kidnapped three women at once.'

'Stop! Enough! Because if he is our man, then there'll be an explanation for everything. Palmans says he's leaving behind a trail. Weinberg's corpse, for instance. True enough, but that's intentional, to send us off in the wrong direction. According to Feyaerts, he doesn't know where he's going. Wrong. Inconceivable. According to our Pol, on the ball as always, today is Wednesday. And despite his great exhaustion, De Mulder has been able to ascertain that he has kidnapped more than one woman. So what? My conclusion: he's back here in Antwerp, where he's been hiding out for hours already in that remote location we were planning to look for today and where, according to my theory, he intends to imprison his victims, so that he can murder them how and when he pleases, preferably on a Monday. That being said, I have to admit I'd rather be completely mistaken and be told he's been arrested, anywhere, even by some bloody gendarme in some godforsaken petrol station in the Tyrol, but . . .'

'Does the fax mention whether Weinberg was murdered?' asks Palmans.

'He apparently died from a heart attack.'

'M doesn't murder men.'

Palmans gets up, walks to the window where he had stood the night before, gazes in the same direction, out over the city, which is shimmering under a bright blue sky, and mumbles: 'There's one detail that's bothering me.'

'Yes?'

'Why was the hijacking of the limousine not reported earlier? Why did we have to wait until this morning to even learn that it was missing? Unless I'm much mistaken, a pretty impressive security team was engaged to protect Miss Palomba at yesterday's premiere.'

'True. Under the command of Colonel Cornelis.'

'Who has asked us to phone him at home as soon as there is any news.'

Van Laken dials Cornelis's home number and turns on the loudspeaker, so that everyone can listen in.

'He claims Ava Palomba personally informed him of her decision not to attend the premiere. He therefore had no reason at all to be ill at ease ... Hallo, Mrs Cornelis? Commissaris Van Laken here. Is your husband home?'

'Mr Van Laken! He's been waiting for your call for hours! I'll fetch him immediately. I think he's out watering the begonias ...'

'Tough life they have in the fuckin' gendarmerie!'

'He's suffering from depression,' whispers Van Laken, with his hand over the mouthpiece.

'Hello? Van Laken? I'm glad you've finally called!'

'You sound a lot more cheerful than this morning. Feeling better?'

'Much! I have to thank you again. Your suggestion that I write my memoirs has given me another idea that's even better. I'm going to write them in the form of a film scenario, which my old friend Vangenechte will undoubtedly want to produce since the leading female role is going to be absolutely perfect for Ava Palomba! I'm going to start it tomorrow. What do you think about that?'

'Words fail me ...'

'You know what the proverb says?'

'No, colonel. What does the proverb say?'

'The proverb says: Contemplation leads to creation.'

'But of course. You'll have to excuse me, I've a lot on my mind today. Until the next time, colonel. And once again ... good luck with your very original project!' Van Laken replaces the receiver and, shaking his head, looks at his bewildered colleagues. 'So, Palmans, does that answer your question?'

'Was that the same Cornelis who led the investigation into the Fouchard case?'

'Which still remains unsolved, yes.'

'The man's totally fuckin' lost it!'

'Yes, Somers. And we're left holding the baby.'

47

'He can't keep up his little game much longer,' says Suzanna. 'The psychological strain might break him at any moment. There's a limit to how much of this emotional tension anyone can take. If I was you, I wouldn't worry too much. All we have to do is wait. Look at me: I'm supposed to be in the Galliera Museum, in Paris, at two o'clock tomorrow. My seat has been reserved for months; number thirteen, my usual seat. And I'm pretty certain I'm going to be there on time.'

'An auction?' asks Ava.

'The auction! Organised by Anne-Aymone Giscard d'Estaing in aid of underprivileged children.'

'For Christ's sake, how can you be thinking about such snobby nonsense! Our lives are in danger and all madame can think about is her goddamned social calendar!'

'I'm talking about fashion, Cindy, and about charity, two concepts totally alien to you.'

'Tell me more about it, Suzy.'

'Well, there's not much to it really. I've got my eye on three lots and if the prices are reasonable . . .'

'Tell me!'

'The first is a sexy little evening dress, a mini, in black velvet with a fluorescent lycra lining and matching tights. An outfit from Thierry Mugler's winter collection '90–'91, worn by Diana Ross during the Grammy Awards in '91. There's also a magical Valentino evening dress and matching scarf, in champagne-coloured silk mousseline, embroidered in gold thread and salmon-pink silk. It's been donated by Her Majesty Shabanou Farah Palavi. She wore the dress only once, at an official banquet in honour of the French President Giscard d'Estaing during his visit to Iran in 1975 . . .'

'Ridiculous!'

'Cindy, I thought you weren't going to say another word?'

'Oh, let her have her say.'

'That craving to possess things! Do you get some sort of kick out of looking at all those expensive rags hanging in your wardrobe?'

'My pleasure has nothing to do with possession, Cindy. I leave that to the collectors. Usually boring, frustrated individuals. My pleasure is in the purchasing. It only lasts a couple of seconds and it hurts a little. Like every pleasure worthy of the name. But I'm afraid that level of refinement is beyond your understanding.'

'And the third lot?' asks Ava.

'The *pièce de résistance*! A "drapage", created by Madame Grès in 1965. A mysterious combination of black silk crêpe and geranium-red mousseline, worn by Her Serene Highness, the Princess Grace of Monaco . . .'

'Grace Kelly?'

'That's right, sweetie. A dress that's simply begging for Mitsouko by Guerlain, if you see what I mean . . . Donated by Prince Rainier. I know I'll find it hard to resist.'

'If we get out of this alive, I'll come with you,' says Ava dreamily.

'And I'll buy you that Mugler evening dress. It's simply made for you.'

'Nice gift! A dress Diana Ross was sweating in all evening!' Cindy snarls, cowering down amongst the clutter on the floor as if she is afraid of Suzanna's reaction, or has seen some danger looming behind Ava that the others have missed.

Ava turns around and understands Cindy's clumsy and futile attempt to hide: Mercury has stepped out of the car. He has left the door open and is gazing around distraught at the scenery, which is slowly becoming familiar. His skin is ashen, his face haggard. For the first time, there is no music coming from the driver's cabin. The oppressive silence increases the atmosphere of paralysis that shrouds the petrified landscape. Mercury pricks up his ears, but fails to hear the slightest sound. Every form of life seems to have become extinct; the croaking of the frogs has stopped, there is not a breath of wind and, as far as he can hear, there is only a deathly, ominous silence. The sky behind the conical slag heaps is threatening and it looks as if it is finally going to rain, today of all days, after centuries of drought.

'What did I tell you?' says Suzanna. 'Things are looking up.'

'Perhaps he has to go to an auction too,' she hears Cindy grizzle at her feet, but she doesn't deem this worthy of an answer. She smears her dry lips with lipstick, as if she is getting ready to leave and wants to make herself more presentable, more human, for the press when they are back in the civilised world. A sweet perfume that reminds Ava of the bowl of peaches in her father's kitchen rises from her handbag.

'Suzy, look!' Ava suddenly shouts. 'He's walking away! He's going to leave us here! And they'll never find us here, Suzy, never!' she screams and bursts into tears. 'Mama, do something, please. I don't want them to find me here in a couple of years like a dried-out mummy.'

'Don't be so dramatic, sweetie. We're the tough type, you and me, the type that survives no matter what.'

'Even if we have to chop up Cindy and eat her piece by piece, like those men after that aeroplane crash in the Andes,' Ava adds, trying to give herself courage, as she gazes anxiously outside.

Mercury walks across the street to the abandoned café on the corner. The windows and the door are boarded shut. He peers inside through the gaps between the planks, but it is too dark inside for him to make anything out. He returns to the limousine, opens the boot, takes out a crowbar, walks back to the ruin and begins to force loose the rotting planks. The door turns out to be locked. He smashes its window with the crowbar, sticks his arm between the shards of glass and hammers on the rusty bolt until the door creaks open.

Inside Café Le Moderne, time has stood still, coming to a halt on 15 July 1963, according to the last leaf of the tear-off calendar on the wall next to a peeling Coca-Cola advert, in which a platinum-blonde American housewife with moist pink lips is whispering 'Come up for a Coke'. Mercury plops down on a bar stool, raising a cloud of fine dark grey dust, and emotionally opens the *Soir Illustré* of 10 July, which is lying in front of him amongst the clutter on the bar. 10 July '63! One day after he was born.

The front page has a faded photo of Giovanni Battista Montini, elected Pope Paul VI by a conclave of eighty cardinals on 21 June. A malicious man, thinks Mercury, a bird of prey. Lee Van Cleef. Leafing through the brittle magazine, he learns that in that same month Kennedy made his famous 'Ich bin ein Berliner' speech to an enthusiastic crowd of four hundred thousand at Checkpoint Charlie; Rouahallah Khomeini was arrested in Tehran; John Profumo, the Secretary of State for War, resigned from the British government and parliament following the exposure of his relationship with the beautiful and enigmatic call girl Christine Keeler; twenty-six-year-old Lieutenant Valentina Tereshkova landed safely back in Karaganda after circling the earth forty-eight times and becoming the first woman in space; a certain Salvatore Maldonato, a butcher in the Rue de la Houille, Charleroi, committed suicide after discovering the body of his wife slashed with a butcher's knife in the bedroom; a Buddhist monk committed ritual suicide in Saigon, dousing himself with petrol and setting fire to himself in protest against President Diem's religious policy; slavery was abolished in Saudi Arabia; and most important of all – but this he already knew – in Hollywood Gregory Peck had finally been awarded an Oscar. He regrets that Richard is no longer with them, because he has forgotten for which role and in which film, and Weinberg would undoubtedly have known the answer.

On the wooden shelves behind the bar, there are still dusty glasses and full bottles of beer and mineral water. In the half-open drawer beneath the till, Mercury finds a bottle opener and opens one of the bottles. He wipes the neck clean with his shirt-sleeve and takes a cautious sip, more out of curiosity than from thirst. The taste of the thirty-year-old sparkling water is as good as ever. He winks provocatively at the pin-up with the pink lips in the advert next to the calendar. Beneath the bar, amongst the empty beer crates, he finds a couple of crocks of jenever and a rare, half-full bottle of Vat 69. He then holds a stinking rag under the brown-yellow water that is dripping from the tap, and uses it to wipe one of the café tables as clean as he can. He pushes up two chairs, dusts them off, places the drink, a plastic vase of artificial carnations and, after rinsing them, two glasses in the middle of the rectangular red formica table top. Shame there is no electricity anymore and that the Wurlitzer is dead beneath its dusty crust. He will have to provide the music himself, pick out a tape from the car and play it on his portable Sony . . .

Mercury stands in a corner of the café and surveys the scene – the way a film director stares in silence at his waiting set, before the sun lamps are turned on and it starts to get warm – and asks himself a thousand questions about the position of the camera for the first, sweeping shot.

48

'Commissaris, there is a man downstairs who says he has to hand over some photos to you, personally,' says a female officer, who according to Palmans must look more than presentable beneath her uniform, despite her shiny complexion, 'Shall I send him on up?'

'Little fucker with a lisp?' asks Somers.

'Yes.'

'Little Monsieur Johnny, the dwarf.'

'Send him on up, Josiane.'

'Yes, commissaris.'

'I hope there's a bit more to see this time. Hey, look who's dropped by!'

VDB shuffles into the conference room. He looks depressed, greets nobody, heaves a deep sigh, automatically takes his place amongst the others, opens his briefcase with a furrowed brow and takes out a brown medicine bottle.

'Well, VDB? Aren't you feeling well?'

'It's contagious.'

'What?'

'Our Marjan's skin complaint. Especially when the weather's sultry.'

Feyaerts and De Mulder simultaneously move their chairs away. Luckily, VDB never shakes hands.

'You have to try and take your mind off it,' says Van Laken, who would like to see VDB leave the room as soon as possible. 'Eczema is usually psychosomatic. The night watchman who found Lova Spencer floating amongst those scorpion things yesterday is coming in for questioning at sixteen hundred hours. Room thirty-four, third floor. Will you take his statement?'

'If there's nobody else,' grumbles VDB, stowing his medication back in his briefcase, which he carefully locks with a tiny key. He passes the photographer in the doorway without even noticing him.

'Come in, comrade!' shouts Van Laken, trying his best to hide his surprise at the appearance of a parrot-covered dwarf by being excessively jovial and far more friendly than usual. 'And? Better luck this time?'

Monsieur Jean brings the tips of his fingers to his lips, kisses them with a loud smack, slides into VDB's empty chair and proudly takes a black and white photo from his shoulder bag.

'Here is your man!'

Van Laken studies the photo closely, without saying a word, without showing the slightest emotion, with an expressionless face he hopes will hide how disappointed he is that Mercury looks so normal, how jealous he is that Courtois had described the monster down to the tiniest details, and how difficult it is to admit that the charming young man in the photo is indeed attractive, the type even Maartje used to fall for, in the past.

'Look at his gaze. The way he's looking at Cindy Beaver. It gives me the shivers.' Van Laken shows the photo of Mercury holding open the door for Cindy to De Mulder, Feyaerts and Somers. 'Well, Palmans, not interested?'

Palmans, who is sitting in his usual place at the window, staring dreamily at the River Scheldt, turns around.

'Yes . . . But I'm afraid we might be wasting our time.'

'How do you mean?'

'Unless somebody recognises him, that photo's totally useless.'

'To me, he just looks concerned.'

'Bashful more like.'

'Yes. Even friendly.'

'Any woman would be attracted to such a man,' says

Palmans. 'He has a mysterious quality, that much is certain. Josiane!'

The blonde police woman sticks her head through the doorway and looks at Palmans with lacklustre eyes and a vaguely bitter expression, something like: don't even think about it, you know I've got a steady boyfriend.

'Come and look at this! We need a specialist opinion!'

Palmans, who never misses a chance to make advances to Josiane despite her coolness, and is meanwhile ogling the always-open third button of her shirt, hands her the photo of Mercury.

'Wow! I wouldn't mind an evening out with him!'

'I thought you were engaged?'

'Sometimes.'

'Do you know who it is?' asks Van Laken.

'No, commissaris. But I'd like to get to know him!'

'Thank you. That will be all, Josiane.'

'What did I tell you?' says Palmans, waving the photo. 'The man drives women wild! I'm afraid you're right, commissaris: this is the man we've been looking for . . . now I'm certain of it.'

'Will you still be needing me?'

Everybody had forgotten Monsieur Jean, whose oversized head is just visible above the table.

'No.'

'To whom do I send my bill?'

'You can arrange that with Mr Vandenbos, room thirty-four, third floor.'

'But don't shake his hand, Johnny my lad! Don't lay a fuckin' finger on him, promise? It's for your own good!'

'I wouldn't dream of it,' laughs the dwarf, blushing. The meaning of Somers' warning escapes him, but he feels so ill at ease in a room full of policemen that he wants to get away as fast as his little feet will carry him.

'Okay. Enough of this chattering, lads. Palmans thinks we

have no time to lose and he is not wrong. Somers, you go to the land registry office as planned. De Mulder, take a couple of men and go over Vangenechte's villa with a fine-tooth comb. And De Mulder, don't forget to grill the maid. I think the lovely Conchita knows a whole lot more about Mercury than she told us on our first visit. Feyaerts, you take this photo and have it circulated via Interpol and also nationally: the gendarmerie, border crossings, petrol stations, airports, supermarkets and so forth. Palmans you go to Suzanna Rizzoni's residence in the Nassaustraat, Courtois has the address, and wait for us there. Rizzoni has a live-in boyfriend who should normally have gone with them, but changed his mind at the last moment. I want to question him personally. I want to know why. Pol, would you ask Josiane to print a couple of copies of the photo?'

'And give her one to hang above her bed, with my compliments,' says Palmans, without moving his lips.

49

Courtois starts the motor of the grey Opel whilst Van Laken is still squeezing his doubled-up metre ninety inside, feeling for the lever that moves his seat backwards, and grumbling about it as usual.

'Nassaustraat?'

Van Laken looks at his watch and starts in amazement: it is half past four.

'I'll drop in at home a moment along the way. And if you drive via the Quellinstraat, stop at Fiori.'

'Fiori!' Courtois exclaims in surprise. 'The only postmodern flower shop in Antwerp!'

'Have you got the photo with you?'

Courtois hands him the enlarged portrait of Mercury, which looks harder and more threatening in the photocopy, lots of white and a little black.

'If that's not a murderer, I'll hand in my resignation.' Courtois finds it unnecessary to respond. Van Laken habitually threatens to resign at the slightest provocation.

At Fiori, probably the most expensive flower shop in the city centre, Van Laken has a rather old-fashioned bouquet of twenty-nine baccarat roses made up. It is almost thirty years since he first met Maartje; in '67 at the round table of Café Den Engel. She can put them in a bucket, he thinks, and take them along to the caravan on Sunday. She had smashed their crystal vase the evening before she left him. But she will have forgotten that by now. Everything is forgiven. She is back. Mercury's days are numbered. A new chapter can begin. At the lake. Just a few more days patience.

'Unusual music,' he says to the retiring young man with a bleached cowlick and shaved temples, who is wrapping the bouquet in cellophane on a frosted-glass table between two designer loudspeakers.

'Corsican polyphonic chants.'

'Strange . . .'

'Postmodern . . . in a way.'

'Doesn't surprise me in the least.' In the past, when Maartje was gone, it would never have occurred to him to talk to a florist about music. In the past, he would have moaned about the hullabaloo going on outside, because Courtois was double parked and blocking the path of a bus.

Van Laken lays the roses carefully on the back seat of the car. Courtois looks around nervously, but does not dare to tell his boss that there are more urgent things to do than buying flowers. Van Laken notices and reassures his assistant: 'No need to pull such a face, Pol! I'll just drop them in and hurry back out. Thirty seconds. That's all.'

'I'm not pulling a face. It's just that the rush hour seems to be beginning earlier and earlier.'

In the Breydelstraat, Courtois pulls up behind a lorry that is unloading beer barrels in front of the Café Brabançonne. Van Laken lifts the bouquet from the back seat and the rather furtive way he disappears with it into the narrow alley alongside the café moves Courtois, who turns off the engine, winds down his window, lights a cigarette and turns on the radio. It is Jacques Dutronc singing 'C'est l'hymne à L'Amour'.

A little out of breath – he lives on the third floor and as usual the ancient lift is out of order – Van Laken is about to stick his key into the Yale lock when he notices that the door of the apartment is ajar.

'Maartje! Lamb-chop!'

No answer. Van Laken can smell coffee. A homely fragrance he is no longer used to. The smell of happiness and simple pleasures. He tiptoes through the living room to the bedroom.

Perhaps she is still lying in bed enjoying the afterglow, understandable, after last night's intense emotions. Maybe he simply forgot to shut the door behind himself this morning. But the bed is empty and the room is filled with the usual chaos. Disappointed, he throws the flowers on to the clammy mattress and notices the pink envelope sticking out from between the folds of the tousled sheets. The love letter she was writing when he phoned her from the office. Van Laken kneels down on the pillow that still smells of Maartje, pays no attention to the peal of thunder outside, rips open the envelope and begins to read feverishly.

Dearest Miel,

Yesterday was no coincidence. I'd been waiting for you outside the Oudaan all evening, because I wanted to talk to you. But when you finally came outside, you were with your colleagues. And then I saw you leaving on foot. You looked so forlorn and miserable I didn't dare to call to you and so I followed you as far as the nightshop, because at first I thought: he's going home. And then when I was suddenly standing there in front of you, dripping wet, I still couldn't find the right words and that broke my heart.

When I came home with you afterwards, it was out of pity, because I couldn't bear to let you walk out into the rain alone. But nothing lasts forever and as you always say yourself: everything always turns out for the best, sooner or later. So now I'm going to tell you what I couldn't tell you yesterday, because when you've got a lump in your throat, it's easier to write than it is to speak.

Dearest Miel,

When I left you in the autumn, it wasn't because I didn't love you, you know I love you, but because you and I never had the same dreams, or rather (and this is difficult to say) because you have never been able to fulfil my dreams. Not that I've ever really asked for much. You see, Miel, I'm a woman who's not very good at being alone and all those years that I was sat at home waiting for you, I had too much time to think.

So is it so much better with your hairdresser? you'll say. Well, it's different. For Nino, I'm there every minute of the day. He makes me laugh. Your stories were always so serious, even horrifying. If you did talk to me, it was always about corpses and blood, about murder and manslaughter. You know, it's the little things that mean a lot, the little tokens of affection, not the great promises. And what were you promising me all those years? A solitary life in a caravan that was never going to go anywhere, a rowing boat on a lake where it is always raining, a poodle and a little patch of lawn, three metres by four, surrounded by tulips in the spring.

I've therefore decided to divorce you. There, I've said it. That's what I'd come to tell you yesterday. And what happened between us last night, that was nothing. You're so different to the cheerful lad I used to know thirty years ago and you're much too old to change. I don't feel any guilt, but I do feel terrible. I'm the villain in our story. But today is Wednesday and I need genuine, warm affection. I'm sure you'll soon find somebody else, a pretty girl who'll understand you better than I ever could. You're still as charming as ever, remember that. I'll never forget you.

Maartje.

P.S. Don't bother looking for the cat. I've taken her with me. She was also stuck here all alone.

Van Laken folds the letter in two and sticks it slowly in his pocket. Then he picks up the roses, sleepwalks to the kitchen, fills a bucket, pushes the flowers into the water without removing their cellophane wrapping, sucks his bleeding index finger and bursts into tears.

When he stumbles groggily out on to the pavement in front of the Café Brabançonne ten minutes later, the rain is gushing from the low black clouds that have built up over the city and the paving stones smell like Maartje's hair, last night, at the bar of the Madonna. The lorry has meanwhile left and Courtois is now parked right in front of the door. Van Laken stares right through him, as he shuffles slowly to the car, as if oblivious to the rain. When Courtois pushes open the door for him, he flops exhausted into the car and stares vacantly at the raindrops splashing down the windscreen and further, at the water-blurred street filled with scurrying phantoms.

'I bet she was over the moon,' says Courtois, who is convinced Van Laken has spent the last twenty minutes making passionate love to his refound sweetheart, whilst he himself sat waiting below, watching the storm clouds gather over the city like a murky blanket.

'I've never met a woman who doesn't buckle at the knees for flowers.'

'I used to have a girlfriend who'd only accept them if they were packed in flat cardboard boxes, like in the American films of the Forties. A difficult lady. Casa Rizzoni?'

'Casa Rizzoni.'

Courtois slaloms gracefully in and out of the busy traffic, sirens blaring, wondering why his boss seems so distracted since his visit to his wife.

'Did you show her the photo?'

'Who?' Van Laken asks, tapping on the side window with the Scrabble block.

'Mrs Van Laken . . .'

'Yes, of course.'

'How did she react?'

'She said he looked dependable and had a good haircut.'

'A good haircut?'

'My wife attaches exceptional importance to haircuts.'

On the Koolkaai, they are cut off by a concrete mixer lorry and forced to wait. Van Laken gets out of the car without explanation.

'Wait here.'

Through the windscreen wipers, Courtois watches him enter the brothel on the corner of the Gorterstraat and begins to regret the pernicious influence Mrs Van Laken has had on his boss's powers of concentration.

The still very young transvestite slides from his velvet-covered barstool, pulls the colourless net curtain across his window and brushes the raindrops from Van Laken's forehead with trembling hands.

'Don't go to any trouble, Lolita. Police. Have you got a telephone?'

'Of course I've got one! Pigs, I can smell them a mile away!' screeches the emaciated youth, throwing his red wig across the room. 'Over there, next to the bed.'

Van Laken sits on the edge of the creaking bed and dials the number of Somers' car. The room smells of lily-of-the-valley and the paraffin stove and is bathed in an even red glow. Teddy bears, whips, a postcard of the Mont Saint-Michel and a poster of Boy George are hanging on the wall.

'Somers. It's me . . .' Van Laken says quietly, holding his hand in front of his mouth, afraid the boy might be eavesdropping.

'So, boss . . . what's new?'

'Somers, I . . .'

'I can hardly hear a fuckin' word!'

'I've got a personal favour to ask of you.'

'Let's hear it.'

'Have you got a moment?'

'Loads. I'm stuck in a fuckin' traffic jam.'

'You too? So much the better. Have you . . . Have you got any stuff on you? You know what I mean . . .'

'No.'

'So you have. Don't play the innocent, Somers. I've known for years that you're a snorter . . . but you're also one of my best officers . . . If you help me out, it will be our little secret.'

'What do you want me to do?'

'You know Nino's, that fancy hairdresser's in the Pelikaan-straat, next to the diamond exchange? Well I want you to go there and drag out the owner, a half Jewish, half Italian runt of a metre sixty, and arrest him for possession of narcotics . . .'

'That I've planted in one of his little pots myself, right?'

'Right. And if he tries to resist, kick the shit out of him.'

'This could have serious consequences . . .'

'So could your habit . . . I'll cover for you.'

'And what do I do with the little runt afterwards?'

'You put him on ice and leave him to me. If you need to reach me, I'll be at Rizzoni's.'

Van Laken replaces the receiver, takes a five hundred franc note from his wallet and hands it to the transvestite, who is trembling so violently on his over-high heels that his laddered fishnet stockings fall down.

'Here, for your trouble.'

'For that price, you are entitled to a little sample, officer.'

'Never when I'm on duty, gorgeous. But I will take one of your cigarettes, preferably a purple one with a golden filter, like the one you're holding.'

50

Mercury is squatting motionless in front of the wide open door of the limousine, with his pistol trained on the three women. He does not know what to say. Ava is seeking protection in Suzanna's arms and Cindy, wishing she were invisible, is gazing in the other direction, as she did when she was a little girl and feared that the white clown in the circus would pick her out of the audience to come into the ring.

'What you're listening to now,' Mercury begins hesitantly, 'is "E il sol dell' anima" from *Rigoletto* by Giuseppe Verdi, sung by Luciano Pavarotti and the soprano Renata Scotto, accompanied by the orchestra of the Rome Opera, conducted by Carlo Maria Giulini. It is an old recording – from 19 November '66, I think, but I might be wrong, I'm a little tired – but for those days, it's the height of technical perfection. I thought you might enjoy it, Mrs Rizzoni.'

'Very kind of you, Mercury. Exactly what I needed,' Suzanna answers ironically.

'The CD lasts forty-seven minutes. It also has excerpts from *La Traviata, Un Ballo in Maschera, Don Carlos, Nabucco, Il Trovatore, Aïda* and *La Forza del Destino*. All of them sung by the very best voices: Callas, Giuseppe di Stefano, Giuliana Raymondi, Fedora Barbieri, Renata Tebaldi, I'm probably forgetting a couple. A veritable feast, at least for the enthusiast.'

'Grazie!'

'Well, I hope that Verdi and especially the sonorous sounds of your mother tongue will remind you of pleasant childhood memories . . . while Ava and I go for a little walk . . .'

Suzanna feels Ava's sharp nails dig into her upper arm

through Sarah Bernhardt's dress. Cindy can barely suppress a sigh of relief.

'Ava?'

'What do you want from me, Mercury?' she groans, barely understandable.

'I want you to get out and come along with me.'

'Don't hurt me . . .'

'I won't hurt you . . . I promise.'

'I'll go with you.'

'You'll stay exactly where you are, Mrs Rizzoni, calmly listening to Verdi with Mrs Weinberg. What I have to say to Ava has nothing to do with you . . . Ava?'

What scares Ava most is the strange mixture of doubt and calm resolution in Mercury's behaviour, as if his schizophrenia is suddenly getting the upper hand, as if the dreaded moment Suzanna had been talking about, the moment when the demon in him awakens, has finally broken.

'I'm afraid you have no choice, sweetie,' Suzanna whispers. 'Do what he says, don't disagree with him and above all, use your talent: a tempted man is a careless man. I'll pray for you.'

Suzanna frees herself from Ava's grip and pushes her slowly out of the car. Mercury grasps her wrist tightly. As he kicks the door shut behind her, it begins to rain.

'Who had to shut up? Who was the vulgar waste of space who was going to be mutilated? You're a bitch, Suzanna, a pretentious, arrogant, know-it-all bitch!' Cindy is exultant, reborn. She stretches, like a cat that is waking up, spreads herself out over the whole width of the rear seat, slides a hand into her jeans and closes her eyes.

The sky is so dark that night already seems to have fallen. Rolling black clouds thunder and burst, pelting down a torrent over the colourless landscape, which glimmers and soaks up the overabundant rainwater like an inky sponge. Ava has left her shoes in the limousine and, without releasing her wrist, Mercury tenderly watches how her delicate feet sink into the ebony sludge, the soft mud slithering between her toes, with their red-painted nails. She rubs her face with her free hand, as if she is trying to wipe away all the squalor of the previous night, the anxious sweat, the tension, the smell of Ted. She opens her mouth, lets the refreshing water flow over her tongue and down her throat, licks her fingers, her eyelashes stick together, her dress is saturated and transparent. Mercury watches her dark nipples stiffen. She throws back her head and smiles.

'Mercury, let me enjoy the rain a moment longer, please . . .'

He releases her arm. The voice of Maria Callas rings out of the limousine: '*E strano . . . ah! Forze è lui . . . Follie!*' Ava stretches out her arms and spins like a top, until she wobbles drunkenly and falls into the ink. *Singing in the rain.*

Mercury helps her up, licks the mud from her cheeks. She lets herself hang limply, like a silvery rag, as if after the purification of the heavenly shower bath, she has resigned herself to her fate and is surrendering herself completely to her executioner.

'Come.' He picks her up and carries her – like King Kong carrying Fay Wray – in his arms to Le Moderne, where he gently sets her down on one of the two chairs he had just wiped clean.

'If people are good to water, then water is good for people . . . What's the matter?'

Ava is gazing around with a dazed look in her eyes. 'I don't understand what you mean.'

'The purer the water, the purer the body. Water low in mineral salts cleanses the body of impurities. That way, the body recovers its natural balance and the spirit rediscovers the well-being and serenity it so badly needs. That's what I was thinking just now, when I saw you dancing in the rain. Sounds familiar, doesn't it?'

'Not to me.'

Mercury picks up one of the bottles from the table in front of him and waves it in front of Ava's dripping face. 'Spa! The advert for Spa Reine! Pure goodness!'

'Just stop it, Mercury. Stop playing with me. I'm not some toy. I know who you are. Whatever you're planning to do, do it quickly, now, immediately. I'm so tired, so tired . . .'

Mercury sits down opposite her, leans over, lays his hand on hers and looks her straight in the eyes.

'You've no idea who I am.' He opens two bottles of Spa and fills the glasses. 'A drop of thirty-year-old Vat 69? A collector's item.'

'No, thank you.' She empties her glass in a single gulp and gazes vacantly at Mercury, who clumsily adds a shot of whisky to his water, spilling it, as nervous as a teenager on his first date.

'Do you know where we are?'

'God only knows. Not far from Charleroi, I think.'

'Still in Belgium?'

'Of course.'

'Why did you stop here? Why didn't you just carry on driving?'

He himself has no idea.

'Ava, have you ever had a dream, a destructive, obsessional dream, something you thought about every moment, something that wouldn't let you go and seemed to become more unattainable, more unreal every day, making you forget about thirst and hunger, an overpowering longing that keeps you awake, an image that reappears every time you close your eyes?'

'In the past, you mean?'

'Yes . . .'

'Not in the past, no. I realised all my childhood dreams quite quickly and easily.' She hopes this doesn't sound too arrogant.

'And now?'

'Now? Toothpaste.'

Mercury laughs. Clinks his glass against hers.

'I don't want to die with a sticky taste in my mouth.' The restrained tone in which she utters this rather melodramatic statement, proves yet again that she is a not unaccomplished actress.

'But who said anything about dying? Sweetheart, could you really think for a single second that I . . . that I was M?' He offers her a cigarette.

Gusts of wind are making the roof creak. Water is beginning to seep through the ceiling. Ava is confused by what Mercury has just said. It sounded so simple, so honest. And the atmosphere in the abandoned café is somehow secure, reassuring. Perhaps because it is thundering and lightning outside. Mercury lights a candle and puts his tiny tape recorder on the table next to the bottle of Vat 69.

'Are you planning to record my death throes?' The tremolo in her voice is perhaps a little exaggerated.

'She sounds like Gloria Swanson in the final scene of *Sunset Boulevard*,' thinks Mercury.

'I can't think without the appropriate music.' He turns on the tape recorder: Tom Waits sings 'Old Shoes and Picture Postcards'. Ava shivers. Her dress is sticking to her skin and the wind is whistling through the broken window of the front door.

'Okay,' she says with chattering teeth, 'I don't know who you are. Suppose I'm mistaken. Can you tell me why you've plunged us into this nightmare? Perhaps you could begin by introducing yourself?' She turns her hand over, palm upwards, an invitation. Mercury plaits his fingers through hers. She realises she may at last be playing the role she has always longed for, and not a single one of her previous partners exuded Mercury's troubled charm. He takes a deep breath, as if he is about to recite a multiplication table.

'My real name is Frank Stavlisky. I'm thirty and I am not a chauffeur by profession . . .'

'Nobody is a chauffeur by profession.'

'Oh, but they are, Uncle Bens, for example . . . But let me finish. When I was three years old, my father, who'd had enough of running a shoe shop, abandoned our family. A cliché. Once, when I became an adult, he sent me a postcard of birds of paradise, from Manaus in the Amazon, where he was trying to make his fortune prospecting for gold. He got the date wrong and the card was mouldy and illegible. It's very humid there . . . And that's the last I heard from him. I studied music and film history, and when my mother died, I went to the film academy in Lodz, Polanski's old school, in Poland, because I still had distant relatives living there. I got my diploma. So on paper, I'm a qualified film director . . .'

Mercury is interrupted by the shrill voice of Cindy, screaming at Suzanna in the limousine.

'Those two will scratch each other's eyes out yet,' says Ava anxiously.

'Let them get on with it. I can use everything.'

Although she does not understand exactly what Mercury means by this, Ava squeezes his hand and whispers: 'Carry on.'

'When I returned from Poland, I was arrested at the airport with fifty grammes of hash in my pocket. I spent eight months in prison, two in Turnhout, the rest in Merksplas. That's where I learnt to live alone, where I discovered solitude and silence, where I tasted isolation. And that's where you entered my life.'

'In Merksplas? In the prison?'

'Yes. Two years ago. Via *Playboy*.'

'My God!'

'I was lying on my bed in my cell — it must have been around Christmas, because it was snowing outside — and when I opened out the centrefold and saw you looking at me from the edge of the swimming pool in that warm, coppery, Californian glow, I felt something I'd never felt before. My heart began to beat faster and erratically, my mouth went dry, my stomach cramped. Playmates usually had little effect on me. But you . . . you were real. You existed. It was as if I could see you breathing. And all of a sudden, I couldn't live with the thought that millions of other men had been looking at the same photo, even worse, that there was probably a man somewhere who shared your life. I was jealous. An emotion I'd never known before. I wanted you all to myself. By the time I was released from Merksplas, I was even more obsessed. I decided to collect every possible sort of information about you: interviews, newspaper cuttings, videos . . . I knew everything about you. I wrote to you several times but I never received an answer.'

'I got so many crazy letters! I couldn't understand what was happening to me. After all, I was nobody, a photo, nothing more, a fantasy . . .'

'To me you were real. You began to act a bit, small roles in trivial, inane productions, nothing for you. I've seen them all: *The Revenge of Alfredo Waldemar Engel* . . .'

'Terrible!'

'*Dancing Divinity, Benidorm Lilly* . . .'

'Stop it!'

'You were always divine, you radiated such purity, such simplicity. I couldn't just watch you go downhill, end up in the porn circuit, without reacting, I mean. I knew if I was ever going to make a film, it could only be with you. Or better said: I'd write you a scenario, my first film, a film that would wash you clean, wipe away your scars, propel you to the highest heights, reveal you to the world as the true star you really are, a film in which you'd be able to display not only your beauty but also all the myriad facets of your talent, a film in which you would blossom, a long bottled-up cry of love . . .'

The cries shrieking from the limousine are anything but cries of love, but Ava is so spellbound by Mercury's declaration that she pays them no attention.

While he has been talking, he has edged his chair closer to

hers. He gently strokes her back and she feels the warmth gradually returning to her body. She relaxes and lays her head on his shoulder. Maybe this is the story he used to gain the confidence of his previous victims, but his voice is so sensual and his hand on her back feels so protective that she can't resist the dangerous pleasure of abandoning herself to her fate.

'So I set to work, but I quickly came to the painful realisation that I couldn't get a letter down on paper. I sat for hours staring desperately at that white sheet of paper on the table in front of me, but each time I put my pen to the paper, my hand cramped and the words just evaporated. No story was good enough for you. There I sat, inadequate, helpless, without imagination, surrounded by your photos . . . To survive, I started smuggling again, from Amsterdam, which in my case was extremely risky. Bit by bit, I sold off my CD collection, my film books, my videotapes . . . I became isolated again. All I could think of was you. I made wild plans to leave for America, to look for you, who knows, even wangle a job on *Desert Flower*. You'd just started shooting *Desert Flower*.'

'You're crazy.'

'You drove me crazy.'

Mercury runs his index finger over her lips, feels the tremor between her shoulder blades, kisses her mouth which opens, finds her warm tongue, the tongue of the woman beside the swimming pool in the photo, tastes mud and honey and his eyes fill with tears. This blessed moment alone has made it all worthwhile.

'Why didn't you come to America? Ted was so different then . . . I'm sure he would have helped you.'

'I couldn't get a visa, because of my record.'

Ava breathes heavily, swallows, tastes mud and honey and whisky.

'But that doesn't explain this absurd kidnapping.'

The husky voice of Billie Holiday is now resounding from the tiny tape recorder: '*In my solitude, you haunt me . . .*'

Mercury stands up, takes Ava by the hand, throws his arm around her waist and, almost imperceptibly, begins to dance with her. The same bloodcurdling screams are still resounding from the limousine.

'I was on the verge of a nervous breakdown. I was taking a bath ten times a day, which in my case indicates that I've sunk about as low as I can sink. I thought about suicide, about Poland . . . And then destiny stepped in and did my deciding for me. First there was M, who hit the headlines with his stage-managed atrocities. Like everybody else, I didn't pay much attention to the first murder, Lolita Moore, the "skinned rabbit". But when he kept on striking and moreover seemed to be uncatchable and to be growing into some sort of disconcerting, terrifying, perplexing folk hero, he started to fascinate me more and more. Serial killers are so un-Flemish that I thought to myself: Perhaps there's material here for an original debut film. I started to compile all the information I could find about him. I was born again, because I had found a topic that could maybe lead me to you. And then when I read in *Story* that you'd be staying in Belgium for an unlimited time and that you were living in Antwerp with your producer, despite the danger to which he was exposing you, then I knew that I too had a guardian angel watching over me. And then to top it all, I heard that there was a job vacancy at Harlow Productions . . . as chauffeur . . .' He kisses her neck.

'You had everything you'd ever dreamed of! Why didn't you come to talk to me?'

'The vital element was still missing.'

'What?'

'I had no storyline. And no imagination. So I had to induce one.'

'And now?'

'Now the scenario is writing itself. You're playing the leading role. Playing yourself. And the supporting roles are turning out better than I could ever have expected.'

'But what . . .'

'I have to admit that none of this was planned.'

'Not planned? And the car then?'

'My intention was to disappear alone with you.'

'What made you change your mind?'

'Ted. I couldn't stand to see you sitting next to that swine anymore . . . And the gendarmes . . . And an attack of . . . let's call it panic . . . but that's another story.'

'And how does your film end?'

'No idea. I'm waiting to see what happens.'

'Really no idea?'

'Perhaps the actress will fall in love with her director?'

'*Déjà vu*. I'm afraid a happy ending is no longer possible, Mercury . . .'

'Frank.'

'Frank . . . and that the gates of Merksplas prison are again open wide for you.'

'Unless you don't press charges, sweetheart . . .'

'Why wouldn't I . . .'

'Have you any idea of the media attention this case is getting? I listened to the news this afternoon. Leading item. Ten minutes.'

'Have they found Richard yet?'

'Yes. But apart from that, they're feeling in the dark.'

'And *Desert Flower*?'

'Shot down in flames. You're in urgent need of some stunt to help you climb back up the ladder. And that's what I'm offering you. Suppose we both reappear, hand in hand, like a loving couple, and announce our film project . . . the producers will be queuing up!'

'Except for Ted.'

'Except for Ted. But the world hasn't exactly been waiting with bated breath for him to make films! Would you want to work with him again?'

'And how are you going to explain that he's now lying . . .

asleep . . . in a flooded cellar full of frogs, somewhere in the vicinity of Charleroi?'

'That's nothing to do with me. It's part of the scenario. Suzanna pushed him in. I was simply an observer. The first, privileged member of the audience. As I already said: the scenario is writing itself . . . Eva, you have to trust me . . . I love you, like nobody else could ever love you.'

'Eva?'

'That's your real name, isn't it? Eva Tuinman?'

'Do you really know everything about me?'

'Everything. Because "tuinman" is the Dutch word for gardener, your first agent, John Ferley, changed the Eva into Ava. Like Ava Gardner, right? Ava was two-dimensional. Eva is three-dimensional. Ava is the photo, the glamour, the glitter. Eva the woman with whom I am dancing, who I'm holding in my arms, who I can feel pressed against me and who I never, ever want to let go . . . The person you love is the person you dream about. And not the other way around. Love really is that simple.'

She throws her arms over his shoulders, presses herself against him, opens her lips and waits for him to kiss her again. In her husky, alcohol-and-tobacco voice, Billie Holiday is singing. '*Lover man, oh where can you be . . .*'

51

Palmans has been parked in front of the polished steel portal of the Rizzoni Factory for more than an hour already when Van Laken's Opel finally appears around the corner of the narrow street, skidding over the wet cobblestones. Palmans gets out of his car, throws the brochure he has been dreamily flicking through – for a weekend break in the Seychelles – into the gutter and watches how the glossy photo of the white beach, slanting palm trees and opal sea floats away on the dark water and disappears down the drain. Paradise is not for him.

'I'd almost given you up!'

'Don't go playing the martyr, Palmans, nobody asked you to wait outside in the rain,' Van Laken snaps and stubs out his cigarette in a crack in the brick façade.

Behind Van Laken's back, Courtois signals to Palmans that Big Mac is back in form and that he had better be careful what he says.

'Seen any movement?'

'Nothing and nobody.'

Van Laken casts a disdainful eye at the gigantic zip-fastener above the door, rings the bell, holds his hand over the lens of the video camera beside the bell, and waits motionless in the pelting rain, his ear pressed against the intercom, a new, sodden cigarette clamped between his lips.

'Hallo?' A husky, coarse male voice.

'Van Laken. Police.'

'I can't see anything on my screen. Perhaps you're leaning . . .'

'I can't see you either. And that suits me fine.'

'Eh . . . Mrs Rizzoni is not at home.'

'That's the reason we've called.'

'Do you have an appointment?'

'I never make appointments.'

'Then I'm afraid . . .'

'Who am I talking to?'

'Arthur Rambo. The poet.'

'Listen here, laddie, I'm sick to the teeth of poets, dancers, hairdressers and arty-farty types in general! You've got exactly three seconds to open this goddamned door before I kick the bastard in!' Van Laken knows he is going way beyond his authority, that he hasn't got a warrant, that Arthur could file a complaint, but it works. There is a little buzz and the door clicks open.

'Wait in the hall. I'll come downstairs.'

Van Laken steps inside, shakes the water from his coat and flattens back his hair with both hands.

'This place smells just like the aisles in the aquarium, yesterday at the zoo,' says Courtois.

'It's you, you smell like a wet dog.'

'All of these lofts are damp. Been empty much too long.'

'No, Palmans, Courtois smells like a wet dog.'

Van Laken has not been in such a bad mood for weeks. Courtois decides to keep his comments to himself.

The glass double door that separates the two successive halls slides open automatically, like a pane of glass splitting silently in two, and Arthur's impressive silhouette appears in the bright backlight. Van Laken, whose anger has gained the upper hand, is ready to pounce, but Arthur is too quick for him.

'Gentlemen, I have to say that this unannounced visit is highly inconvenient.'

'Shut it, Tarzan!'

Palmans discreetly squeezes Van Laken's arm and whispers in his ear that he has to calm down, whatever the cause of his annoyance, that Mr Rambo is not obliged to receive them, that they have no proof he has done anything wrong and that they therefore certainly cannot treat him as a suspect.

'Excuse me,' mumbles Van Laken, 'thunderstorms always make me nervous. And closed doors even more so. Are you going to invite us inside, or are we all going to stand here dripping in the hallway?'

Palmans only now notices that Arthur is as wet as everyone else and was probably taking a shower when the bell rang. His imitation leopard bathrobe is hanging open over his broad chest and he is wearing black vinyl briefs covered in zip-fasteners. Nobody normal takes a shower in his swimming trunks . . .

'Two minutes, that's all.' Arthur turns around indignantly and hurries through a bare, gently sloping corridor of whitewashed concrete, closely followed by Van Laken – who, because he is three times skinnier, seems even taller than the colossus in front of him – and Courtois, who pinches his nose to indicate to Palmans that there is something rotten in the state of Rizzoni. On the first floor the corridor opens out into an immense space, dotted here and there with black leather sofas, palm trees in wicker baskets, abstract sculptures and futuristic TV sets, all reflected in a sea of blue-green marble. Arthur flops arrogantly into one of the sofas and gazes piercingly at Van Laken, who is staring open-mouthed at the works of art.

'The work of friends. Tinguely, Nikki de Saint-Phalle, Panamarenko and Szukalski. I'm listening.'

Van Laken signals to Courtois to show Arthur the photo of Mercury.

'Do you know this man?'

Arthur casts a disinterested eye over the photo, rubs his oiled pectorals and then drops the photo on the gleaming floor.

'Never seen him before.'

'But I think you have. Didn't you see Mrs Rizzoni getting into Vangenechte's limousine yesterday?'

'Who's Vangenechte?'

'Ted Harlow.'

'That's not Ted Harlow.'

'It's his chauffeur.'

'I don't pay much attention to the staff.'

'I can understand that. Have you had any news from Mrs Rizzoni?'

Arthur's exaggerated self-confidence finally seems to lapse for a moment. He feels for the pack of Chesterfields on the back of the sofa, takes out the last cigarette and lights it with a golden Cartier.

'Listen, we're modern, broad-minded people. My girlfriend enjoys her freedom how and when she feels like it. I don't need to get worried. I trust her one hundred per cent. And besides, just between you and me, Van Laken . . .'

'Mr Van Laken . . .'

'Mr Van Laken, you know as well as I do that women always return to their nest.'

'That's true, isn't it, commissaris?' Courtois adds eagerly, trying to break the tension and remind Van Laken of why he was so good-humoured this morning.

'Is this fancy dress outfit your normal working attire?' Van Laken continues, as if he has not heard Courtois' remark.

'Commissaris, may I know the real reason for your visit? You've interrupted me in the middle of a verse I was endeavouring to fine-tune.'

'Endeavouring to fine-tune . . . Fine-tuning a verse . . . These poets express themselves so elegantly, don't you think so, Palmans?'

Palmans nods wearily.

'The reason for our visit, Mr Poet, is that we have good reason to believe that Mrs Rizzoni is in danger of her life. I assume you have already heard of M?'

'M? Like the letter M? No, I've never heard . . .'

'Strange.' Van Laken drops his soaking wet coat on the

floor, sits beside Arthur on the sofa, crosses his legs, stretches and gazes around with a smile, like somebody who is paying a first visit to friends and is waiting for the lady of the house to appear with the appetisers.

'Cosy little flat . . .'

'Commissaris, I'm afraid your time is up.'

'Rambo. Arthur Rambo. A pseudonym, I assume? Your pen name?'

'Right.' Arthur stands up resolutely, flexes his shoulders and closes his bathrobe. 'This visit is over. I'll show you to the door.'

'Really cosy here, isn't it, Courtois? It's not because you have a pile of money that you automatically have the necessary taste . . .'

Courtois no longer knows how to react – Van Laken is losing it, that much is certain. He looks at Palmans questioningly.

'I think we're all done here.'

'You might be, Palmans, but I'm not. I'm staying a while. Certainly while it's still pissing down outside. I find this gentleman an exceptionally charming person, somebody I'd like to get to know better. And I suddenly have dozens of questions.'

'What do we do in the meantime?'

'Whatever you like, Pol. Sit down, Mr Rambo. After all, you are at home.'

'I'm staying,' says Courtois, who does not dare to leave Van Laken alone with Arthur.

Arthur is so confused by Van Laken's inexplicable attitude that he meekly sits down on the edge of the sofa.

'If you don't need me anymore, I'll go back to the office. There may be news.'

'Good thinking, Palmans! Keep us informed. You know where we are.'

'I'll find my own way out.' Palmans awkwardly says his goodbyes and hurries outside through the concrete shaft.

'From now on, I advise you to answer all my questions extremely carefully.'

'I'm calling my cousin. He's a lawyer.'

'Have you got anything to hide?'

'No.'

'Well then . . . A few innocent questions . . . Pol, will you take notes?'

The nearest sofa is some ten metres away, hidden behind an iron pillar, so that Courtois is obliged to squat where he is, his notebook balanced awkwardly on his knee. What is Van Laken up to? What has got into him? What is he keeping quiet? Why is he behaving so strangely? Either he is in urgent need of a holiday, or Maartje's unexpected return has unhinged him completely, or maybe this is another one of his highly individual strategic moves, that nobody understands but himself. Courtois listens enthralled.

'You see, Pol, there are a couple of details about Mr . . . Mr . . .?'

'Wouters.'

'Got a nice ring to it. Wouters! . . . about Mr Wouters that rather trouble me. He claims, for instance, not to have seen Mercury and says that women always return to their nest. And nothing could be further from the truth. That sounds arrogant and throw-away. Secondly, he must be about the only normal person in Flanders who has not heard of M. Thirdly, he's wandering around in his swimsuit, when it's pouring with rain outside and the beach is more than a hundred kilometres away. Fourthly, he smells like a swamp.'

'The smell I mentioned when we came in here?'

'Yes, Pol. And sorry about that wet dog remark. Our Mr Wouters is therefore lying. And I want to know why.'

'Poets of good standing seldom reveal the naked truth, choosing instead to conceal it behind an exotic flourish.'

'Beautifully formulated! But you don't look like a poet. And I doubt very much that you're of good standing.'

'So what do you think a poet should look like?'

'Thin, pale, impoverished and with a gleam of intelligence in his eyes.'

Van Laken's uncompromising, provocative tactics seem to be working. Arthur is beginning to fray at the edges.

'I'll ask you again, is this your normal working attire?'

'Yes.'

'Did you see the man in that photo when he came to pick up Mrs Rizzoni yesterday?'

'Yes.'

'Did you notice anything unusual?'

'Such as?'

'Did he seem to be trying to hide himself?'

'No.'

'So why did you initially claim not to recognise him?'

'Because I didn't recognise him.'

'Do you happen to have a cup of coffee?'

'No.'

'Aren't you worried?'

'Yes . . .'

'So why didn't you contact the police?'

'Because I was asleep. And because I don't like cops.'

'And why is that, Mr Wouters?'

'It's in my genes.'

'Like the poetry?'

'Right.'

'Mr Wouters, what exactly is the nature of your relationship with Mrs Rizzoni?'

'Why?'

'You don't fit in here.'

'I'm her lover. Does a lover have to fit in?'

'Lovers never fit in, Mr Wouters. Another little question: do you ever smear yourself with a special oil? You're shining like a shop-window dummy.'

'Yes.'

'And does that oil smell of stagnant ponds?'

'I don't notice the smell anymore. But I've never had any complaints.'

'One final question: why did you claim never to have heard of M?'

'To keep the conversation brief.'

'Unsuccessfully. So you do know who I mean?'

'I've read about him, like everybody else, in the newspaper.'

'You see, Mr Wouters, we've meanwhile discovered his identity.'

Arthur stands up menacingly, casting his shadow over Van Laken. Beads of sweat are rolling from his chin, down his neck and over the tattoo on his chest. If this chap loses his temper, he could chuck us out of the window with one arm tied behind his back, thinks Courtois, who is feeling more and more uneasy. Van Laken continues to sit in the deep sofa totally unperturbed.

Arthur picks up the photo of Mercury and studies it carefully.

'You think Suzy's absence has something to do with . . . something to do with this M?'

'Undoubtedly.'

'Is this his picture?'

'Yes.'

'Ted Harlow's chauffeur?'

'Ted Harlow's new chauffeur.'

'Suzy's not his type. She's not in danger.'

'Well she is your type . . . But no, I don't think he's set his sights on her. And I keep hoping she'll simply resurface and telephone you. Women can be so unpredictable . . .'

The urgent ring of a telephone echoes from somewhere in the room. Arthur rushes to a low table – four bronze legs with a Perspex top – and retrieves the cordless phone from beneath a toppled pile of fashion magazines.

'What did I tell you!' shouts Van Laken, stretching and folding his hands behind his head.

'Don't you think we ought to be going?' Despite his admiration, Courtois feels his superior's little performance has gone on long enough and has not actually achieved very much.

'It's for you, commissaris!' Arthur's loud voice echoes around the concrete walls of the loft. Like in an empty warehouse, thinks Van Laken.

'Yes?'

'Somers here.'

'I'm listening.'

'The cat's in the bag.'

'How did it go?'

'None too easily . . . The little shit had no idea what was going on.'

'The little shit! Well put! An obnoxious little runt, isn't he?'

'Not especially . . . Didn't want any scandal in front of his clients. And his woman was really pissed-off . . .'

'I know her . . . a quick-tempered type.'

'I should say . . . And her daughter . . .'

'It's his daughter. She hasn't got any children. Where is he now?'

'Here, next door.'

'And where are you?'

'At the fuckin' office.'

'Thank you, Somers. Stay where you are. Palmans is on his way. If anything comes up, you can call me at this number.'

'No news?'

'Nothing definite . . . just a couple of hunches.'

Van Laken hands the phone back to Arthur, who has been anxiously trying to follow the conversation from a distance.

'If I understand correctly, you're planning to set up shop here?'

'We've got all the home bases covered ... men at Vangenechte's, at De Rosier and now also here with you. I'm comfortable here. And my friend Courtois will keep me company.'

Van Laken begins to leaf rather distractedly through the book that was lying on the floor next to the sofa, Jullian's book about decadent dreamers, a book filled with sumptuous paintings by Rochegrosse, Gustave Moreau, Odilon Redon, Jean Delville, Alexandre Sion, J.F. Wagner, William Rimmer and other artists he has never heard of. A book filled with visions from antiquity, winged women, black angels, Amazons, voluptuous nymphs, sadistic mistresses, elves, chimaeras and Sphinxes. His eye is caught by a voluptuous portrait of a woman by a certain Franz von Stuck which reminds him of the photos of Suzanna Rizzoni in the hall. He begins to read aloud the chapter on 'psychopathia sexualis', on page 106, to the left of the painting: 'Swinbourne gives us the most eloquent pictures of the merciless woman. His women are of course the empresses, whose slave the masochistic poet would have liked to be ...'

He turns towards Arthur.

'Mrs Rizzoni sometimes reminds me of an empress. How about you? And now my assistant and I would appreciate a cup of coffee ...'

52

'Don't cry, you're the gentlest man I've ever met. It was good, believe me. It was my fault too, I know it, I can be so clumsy, the first time. I love it when you caress my thighs, come now, stop crying . . .'

Plump raindrops are spattering with a dull thud on the broad rhubarb leaves which are protecting Ava and Mercury like a safe but leaky roof and Mercury is reminded of the aqueous, menacing soundtrack of John Boorman's *Duel in the Pacific*. Ava is lying on her side, leaning on her elbow, naked, one knee raised. She looks like an abstract painting by Soulages: the dark smears of mud standing out against her milk-white skin. On her head, the mud has caked into crusty islands, sown with tufts of hair. Mercury looks at her hand, which is playing with his balls: the red is flaking from her nails. And then at her: even now, she looks like the tanned woman on the edge of her swimming pool, who had made eyes at him from a glossy magazine and whom he has to forget.

'I'm so embarrassed I could die.'

'If it doesn't work the first time, you just have to try again Frank . . . And you have to admit, these aren't exactly the ideal circumstances. Normally I'm different . . . less emotional.'

'I dreamt of this too long.'

After their dance in Le Moderne, it was Ava who had taken him by the arm. They had strolled through the deserted streets of the mining town like newlyweds through Venice – without talking, cuddled up against each other so tightly that he could feel her every tremble ripple through his body – until they found the little brick walled garden, where wild rhubarb was growing: tall, firm plants under which they could hide their budding love from the world, as if under a tropical canopy of green rubber.

It was also Ava who had gone to lie under the fleshy plants, had taken off her dress and stockings, had stretched out her arms invitingly to her executioner and pulled him gently towards her. And he had bent trembling over his fantasy and lain himself weightlessly down on top of her, cautiously, trying not to startle her, as if he wanted to delay the moment he had been longing for, scared of disappointing her and losing her so close to success, confused too because he himself was suddenly having to play a role in his film.

It was Ava who had undressed him. And when his hand disappeared between her thighs, she had squeezed her legs together, a hot, slippery vice, and had moaned like in the final scene of *Desert Flower*. He had kissed her over her whole body – concentrating a little more around her nipples, in her smooth fragrant armpits, the curve of her hips and the velvet of her groin – had licked the mud from her navel. His tongue had then ploughed her until she had grabbed him wildly by the hair to push him from between her legs and to come, silently, with her mouth wide open. She had then spread and pulled back her legs, the universal V for victory, and leaning on his trembling arms he had lowered himself on top of her, so that he could melt inside her. A thousand times he had tried to imagine this blessed moment, a thousand times he had projected this scene onto the screen of his eyelids, but his longing and his anxiety were so overpowering that he had collapsed on her quivering body, his flaccid penis resting in the kiss of her labia.

Ava had rocked him in her arms, comforted him as if he were a child, drunk the tears from his cheeks.

And then the fear had resurfaced. Perhaps this was the turning point, the moment of desperation, when, doubled up with shame, crazed with humiliation, he strangled his victims.

For a moment, she had lain motionless, thinking of her father, to whom life had also been a mystery, but when Mercury had rolled on to his back amongst the rigid, hairy stalks, burying his face in his hands and begging for forgiveness, she had sworn, not without pathos, that she wanted to share the rest of her life with him.

'Frank . . . I'm so cold. It's time we went home.'

'So is this the end?'

'No, silly, it's just the beginning. Hey, what's that?'

Ava points to a dark, heart-shaped mark on her right hip.

'A beauty spot. Why?'

'I've never noticed it before.'

'You're kidding, you've got four. All four in the shape of a heart.'

Mercury kisses her on the side of her right foot, in the hollow of her left knee, on her right hip and in her neck, just below her right earlobe.

'One, two, three, four . . .'

Ava laughs and is reaching for what remains of her Armani evening dress, a shapeless, sodden rag, when she suddenly thinks she hears a strange rustling amongst the rhubarb stalks, not far from the place they are hiding.

'Hush . . . Do you hear that scratching noise?' She presses herself closer to Mercury.

'Yes.'

Without moving a muscle, they listen tensely to what might be an unexpected sign of life in this dead landscape.

'It sounds like . . . clucking.'

'It is clucking, look!'

A skinny, black chicken sticks its head around the stiff stalks, sees the entwined couple, starts, and fluttering in panic disappears back into the dripping undergrowth.

'Rome!' says Mercury.

'Rome?'

'The chicken of Pope Honorius. The saintly man was

convinced his destiny was linked to that of a black hen he had called Rome.'

'You're so well-read,' whispers Ava, shivering with pleasure, and bites him playfully on the ear.

53

'I want to phone my salon!'

'This isn't a fuckin' telephone exchange.'

'If that's your attitude, I demand the presence of a lawyer.'

'And I'm afraid you're going to need one later. A fuckin' good one.'

'I want one now, immediately!'

'Don't go getting your fuckin' toupee in a twist. Sit back down on your chair.'

'But I've done nothing wrong!'

'Come on, we've all done something wrong. Even me.'

'They're trying to ruin me, that's what it is!'

'Who?'

'How should I know, my rivals . . . Alexandre, Desange, Paolo Coiffure . . .'

'Yeah, right. And what about the fuckin' mafia?'

'Somebody's out to get me, that's obvious.'

'You're going to make me cry.'

'I'm the victim of some sort of plot.'

'Yeah right. And the coke in that pot of cream, I suppose I fuckin' planted it?'

'I never said that! But somebody hid that filth there . . . Besides, how did you know it was there?'

'A telephone call. Cup of coffee?'

'That depends on how much longer I have to stay here.'

'That's for Big Mac to decide. But it could be quite some time. Drugs are no fuckin' laughing matter.'

'That's for whom to decide?'

'Commissaris Van Laken. Coffee or no coffee?'

Nino turns to stone. Suddenly understands. Does not dare to believe that what he suspects might be the truth. Could Van Laken have hatched this plot? Is this his revenge, because his wife has now left him for good? Is this desperate deed of a sick man the price he must pay for his happiness with Maartje? Nino hopes he is wrong. If not, then he is up shit creek without a paddle: his word against that of two respected police officers, a hopeless case. He breaks into an anxious sweat and the handcuffs suddenly seem tighter than ever.

'What's up? Hot flushes?'

Nino does not reply. He just stares through the bars of the little window above the filing cabinet, at the sheet of rain, outside.

54

To show that all danger has evaporated, Mercury and Ava stroll arm in arm back to the limousine, a dust and mud-spattered toppled monolith, inside which it is ominously quiet.

'I think they've finally made their peace,' laughs Mercury.

'Or perhaps they've fallen asleep . . . after all that screaming.'

'Eva, you explain the situation to them. And if they agree to our plan, then I'll set them free and we'll all drive back to Antwerp together, okay?'

'Okay. And Ted?'

'Ted is a problem Suzanna has to solve. That's the way it goes in my scenario. Here, hold this. It will reassure them.'

Mercury hands his pistol to Ava and opens the door.

Cindy's limp body flops backwards out of the car and her head thuds into the mud at Mercury's feet. Her mouth is wide open, torn in the corners. Her teeth and her tongue are black with vomit. The broken neck of a crystal decanter is sticking out of her neck, a gaping wound which immediately fills with dark, muddy water. Her left eye seems to have melted. Her T-shirt has been torn to shreds and her blood-smeared breasts are furrowed with deep slashes.

Ava turns away her eyes, her stomach revolts, she has to vomit but can only bring up air and bile and threads of saliva.

Suzanna, glistening with blood, is cowering in the back of the car. She gazes at Mercury with imploring eyes – the eyes of Melinda Mercouri in *Medea* – her mascara has run, her chin is trembling, she is a hundred years old. She curls her upper lip, bares her teeth, opens her mouth but cannot make a sound. She looks like a shrivelled clown, Professor Unrath at the end of *De Blauwe Engel* – Mercury has seen too many films – shakes her head as if she wants to say no . . . No what?

'Mrs Rizzoni! What in God's name has happened?' Mercury picks up Cindy's ashen body and tries to push her back into the car, but she doubles over and flops back into the mud. Suzanna sticks out her hands, as if she is trying to push away the carcass. Blood is oozing from a deep cut in the palm of her left hand. Her voice is unrecognisable, as deep as on a soundtrack that is being played too slowly.

'It's not what you think . . . Cindy went crazy, a wild thing . . . too much coke. Didn't you hear me screaming for help? She attacked me with a piece of broken glass . . . for no reason . . . Look!' She shows them her right ear, which is bleeding profusely. 'She was hysterical . . . we fought . . . I accidentally hit her eye and then . . . then she cut her own throat . . . severed an artery . . . It was terrible, the blood gushed all over me, I was blinded, I wasn't able to stop her . . . God, why didn't Arthur come along! Mercury, we have to get away from here . . . This nightmare has gone on long enough. I have to have treatment . . . have to be in Paris tomorrow . . . it hurts, it hurts so much . . .'

'Come,' says Mercury, grasping her by the wrist, 'I'll take care of you. There's water in the café. Come, Mrs Rizzoni. Please. Don't be afraid, I won't hurt you. Eva, tell her who I am.'

'You can trust him, Suzy, he is not who you think he is.' Ava crawls laboriously to her feet without looking at the limousine. 'My God, Frank, what did you set in motion here . . .'

'A scenario.' Mercury seems to have lost all contact with reality, to be experiencing the situation as if he has tumbled into a film in which everybody is giving their role all they've got, as if he does not realise that Cindy is really dead, that Ted was really pushed to his death, as if he believes that Ava is truly in love with him.

Suzanna puts on her sunglasses and steps out of the car, moaning. Mercury notices that she has covered her face with a thin layer of powder in a futile attempt to cover the blood spatters and smears of mascara. A mask reminiscent of certain tropical fish. Of scorpion fish, to be precise. Her lips have been clumsily painted and her mouth resembles the rectangular sneer of Joan Crawford.

'It's over,' whispers Mercury, as he helps her across the street.

'Suzy, give me a piece of gum, will you? My mouth tastes of bile and putrid earth.'

'I haven't got any gum, sweetie . . .'

'So what are you chewing?'

Surprised, Suzanna takes a glistening, fleshy, dark brown morsel from her mouth and rolls it between her fingertips, with their broken blue artificial nails.

'I think I've bitten off her nipple.'

55

' "If I surrender myself to the whore-suckers, then the fever envelops me even more fragrantly in its most refined tremblings!" Who knows the name of the hairdresser who wrote this?' Van Laken is quoting aloud from the Jullian book, through which he has been yawningly leafing for the past half-hour.

'No idea!' shouts Courtois from the black leather Le Corbusier sofa, next to the Bang & Olufsen, in another far-off corner of the loft.

'Some guy called . . . Rollinat. Or what about this: "Hail Thee, O, most occult, O, most profound carnality, melancholy star of the purple heavens of the world!" No? Wait . . . Samain, Mr Samain! Frustrated little buggers, the lot of them, if you ask me! Who in God's name reads this rubbish!'

'Mr Wouters, apparently.'

Arthur comes into the room carrying two cups of steaming coffee, which look ridiculously small in his gigantic paws. He turns on the light; dozens of quivering neon tubes.

'Do you read this rubbish, Mr Wouters?'

'No. Mrs Rizzoni does. It's giving her inspiration for her new collection, which, as far as I know, will have a Pre-Raphaelite flavour. Naturally it requires a degree of culture and feeling from the reader.'

'Naturally. May I make a quick call to headquarters?'

Arthur, who wishes to avoid any unnecessary argument because he has realised that he is stuck with the two detectives for a while, hands Van Laken the cordless phone.

'I take it you've no objection to me withdrawing to my study in the meantime?'

'Act as if you're at home, Mr Wouters. Hallo? Somers? Any news?'

'None worth mentioning. They thought they'd spotted the limo at the German border, but it wasn't ours . . . And it's now definite that Weinberg died of a heart attack . . . What else . . . oh, yes, Cornelis wants to speak to you, urgently. He was in a right fuckin' panic.'

'What for this time?'

'He wants the address of Tattoo Joe's in Antwerp . . . Wants to have *Ava drives a Harley* tattooed on his shoulder . . .'

'Poor bugger.'

'And this little shit is blowing all his fuses.'

'Give him a valium. And don't hesitate to call me as soon as there's any news.'

'Where are you?'

'Still at Rizzoni's.'

While Van Laken has been telephoning Somers, Courtois, to pass the time, has picked up a video cassette from the top of the TV and inserted it into the built-in VCR. Snow appears on the screen, followed by a hazy, static shot of what appears to be some white surface. The date and hour of recording are printed at the bottom on the right: 07.01.93–23h18. A home video, thinks Courtois, who considers turning it off. Who knows what intimate scenes it might contain? But in that case, Wouters surely wouldn't have left the cassette just lying around. After about ten seconds, the picture comes into focus and Courtois realises that the hazy surface is actually a wall, covered in white porcelain tiles. Probably some avant-garde film, he thinks, with nothing much more to offer than a static shot of a spotless wall. But suddenly, a helmeted, black–leather–clad person appears in the left of the picture, pushing a side of beef dangling from a hook along a rail. The mysterious motorcyclist repeats this same operation five times, mechanically and without much effort, without looking once at the camera, until the whole screen is hung with bloody carcasses. To be honest, Courtois would rather be watching an exciting thriller, but there is only the one cassette and he refuses on principle to watch *The Price is Right* or any other rubbishy television. The screen is empty for a moment and then the leather-clad man reappears. This time he is dragging a light-grey plastic sack across the floor. There is no music, so it is not some modern ballet. The digital clock jumps from 23h26 to 23h27. More out of curiosity than out of interest, Courtois continues to watch. God only knows what possesses these culture snobs. They claim that everything is art, that everyone is a genius, and they don't even know what the bark of a beech tree looks like. At such moments, Courtois, who is a farmer's son who has 'made good' in the city, misses the simple pleasures, like those childhood summers on the farm, when he was allowed to stay up late to play with the dogs and the ducks. But so long as his boss has decided to settle down in Rizzoni's flat, he has no choice.

The man on the screen takes off his helmet and shakes free a luxuriant shock of hair, which tumbles over his shoulders in thick locks. The camera zooms in clumsily. The man turns around, in close-up, and to his great consternation Courtois realises it is actually Suzanna Rizzoni. She smiles, baring her teeth. A ghastly grin. By now, Courtois is sitting on the edge of the sofa. What could this be? A happening? A fashion show?

Cut. Back to the overall picture: Mrs Rizzoni slices open the plastic sack with a razor. Courtois wants to call Van Laken, but his jaws are locked. With her black motorcycle boots, she rolls the naked body of a young girl out of the slashed sack, grabs her by the hair and turns her face towards the camera. The picture wobbles. 23h52. Mrs Rizzoni is planting a meathook through the girl's chin. She is having some difficulty, she has to twist and turn it, but finally she finds the fleshy spot and the hook slides through the mouth, the nose and up into the right eye, pushing it out of its socket. 23h56. Mrs Rizzoni attaches a chain to the meat hook, throws the chain over the rail and hauls up Lolita Moore's body until it is dangling amongst the sides of beef. 23h59. Mrs Rizzoni slices into Lolita's forehead with the razor, just above the eyebrows, from right to left, then extends the incision above the left ear, around the back of the head, above the right ear, and back to the socket with the hanging eye. There is no blood; corpses do not bleed. She then rolls the scalp from the skull and places the besmeared, blonde wig on her head to see if it fits. 08.01.93—00h04. Close-up. Mrs Rizzoni tugs the scalp down over her head, like a hairy bathing cap, pouts her lips, flutters her eyelashes and poses flirtatiously for the camera.

Courtois presses the pause button.

'Emiel!' He doesn't even realise he has called his boss by his Christian name.

'Yes, Courtois? Is it the homely atmosphere that's making you so familiar?'

'Come and look at this! Quickly!'

Van Laken shuts his book, gets up with a sigh, walks diagonally across the room and leans with both arms on the back of the sofa in which Courtois is sitting staring at the flickering image on the screen as if he has been turned to stone.

'Look then!'

'I'm looking, Pol, I'm looking!'

'Wait.' Courtois picks up the remote control and puts the video back on play.

00h32. Mrs Rizzoni has already skinned Lolita's body as far as the hips. The girl's skin is hanging in shreds, like a tattered dress, over her thin legs. 00h37. Mrs Rizzoni carefully snips away the labia with nail scissors and lays them beside the scalp on the tiled floor. 00h39. Two black rubber gloves wrench open the mutilated vagina. 00h40. Close-up of a small knife making tiny incisions to the left and to the right of the mangled hole, so that the gaping wound can be torn open even further. 00h41. Mrs Rizzoni holds a Scrabble block with the letter M in front of the camera and then pushes it deep inside Lolita, so deep that her hand disappears up to the wrist in the raw meat. Snow. 00h43. Mrs Rizzoni turns to the camera, licks the black blood clots from her rubber fingers and grins to reveal her long, dirty teeth, like a werewolf at full moon.

'Goddamnit . . . Goddamnit . . .' Van Laken's fist closes like a vice on the Scrabble block in his trouser pocket. He lights a cigarette without noticing he has lit the filter. He is so stunned by the loathsome spectacle Courtois has shown him that he is at a loss as to how to react and simply stares dumbstruck at the snow on the screen.

'Commissaris!'

'Goddamnit! . . . Don't ask me how, but as soon as we came in here I knew we'd been betting on the wrong horse.'

'What do we do now?'

'Have you got your gun?'

What a question! Naturally Courtois has his gun. He sticks his hand inside his jacket.

'Give it to me . . . I left mine with Maartje. That woman will drive me crazy yet. Phone Somers, explain the situation . . . have him call the public prosecutor's office . . . request reinforcements . . . and don't let go of that video cassette. I'll take care of our film director.'

Van Laken is dripping with sweat and trembling like a leaf. With joy. With excitement too, because yet again, by simply following his intuition and tempting fate, he has made that vital breakthrough. He is on the verge of solving the most difficult case of his career. His unorthodox modus operandi now seems definitely infallible. He had been mistaken about Mercury, of course, but he had already suspected that the moment he had been confronted with Arthur in the doorway. For some unknown reason, Arthur and his putrid body odour had raised his suspicions. Why else would he have decided to hang around in the loft? It is as if his sixth sense had been whispering to him that he was close to the solution. And has he not repeatedly remarked that the serial killer probably had an accomplice? Has he not talked about large, empty places, warehouses and packing sheds, as if he had seen this very loft in some mysterious vision? Naturally, there are still a great many loose ends to be tied up. Why Suzanna Rizzoni had signed her murders with the letter M, for instance. But those worries are for later.

'Mr Wouters! May I disturb you a moment?' Van Laken could naturally shoot the monster down on the spot, but that is too good for him. And besides, in that case, the numerous questions that are still arising would probably go unanswered. Moreover, Wouters probably knows where his girlfriend is hiding, what she is planning for her hostages, and especially what she has dreamt up for poor Ava Palomba. The fact that Wouters had not attended the premiere is undoubtedly part of some new, diabolical plan that Mrs Rizzoni has worked out. And who knows, the limousine might even be parked downstairs in the underground garage, as he had already postulated in one of his theories.

An irritated Arthur walks into the brightly lit room, a wet towel wrapped around his head like a turban.

'Haven't you the slightest understanding for people who are trying to write?'

'For poets, you mean?' Van Laken has totally regained his self-control. He realises he has no chance against the roaring giant in front of him, unless he can first gain his confidence. 'But of course I do! Respect even. The meanderings of the creative process have always fascinated me. But there are still a few details I would like to have your opinion on.'

Arthur remains standing in the middle of the doorway, to make it clear to Van Laken that the area behind him is private territory. Van Laken nods towards Courtois, who is telephoning with his back to them in the far corner of the loft.

'I hope you don't mind ... My colleague has a couple of urgent calls to make. Naturally we'll reimburse you ...'

'That won't be necessary.'

'Thank you, Mr Wouters. Eh ... Mr Wouters, what exactly are your poems about?'

'About love and death. What else?'

'I'm sure I don't know.' Van Laken would like to answer: disembowelment, plucked-out eyeballs, torn-off hands, twisted-off heads, ripped-open livers, severed labia, but first he wants to toy with Arthur, like a cat does with a rat before it rips out its throat, as a sort of reward, after eight months of uninterrupted detective work.

'Do you have any hobbies, besides your writing, Mr Wouters?'

'Body-building.'

'Body-building ... not crossword puzzles?'

'All good poets solve the occasional crossword puzzle.'

'Scrabble?'

'Seldom.'

'But you do have a set?'

'I think so.'

'Feel like a game?'

Arthur begins to breathe quickly and nervously. Van Laken's hand tightens around the gun in his trouser pocket, his finger on the trigger.

'Have you really nothing better to suggest? My girlfriend's life is in danger and what do the police do? Drivel on about board games. If I was to tell people this, nobody would believe me!' Arthur turns to go back into his study.

Van Laken suddenly realises that the putrid odour, the decaying stench of mould and stagnant water, is coming from the corridor behind Arthur, and without waiting any longer, he takes the Scrabble block from his pocket and holds it, trembling, a few centimetres from Arthur's face.

'I've even brought along the missing piece!' He then aims his pistol at Arthur, the barrel touching him right between the eyebrows just beneath his turban. 'Mr Wouters, you're under arrest for complicity in the murder of Anna Maria Zonhoven. You have the right . . .'

Van Laken is unable to finish his sentence, the sentence he loves to utter more than any other: Mr X, you are under arrest for et cetera, et cetera. With one arm Arthur throws him to the marble floor with supernatural strength and then disappears down the corridor, howling like a wounded dog. Courtois rushes over, helps Van Laken to his feet and then follows him down the corridor, which ends in a steep, concrete staircase that leads to the cellars. The stench of brackish water and fungus grows stronger and mingles with something that smells like ether. The stairs are slippery and it is quite dark in the narrow stairwell, so Van Laken steadies himself with one hand against the mossy wall. It feels as soft as velvet. The further they descend, the more the temperature rises. A second, low corridor, in which Van Laken has to stoop so as not to bang his head against the network of pipes, opens out into a murky, vaulted cellar, where Arthur is waiting for them, his outspread arms shielding the glass wall of a gigantic, half-filled aquarium that covers the entire width of the rear wall like a film screen and fills the cellar with a flickering green glow. The stink of humus, medication and fermenting putrefaction and the almost tropical, humid heat are unbearable. The water in the aquarium is so cloudy that Van Laken is unable to make out what vermin might be swimming around in it. In the middle of the cellar, picked out by a brighter, whiter spotlight, stands a marble butcher's slab covered with glass jars and surgical instruments. Van Laken holds his pistol in front of himself with both hands and approaches Arthur hesitantly, testing the slippery floor with the toes of his shoes, and he knows, he knows what he is going to find in the aquarium. His blood pounds through the swollen veins of his temples, the pressure in his skull is appalling, but he does not even feel the migraine. He tries to swallow but he cannot, his throat is as dry as it was so long ago when he dived in to bed for the night with Maartje.

Courtois picks up one of the jars and holds it up to the light above the marble slab.

'And?' Van Laken asks, without turning around.

'Cocks. I mean, penises, preserved in formalin.'

'This has all got nothing to do with me!' Arthur screeches, and then, much quieter, whining like a child: 'It's Suzanna . . . She's so lonely . . . I help her to survive . . . Suzanna is a marvellous creature, a sphinx, a phoenix . . . Nobody will ever understand her . . . She's my mother, my muse, my mentor, my Madonna, my Medusa, my Mona Lisa, my mask . . .' Arthur begins to sob convulsively, like a monstrous, oiled baby, shuddering in the bilious green glow of the aquarium. 'I just held the camera, that's all . . . and most of them were already dead. I can't stand the sight of blood . . . I didn't touch a single one of them!'

'Why was it always on a Monday?' Van Laken asks, almost amicably.

'A commemoration . . . Suzanna loves traditions, loves rituals . . . She punished her mother on a Monday. She was fourteen and ever since . . . She loved her father very much. She did it for him, she said, to free him. Poor Suzy . . .'

'What does the letter M mean?'

'That, I can't tell you. I hope you'll try to understand.'

'But of course. Is Mrs Rizzoni here by any chance?'

'I don't know where she is. But I'm not worried. I know she's immortal.'

'What's in that aquarium behind you, Mr Wouters?'

'Those are my angels . . . Suzanna gave them to me, all five of them, because I've helped her so well. You mustn't touch my angels, they're mine, they're mine alone. They'll only eat from my hand. They love sweet things . . . cream horns, cream puffs, millefeuilles, eclairs, that sort of thing, sometimes a piece of Turkish delight . . . They're called Bonbon, Caramel, Choc-ice and Chocolate. The youngest is provisionally called Ophelia, because he looks more like a water nymph than an angel. They're hiding because they don't know you . . . They're so timorous . . .'

'We'll take good care of them, Mr Wouters. But now you have to come along with us. Cuff this gentleman, Pol, we've lost enough time already.'

An emaciated, wraithlike figure, with long, straggly blond hair, appears behind Arthur, up to its hips in the water. It presses its protruding ribs against the wall of the aquarium and peers with enormous, lifeless eyes through the algae on the thick glass, trying to make out what is going on in the twilight of the cellar. Van Laken, who has looked at his photo so often, immediately recognises the shadow of Karel Verbiest, the young escort-boy who had been kidnapped in the Van Putlei on 11 February.

Arthur turns around, taps on the glass with his nails and begins to sing in an artificially high voice:

'"Afore the park turns twilight blue − the chubby cherubs canter − as sunset sheds its rosy hue − o'er lily and oleander . . ." The melody is mine, the text is loosely based on Stuart Merrill . . . They consider it their song.'

'Come, Mr Wouters, it's time.'

'But I can't possibly go with you! Without me, they don't have the slightest chance of surviving. They need warmth and humidity. Bright light could burn their eyes! Look how delicate they are. You still don't understand, angels need very special care!' Arthur falls to his knees sobbing and slowly unwinds the towel from his head.

'There is indeed much we don't understand, Mr Wouters.

As you yourself remarked, we are only simple souls. But you are coming with us anyway. Now, immediately . . . Pol!'

Courtois helps Arthur to his feet, but when he tries to cuff him, he is blinded by a lightning blow to his left eye and falls backwards, hitting his head against the edge of the marble butcher's slab. Van Laken shoots without hesitation. A first bullet tears through the bronze armour of Arthur's stomach muscles, just below the navel, but he seems not even to feel it; a second hits him right between his eyes; and a third, by accident, hits the glass of the aquarium which cracks and then, under the enormous pressure of the water, explodes like a gigantic television. A devastating tidal wave surges through the torture chamber. Van Laken is swept off his feet by the flood, but is able to grab hold of one of the pillars that support the vault. A deathly silence gradually fills the cellar.

Courtois, whose head is bleeding profusely, is leaning groggily against a brick wall, with Arthur's body pressing down on his legs like a stranded whale. The emaciated bodies of the five boys are floating here and there amongst the algae and the excrement like dead fish in a shallow pool. Van Laken crawls dizzily to his feet, steadies himself against the pillar and surveys the chaos. He then wades through the stinking pool to one of the boys and recognises Ludo Meirmans, alias Beverly Hills, whose unchanged silicone breasts look even more monstrous than before on the skeletal body. He tries to help him to his feet, but it is a hopeless task. The poor wretch has been in the water too long and his legs are too weak to support him. He slides out of Van Laken's arms like an eel.

'Ludo?'

The young transsexual nods his head. His eyes roll in their sockets. He tries to move his stiff lips.

'It's over. Don't be afraid. We're going to help you. This evening, you'll be sleeping in a huge, soft bed.' Over the course of his long career, Van Laken has had to deal with a great many horrifying situations, but the sight of this limp, wrinkled, helpless larva, lying groaning in his arms, is the first to bring a tear to his eye.

'Are you trying to say something?'

The boy opens his mouth, a suppurating, bottomless pit from which the tongue is missing. Van Laken closes his eyes a moment, tastes coffee mixed with bile in the back of his throat. Then, with a green, imploring finger, Ludo Meirmans points to his abdomen: his genitals have been removed and replaced by a clumsily thick-stitched zip-fastener. The world renowned 'Rizzoni Touch'.

56

Mercury closes the First Aid box after having disinfected and dressed the palm of Suzanna's hand. It had been a fiddly job, because a minuscule but stubborn splinter of glass had been lodged in the wound.

'Did it hurt a lot?' asks Ava.

'No idea, sweetie. Sometimes I'm completely impervious to pain. At least, to physical pain.'

'Luckily.' Sometimes Suzanna sounds so hard.

'So. This is the romantic love nest where he seduced you,' laughs Suzanna. 'Le Moderne in . . . Where exactly are we, Mercury?'

'I think not far from Charleroi, madame.'

'Not far from home, as mama used to say . . .'

'Would you like some more water?'

'Oh yes, sweetie! You're an angel!'

Ava opens a bottle of Spa and hands it to Suzanna. 'Well, Frank, what do you suggest now? After all, it's your scenario.'

'My scenario?'

Ava is mistaken. So far he has not been the author. He had simply brought about a short circuit. He had not been able to foresee its consequences. His characters themselves have provided the dramatic outcome. Ava's question comes so unexpectedly that he does not know what to answer.

'What do you two suggest?'

'I think we ought to free Ted and take him with us. We'll only feel guilty about him otherwise.'

'Ted! Jesus! I'd forgotten about him!'

'Suzy!'

'Okay by me. And we can roll Cindy up in my cape and stick her in the boot.'

'I still can't believe it.'

'This may sound hard, but I think I've seen enough bodies and blood for the time being.'

'And you promise not to press charges? It was our idea, Ava's and mine, a publicity stunt that unfortunately went very wrong . . . agreed?'

'Agreed, darling.'

'It's the truth.'

Mercury stands up and sticks his radio and the First Aid box under his arm.

'Within half an hour, we'll be in Charleroi explaining everything to the police.'

'Why don't we simply phone home to say we're on our way?'

'They'd arrest us immediately, Suzy. Our wisest move is to turn ourselves in.'

'But I'd so like to talk to Arthur. You two wouldn't believe how much I miss him, my Panther.'

'Later, Mrs Rizzoni. That could spoil our plan. Another thing: if Ted contradicts us, which he is certain to do . . .'

'If he is still capable.'

'It's three against one. They'll have to believe us.'

'Are you taking something to drink along the way?' Suzanna asks, as she follows Mercury to the door. Ava disappears behind the bar and squats down to rummage amongst the clutter for the last full bottles.

Outside, Mercury stops beside the wreck of the blue Simca to search in one of his pockets for his car keys. Suzanna takes advantage of this moment of inattention to quickly and furtively pick up one of the planks Mercury had wrenched from the door of Le Moderne with the crowbar and slam it against his head. She lets it fall, but the splintered plank dangles from a rusty nail that has pierced his ear and is lodged in his skull. Mercury turns around, stunned, not understanding what has come over Mrs Rizzoni. He totters, his eyesight blurs, the sounds around him fade away, it suddenly becomes quiet, very quiet and cold and dark. He falls to the ground and sinks into the mud. Suzanna takes the pistol from his trouser pocket and, before Ava can intervene, fires twice into Mercury's heart. Ava drops her bottles and runs outside screaming, tries to throw herself on top of Mercury, but Suzanna grabs her so tightly by her arm that she almost tears it off.

'Suzanna! Have you gone crazy too? Let go of me! You're hurting me!'

'Haven't you understood anything?' Suzanna screams back, shaking Ava violently. 'I save your goddamn life and you . . . you keep on living in your dream world, like some lovesick goose. Goddamnit, Ava, don't you realise who that bastard was?'

'I know who he is! A shy, gentle man, an artist, a real one, who loves me, like nobody else has ever loved me!'

'Ava! For Christ's sake, wake up! And I thought you were playing a part, just like me!'

'You've made a terrible mistake, Suzy! I'll never forgive you for this!'

'It's you who's making a terrible mistake, you horny bitch! He's blinded you! Just like all his previous victims!'

'Not true!'

'Oh no?'

'Prove it!'

'You want proof? You really want proof? He murdered Ted! Strangled him! And then he bit off his balls and threw them and your drunken pimp into a flooded cellar, amongst the frogs! And while Ted was sinking, he came! Is that enough?'

'You're lying!'

'And he left behind his signature. Do you have to see it with your own eyes? Come!'

Suzanna takes Ava by the throat and drags her roughly to the house next to Le Moderne. She pushes her into the hallway, grabs her by the hair and forces her to her knees beside the closed wooden hatch.

'Here! Look! I was watching when he wrote it!'

Ava looks at the letter M in the dust at the edge of the closed cellar hatch and shudders. She begins to tremble violently. Gazes desperately at Suzanna. No longer knows who she should believe. And bursts into helpless tears.

'He was so romantic, so well-read, so right . . .'

'They're the most dangerous, sweetie, the most vicious.'

Ava now thinks she hears a faint sound that resembles croaking, deep within the cellar.

57

All the streets around the Rizzoni Factory have been closed to traffic. An army of policemen is keeping the curious and the press at a distance to allow through the never-ending ballet of ambulances and official cars. Van Laken is sitting on the bonnet of the Opel, wrapped in a khaki blanket, shivering and drinking long swigs of cognac from the hip-flask Somers has pressed into his hands. Courtois, who has been talking to Dr Plouvier, comes and stands beside him and leans on the wing. He has a bandage around his head and is wearing sunglasses to hide his split eyebrow. The two men stare right through each other with the burnt-out eyes of those who have descended into hell and by some miracle been returned to the living. It is no longer raining. A sultry night is falling. The café terraces around the Groenplaats will be buzzing with carefree cheer until late. But Van Laken and Courtois are at a loss for words. What they have seen in the cellar demands total silence.

Van Laken looks like a political prisoner who has just escaped from a concentration camp. The last forty-eight hours have broken him for good. The blue glare of the flashing lights makes his features even more gaunt.

'What did Sax say?'

'All five are still alive. But they're starving and totally exhausted. They're suffering from bronchitis or pneumonia. Their wounds are so infected he fears gangrene may set in. And all five . . . eh . . . the tongue and so on . . . you know.'

'Has he already examined the jars?'

'He's looked at them, yes. Like I said, five tongues and four penises . . . in formalin.'

'Four?'

'Yes. The black one's is missing.'

'Black Peter? That's cutting a long tail fuckin' short!'

'Shut it, Somers! Not this evening, understood?' Courtois, who has trouble with Somers' dubious humour at the best of times, grabs him by the collar and pushes him away.

'Come on, lads, calm down. And Somers . . . Pol's right. This is no time for jokes.' Van Laken shakes the last drop of cognac into his mouth, lets it glide over his tongue and down his throat. 'It simply proves that Zsa Zsa Morgan was also murdered by M.'

'Do you know what that fuckin' M means yet?'

Van Laken shakes his head tiredly. Lights a cigarette.

'No. And as long as Mrs Rizzoni is out there, the mystery will remain unsolved. I understand less and less exactly what happened in that limousine yesterday. But after what we've discovered here this evening, I have to say I fear the worst.'

De Mulder appears from behind the ambulance in which young Jos Maartens, the flamenco dancer, the son of Sergeant Maartens of logistics, is being given first aid. He walks up to Van Laken and lays his arm over his boss's shoulder, an intimacy he would never normally permit himself.

'Incredible . . . Congratulations, chief.'

'You don't have to congratulate me. It was pure coincidence and the case is far from solved. Have you found out anything in the meantime?'

'I grilled Conchita.'

'And?'

'She caved in, admitted she'd had a sort of loose relationship with the previous chauffeur. Strange chap, by the way, that Dieudonné . . .'

'In what way?'

'Lived a double life. And above all: enormous gambling debts.'

'Why did she keep that quiet?'

'To protect him apparently.'

'To protect a corpse?'

'Conchita doesn't know he's been murdered. She still thinks he's run off with some other girlfriend.'

'Of course, sorry . . . I'm exhausted. And are there any clues?'

'We're asking around. Seems to be a definite case of gangland score-settling.'

Somers looks compassionately at his boss, whose teeth have suddenly begun to chatter.

'You'd better grab a couple of hours rest with the missus, chief. There's nothing much more to be done around here. We can round things up with the lads from the public prosecutor's office.'

'Thank you, Somers, but I won't be able to sleep until that damned limousine has been found. Pol, are you in any state to drive me to the Oudaan?'

'I've driven half asleep before.'

'Commissaris! Commissaris!' A policemen, whose belly has grown too big for his uniform, runs waggling out of the building.

'Yes, Debelder?'

'A woman just called. Had a deep voice. Wanted to talk to a certain Mr Arthur!'

'Italian accent?'

'Now that you mention it . . .'

'And?'

'Who am I talking to? she asks. Surprised. I answer: Officer Willy Debelder, fourth district. Is Mr Arthur Rambo there? she asks. Yes, I say, but it's rather difficult for him to come to the phone right now. It's quite a mess here. Careful, I think, play for time, Willy, play for time. Can I take a message? I ask. A ruse. And then she hangs up and I say to myself: Willy, my lad, this could well be important. And I rush outside to tell you. And that's it.'

'Thank you, Debelder. Lads, she's getting nervous. And she's missing her partner. She'll definitely try to contact him again. Feyaerts, have her phone tapped. We'll install ourselves upstairs in the loft. It's cosy, and there are plenty of good films. Besides, I still have to finish reading my book.'

58

'I won't hurt you, not today. At my feet lie legions of corpses I've beatified. And not one of them begged for mercy. Together we'll fight evil with evil. Spread your legs, sweetie . . .'

Ava is squatting in the back of the limousine, above the small television, naked except for her evening shoes, no longer sure whether she is still alive or has already landed in hell. Suzanna is lounging opposite her, on the dark stain where Cindy bled to death. She is staring fixedly at the screen beneath Ava's vagina, watching the scene from *Desert Flower* in which Ava is squatting in almost the same position above the contorted, ecstatic face of a black slave girl. She passes Ava the pot of honey.

'No amount of salve could soothe away this shame. But rub yourself with this anyway, sweetie . . . It will ease the consecration . . .'

Ava takes the pot of honey in slow motion, as if in a languid dream, hears herself mumble 'thank you', sticks in her muddy fingers and begins to smear herself with the sticky gunge, first her head, until her hair is sticking to her skull like a gooey cake, then her neck, her breasts, her armpits, her belly, her groin.

'Now the lips . . . spread the lips . . . open the gates of Gomorrah. I want to see your fingers disappear into the fount of depravity, into your injured, defiled lily, into the stinking cesspit of iniquity . . .'

Ava begins to stroke herself with a slithering finger.

'Lick! Lick your fingers! Taste the salty sap of shame! The putrid taste of corruption!'

Ava carries out the orders willingly; she is floating, weightless. This is not of this world. It is as if she has transcended the horror and entered another dimension, the dimension of eternal darkness, the dimension of consummate terror, where fear and pain become blurred and that which is most abhorrent is experienced as normal. It is probably the devil who is lying opposite her.

The honey trickles slowly down the TV screen, over a close-up of Ava's mouth, which is gliding, lips fluttering, over John Drake's tensed, tanned, white-sand-speckled belly. Ava opens her legs wider, spreads her labia with her left hand, smears the honey on the pink, pulsating flesh in between with the right. Making Suzanna so horny that she loses her self-control is her only hope of awakening from this nightmare alive.

'Look, Suzy. Look at my honey pot . . . It's for you, only for you . . . Eat me. We're alone in the world, you and I, nobody can see us, come . . .' Ava urinates and the golden rain mixes with the honey on the screen. 'Drink me!'

'Bonbon, Caramel, Choc-ice, Chocolate . . . oh, it will never work without Panther . . .' Suzanna kneels down in front of Ava. She glides the tip of her tongue momentarily over the TV screen and then she begins to pant and rave.

'Fearful delight! . . . Lacerated bitch! . . . Steel-blue twilight! . . . Liquid past! . . . I am the swan, the feverish sorrow that loses its way in hairy jellyfish! . . . Monday! . . . Wait until Monday, wait for Arthur . . . and suffocate between the unclean folds of my most beautiful slave girl . . . poisonous-slave-girl-of-muddy-honey! . . . Leave-behind-no-traces . . . Never . . . Traces of Javanese purple . . . of Venetian slime . . .' She grabs Ava by the thighs and pushes her legs in the air. 'O magnificent, besmeared, perfumed fungus . . .'

'Why Monday, Suzy, why not now?'

'Monday is the red–letter day of chastening, sweetie.'

'Why?' Ava runs a scented finger over Suzy's lips, the same finger with which she is rooting between Mexican thighs on the screen.

'You were supposed to be my masterpiece, the crowning glory of my work. But now everything is ruined.'

This is the first comprehensible sentence Suzanna has uttered. Ava seizes the opportunity.

'Tell me everything, Suzy. I want to understand. Nobody can live with such a crushing secret.'

Suzanna throws herself back on the seat, her dark gaze fixed on Ava's motionless body.

'Look.'

With both hands, she clasps the bottom of her torn dress and slowly lifts it, over her calves, her knees, her thighs. She is wearing the tattered remnants of real silk stockings, old-fashioned stockings with a seam. Above her black–lace garter, her skin is pale and waxen. Her right hand disappears deep into her Calvin Klein underpants and pulls out a dark, sinewy penis which immediately uncurls between her fingers. With the other hand she slowly slides her wig from her shaved head.

'Suzy? . . .' Ava tries to slide down from above the TV set, but Suzanna points the pistol at her.

'Don't move, sweetie . . . don't arouse him, he has your fate in his hands.'

'Suzy!'

'Suzy doesn't exist! Everybody is looking for Suzanna Rizzoni, but she is just a name, a label, a puppet, a costumed phantom, an illusion, a vision . . . And that's why she's immortal!'

'But who are you then?!'

'Maldonato! . . . Sometimes . . . Little Marcello Maldonato, who slumbers inside me. Marcello Maldonato who used to be forced by his mother to dress as a girl and pose in the scullery, amongst fat, greasy, sweaty, hairy men, for the "artistic"

photos she called her "still lifes"! While papa had to watch
from his wheelchair! People are never what they seem . . .
Shatter their golden masks and they spatter you with shit!'

'I don't understand . . .'

'She was the first one Marcello executed! The herring-eater!
The Dutch whore! On a Monday night, at full moon. He was
fourteen and ever since, he's lived inside me, little Marcellino
. . . The sweet little devil chooses my clothes, guides my hand,
shows me the way to the light . . .' Suzanna is gently rubbing
her penis, causing it to swell.

'But, Suzy . . . all those other, innocent girls . . .'

'Innocent? They were the pus, the fungus, the boils that
blemished his immaculate, flawless beauty! Marcello had a
mission and I let him fulfil it . . . for the pure pleasure of it.'

'Why Ted?'

'Because he had defiled you and you had enjoyed it!'

'Mercury . . .'

'Mercury was a tiresome amateur who got in Marcello's
way. Excrement, bile and blood! You don't smell of it so
much! Marcello can sometimes get very jealous, you
know . . .'

'Mercury smelt of cinnamon.'

'Living, dying . . . Melodramatic intermezzi. Don't worry,
sweetie, I shall let you taste the sensuality of the drama and
before we part company, reveal the Great Mystery . . .'

'But I . . . I'm your friend, aren't I? Surely I'm different?'

'All of them were Marcello's girlfriends. He was so
desperately in search of love. And as far as you're concerned,
sweetie, just look at yourself: you're just like all the others, a
panting, dripping, ripped open slut!'

Ava looks at the bronze veins of Suzanna's swollen penis,
which is protruding stiffly from between the roses of Sarah
Bernhardt's dress, and after all she has been through, she is
capable of doing anything to save her life.

'Fuck me.' She throws her arms around her thighs and pulls

back her knees to her shoulders. Like in the final scene of *Benidorm Lilly*.

'Strange. Those were the exact last words of all the whores who went before you, sweetie. You see, you do belong to that pack of barbarian bitches! Marcello is never wrong!'

'Fuck me, Marcello.' Ava is now feigning exaggerated arousal, as she does in her films, in which she performs the most bizarre sexual acts as if they were everyday pastimes. Suzanna kneels back down in front of her friend. Dusk is falling outside and the glare of the TV screen colours her contorted face blue, then green, then purple, then pink. She takes the pistol from the back seat and rubs the cold weapon over Ava's clitoris. Ava looks at Suzanna's shaved head and notices the tattoo: a red capital M, with the two legs pointing towards the forehead.

'Of course Marcello's going to fuck you first, sweetie.' Suzanna pushes the chromium-plated barrel of the pistol into Ava's vagina, releases the safety catch, slips her index finger over the trigger and begins to slide the weapon slowly to and fro, in and out, in and out. The gun could go off at any moment. Ava closes her eyes and prays.

'Look at me, mama. Look at Marcellino . . . Mama!'

Ava opens her eyes again. Suzanna is gazing up at her imploringly, from between her legs: tears are leaving black trails in the plaster of her cheeks. She has dropped the pistol and is holding her flaccid penis in both hands. The heels of Ava's stilettoes are pointing at her staring eyes. Suzanna is waiting. Is this what she wants? Ava summons up all her remaining strength and kicks the two black-lacquered spikes into Suzanna's eyes, churns, twists her heels, something cracks, she pulls back, blood gushes from the eye sockets, Suzanna holds her fingertips to the fresh wounds, utters a bloodcurdling shriek, like a wounded animal of prey, feels around wildly, calls for Arthur. Red froth bubbles from her mouth. She crawls out of the car on her hands and knees, stands up roaring, her monstrous silhouette with its undersized head standing out against the red glow of the setting sun. Ava takes the sticky pistol from between her legs and fires at the Beast, but the bullets seem to go right through it. She aims at the breast, the stomach, the head, empties the magazine, but the blinded monster remains unharmed and begins to dance, laughing and hawking, with the mousseline of her dress fluttering around her like transparent wings in the twilight. Evil cannot be destroyed, thinks Ava, she is immortal . . .

'Eva!'

'Frank?'

It is the weak voice of Mercury, who is stumbling towards the limousine with a deep wound on his left temple. 'Don't bother! They're blanks. I switched all the bullets myself last week . . . To avoid accidents!' he laughs feebly. 'Hurry!'

Ava drags herself back into the car, completely exhausted, and lays her head on Mercury's shoulder as he starts the engine.

'It's going to be a good film,' he says, 'with a happy ending, the way it should be.'

The limousine makes a wide turn and then stops at about a hundred metres from Suzanna, who is spinning around slowly, like a wounded eagle with outstretched wings, in the middle of the road, her bald head hanging backwards, an ecstatic smile on her lips, her emptying eyes pointed at the sky.

'This calls for the right background music,' Mercury says excitedly, as he presses the button of the CD player. A crystal-clear female voice fills the limousine:

In dämmrigen Grüften
Träumte ich lang
Von deinen Bäumen und blauen Lüften,
Von deinem Duft und Vogelgesang.

Nun liegst du erschlossen
In Gleiss und Zier,

Von Licht übergossen,
Wie ein Wunder vor mir.

'The first of *The Four Last Songs*, by Richard Strauss,' he mumbles. 'Performed by Kiri Te Kanawa, accompanied by the London Symphony Orchestra, conducted by Andrew Davis.' Then he puts his foot down, the wheels spin, a cloud of black smoke belches from the exhaust pipe and the evening suddenly smells of oil and burning rubber. The car squeals into motion, accelerating, straight towards Suzanna. She hears the limousine approaching, turns around, waves, an absurd little childlike gesture, like a small boy waving goodbye to his mother on a railway platform in August. The impact is terrible. Suzanna flies over the bonnet like a dislocated doll and thuds down behind the car, a nondescript, twitching heap of green in the coal–black mud.

Van Laken, Courtois, Somers and De Mulder, are sitting in the Rizzoni loft watching the videotapes of the murders when, at around nine-thirty — during the sequence in which Suzanna, dressed in an elegant double-breasted Armani men's suit, is arranging Peggy 'Sue' Laenen's twisted-off head amongst the perfume bottles on the dressing table in her bathroom — the long-awaited news finally arrives: Conchita has received a telephone call from Ava. She had called home from the limousine, somewhere in the neighbourhood of Charleroi, and told her maid the outline of her confused story. It was Suzanna, her best friend, who had hijacked the limousine in an inexplicable fit of insanity, in order to slaughter her hostages one by one with infinite cruelty; first Richard, then Ted, then Cindy, then Mercury, but he turned out to be only wounded and had saved her life at the last moment. Together, they had finally succeeded in overcoming Suzanna. In this version Mercury played the part of the hero, the guardian angel, which rather annoyed Van Laken who had imagined him very differently and for twenty-four hours had considered him to be the prime suspect. Moreover, he had not really solved the case and he was stuck with three new bodies. A success it was not.

'Okay, lads, that's it. Thank you. I'm going home. It's not my day today.' Van Laken sounds frosty and gets up as if he has just been watching a boring film. 'I think we've all earned a weekend's rest.'

'I suppose you'll be going to the lake, chief?'

'If my wife has no objections, why not?'

Van Laken can hardly walk home in his damp clothes, so Courtois offers to drive him. He drops him off in the Breydelstraat at around ten p.m. His hollow-cheeked boss has fallen asleep during the journey so he has to shake him gently awake after he had double-parked the car in front of the Café Brabançonne.

'So. Until Monday.'

'Till Monday. And have your head looked at. And, Pol, thank you. Without you I probably wouldn't have survived. You know where you can reach me.'

Van Laken gives his assistant a friendly pat on the shoulder and clambers out of the car. As he edges his way across the pavement, hunchbacked, through the festive passers-by and disappears into the dark hallway, Courtois watches him, the way you watch somebody who is disappearing from your life forever.

The lift is naturally still out of order, so Van Laken begins to clamber slowly up the creaking stairs. Between the second and the third floor, the light goes out, but he knows the stairs like the back of his hand and trudges on through the darkness like a blind man. Another five steps and then he will feel the light switch, on the wall, to the left of the door of his flat.

'Miel?'

Van Laken stops dead in his tracks. That was the voice of Maartje, when she was twenty.

'Maartje?'

The light in the stairway flicks back on. Maartje is sitting on the last step, clasping the gun he had left in the flat tightly in her two hands and aiming it down at him between her knees.

'Maartje!'

She closes her eyes, pulls the trigger, is startled by the bang and the recoil. The bullet penetrates his open mouth and bores through his skull, spattering it open like an overripe pomegranate.